Escape

James R. Hughes

PRESS

For Lillian, my Spanish bride.

Chapter 1
(Valladolid, 1554)

The Office of the Inquisition returned to Valladolid, the capital of Spain, on Wednesday, October 17th, in the year of our Lord, 1554.

It had been an exceptionally dry summer and fall that year and the rains were late, but on the Monday before the Inquisition arrived it had finally begun to rain, and it had not stopped for three days. It felt colder than usual. Anyone who didn't have to venture out stayed indoors. Even the children were missing from the streets. Usually all the children in town — at least it appeared that way — could be found playing their disorganized games in the small plaza in front of Bartolomé's house. There were no children playing that day and Bartolomé missed their clamour. Often, when he returned from his tutor's quarters, he would sit on the porch and watch them play 'get the hat', 'follow the leader', 'tag' or 'running the gauntlet'.

That afternoon Bartolomé was standing in the open doorway of his father's workshop watching the rain stream down. On Monday when it had started to rain, the smell from the street was terrible, but after the three days of heavy rain, the gutters were flowing faster than the Rio Pisuerga in the spring. Bartolomé breathed deeply. The air was finally clean.

As he turned to go into the workshop, he heard the faint tinkle of harness bells and an odd rumbling sound. He stepped back onto the porch and saw the first of the travellers coming around the corner of his street into the plaza.

The monks and their court-appointed guards passed by. A few of the monks were riding donkeys. A captain was on horseback. The rest of the monks and soldiers were on foot. The monks were huddled together in a black wet lump that slopped and gurgled like sludge down the Rio Duero. The soldiers attempted to keep in formation, but it was obvious that the rain had weakened their resolve. Behind this soggy group, followed about a dozen enclosed horse-drawn carriages with black curtains covering their windows. Presumably, these carried the officers of the Inquisition. The stream of carts continued to rumble by Bartolomé's house for as long, it seemed, as the rains had been falling. The carts were pulled by strong, but bored, oxen and tired ponies. A few of the carts had enclosed boxes, the rest were open. Bartolomé could not see what was in any of the carts since even the open ones had large canvas coverings over the hidden cargo. From accounts elsewhere, one could guess what un-mentionable horrors were in the carts.

On any other day, the whole city would have flowed into the main plaza expecting to see a parade, but on that day, no one appeared to care. Rather, it was almost as if the people thought the plague had arrived and had locked their doors to keep it out.

As the last of the carts passed his house, Bartolomé felt a chill run down his neck and back. The temperature had dropped again. He went into his father's workshop, closed the door, and attempted to warm himself by the small charcoal furnace his father kept burning most of the time for melting gold.

The next day a proclamation was found posted on the doors of Santa María la Antigua, the city's main Cathedral, and on the doors of all the churches throughout the city. It denounced a long list of heresies that were to be reported to the Inquisition, provided processes for reporting heretics, and itemized the specific punishments that would be exacted on those who did not report heretics. On the way to his tutor's, Bartolomé read the proclamation.

He arrived late at the home of his tutor, Doctor Pedro Ortiz de Tendilla. He opened the door without knocking and entered the small room on the main floor that was used as a classroom. The other three students of Doctor Ortiz were already there. Doctor Ortiz, rubbing his short white beard and peering over the top of his reading spectacles said, "You are late, Bartolomé Garcia. What has kept you? Did you sleep in?"

"No Sir, I am late because I stopped to read the proclamation posted on the church door."

"What proclamation is that?"

"The one from the Office of the Inquisition. It declares to be heresy all kinds of things including reading the Bible, owning books by someone named Martin Luther, and a long list of beliefs. The proclamation commands us to tell the Office of the Inquisition if we suspect anyone of reading the books, or holding to these beliefs. Why have they declared these actions heretical? How can reading the Bible be a heresy?"

"I don't think that this is the right time to discuss the proclamation of the Inquisition," replied Doctor Ortiz. "Possibly, later, if you have completed your Latin assignment we can discuss it. Please sit down and open Nebrija's *Introductiones Latinae*."

Doctor Ortiz tried to be gruff but his students knew that he really loved them and he loved teaching. He was an old man. They didn't know how old, but he was well over sixty, probably closer to seventy. He was from Tendilla in Alcarria, a despised region of Castile of which the proverb spoke, "The Alcarria is a nice country where people do not want to go." However, being from Alcarria hadn't affected his ability to learn or teach. His students had never met anyone who they considered as learned as Doctor Ortiz. They were in awe of his broad range of knowledge and of what he had experienced in his travels throughout Europe.

The Latin class dragged on. The other students struggled to memorize the irregular verbs they were considering. Bartolomé's mouth participated in the singsong of the memory work, but his mind was elsewhere. It really didn't matter if he paid attention at that moment; he already knew the material they were supposed to have memorized. He was a good student and usually interested in his studies. He had picked up Latin quickly when first introduced to it, and showed an ability to learn new languages easily. To challenge him, Doctor Ortiz had given him more work than the other students and then had introduced him to Greek. When he had begun to read Greek with the help of a Greek-Latin lexicon, Doctor Ortiz had continued to challenge him by having him learn Hebrew. Doctor Ortiz hoped that if Bartolomé applied himself to the study of languages he might someday contribute to the Church in the way Erasmus had with the publication of the Greek New Testament in 1516 or Cardinal Ximenes had when he published, in 1517, the *Alcala Polyglot Bible* that contained Hebrew, Greek and Latin texts of the Bible. However, Bartolomé had expressed other ideas—specifically about studying law.

Bartolomé had not thought much about the Inquisition before. It was remote from his life as a student preparing to attend university. Watching the inquisitors come into the city the previous day, and reading the proclamation started him thinking in new directions. He wanted to know why the things that had been banned by the Inquisition were wrong.

"Bartolomé! Pay attention." said Doctor Ortiz, slapping his pointer on the table to bring Bartolomé back to the class.

"Sorry Sir, what were you asking?"

"I did not ask you a question, Bartolomé; we have now completed our review of the verbs. I suggested that we turn now to study Fuchs' *Herbal*. Bring your stools over here, and sit around me, so that you can see the prints."

The four students gathered round his table where he held open the large book and started to explain the characteristics and uses of a number of the herbs. Doctor Ortiz was very good at illustrating his lessons and called on his personal experience to make them interesting. He told them how one herb, Feverfew, had been used by a monk to clear up his headaches when he was in the scriptorium and how Plantain had been rubbed on the burns of a soldier whose flintlock had backfired.

After they had learned about six or seven of the plants, Doctor Ortiz closed the book and said, "I was thinking that we would go on a field trip Saturday morning, if this rain lets up. You should learn to identify some of the more common herbs in their dormant state—especially those with useful roots and leaves. It is easier to recognize them when they are flowering but you should be able to identify them at any time of the year."

Two of the students groaned. Francisco said, "Why do we have to learn to identify these plants? We can buy them at the apothecary. What use is it going to be for me to know how to collect them in the field? I am not going to be a doctor. I am going to join my brother as a soldier and fight the French!"

"Francisco, learning botany is not a waste of time. Even if you are a soldier, you will find this study useful. You could be on the battlefield with a wounded friend and knowing about botanicals could save his life. Also this kind of study expands your thinking and makes you curious about life."

"The only life I'm curious about is the kind that walks on two legs, has nice breasts, and smiles in a pretty face!" The other boys laughed.

Doctor Ortiz ignored the boy's comment and said, "Ok, I will make Saturday's field trip optional. You don't have to come unless you *want* to."

In general, Doctor Ortiz held classes on Saturday morning, but sometimes he let the boys have time off. He was not a strict disciplinarian and tried to cultivate in his students an interest in learning and an ability to construct clear, logical arguments, rather than beating facts into them. He believed in the importance of memorization but balanced his lectures, and the routine of memory work, with debate and discussion.

Bartolomé was the only student who indicated that he wanted to go on the field trip. The other boys did not tease him for wanting to go. He was never pretentious with them and they considered him their close friend. They did not envy his scholastic abilities. They respected him for being an exceptional student, while still being able to share fun times with them.

After lunch, the class addressed the other subjects for the day including rhetoric, logic and mathematics. They never studied music. Doctor Ortiz had made it clear when Juan Garcia, Bartolomé's father, had contracted with him, that he had no ability in music. This was one of the seven liberal arts that Bartolomé would have to learn elsewhere. In fact, his total inability to sing was one of the reasons he had never gone into the Church.

Bartolomé applied himself to his studies for the rest of the day and the next, and did not think any more about the Inquisition.

On Friday evening, he asked his father if he needed him to do any duties around the workshop on Saturday. "Doctor Ortiz wants to take us out of the city to learn to identify herbs."

"That is fine, I won't need you. However, when you return, can you break up some of the larger pieces of charcoal and bring in a few more pails full?"

"I can do it right now — and could I borrow the horse tomorrow? Doctor Ortiz will likely want to take his donkey, and we can go farther if I don't have to walk all the way."

"You may use the horse, but please be back by three o'clock. I have been asked to go to your grandfather's for the evening and the horse should be allowed to have a few hours rest before I go."

Bartolomé changed into some old clothes and went to the shed in the courtyard to break up the largest pieces of charcoal. Even though he tried not to make too much of a mess, everything including himself was covered in black dust. By the time he had finished, he was ready for a hot bath. Unlike some of his peers, he did not think it was a sign of masculinity to take as few baths as possible. His father had taught him, from the time he was a child, that it was only an oldwives' tale that taking baths caused illness. Since he was a little boy, being reared by his father, he had always liked stepping into a tub of hot water on a cold evening and then rubbing down with a clean linen towel.

The next morning the rain had finally stopped, but it was still overcast and cool. This would be a good day to go searching for herbs.

Bartolomé met Doctor Ortiz at nine o'clock. Doctor Ortiz had his donkey, Flor, ready for the trip. He did not use a saddle, but had placed a blanket over the donkey's back. He also had a pair of old leather saddlebags that he had draped over the rump of the donkey. When Doctor Ortiz sat on the donkey, it was a comical sight. Doctor Ortiz was of average height, but Flor was somewhat smaller than a typical donkey, and the Doctor's feet almost touched the ground. Bartolomé had to bite his tongue to keep from laughing as Doctor Ortiz, with a creaky struggle, finally settled on the back of the donkey.

They headed north of the city. There were wilder, unfarmed, areas in that direction where they could look for herbs. As soon as they had left the city, Doctor Ortiz said to Bartolomé, "I don't want you to think that I was ignoring your questions about the Inquisition on Thursday. I was being careful not to discuss the prohibitions of the Inquisition with the other students. Cambranes, in particular, is not discreet. He might say the wrong thing at home or with his friends. In a spirit of enquiry, we might discuss a subject, and then find that we are called up on charges of heresy. I was hoping that you and I would find some time alone to discuss this matter, but I didn't want to suggest that, as it might have been misunderstood. When I proposed this field trip,

I was certain that if I made it optional, Cambranes, Francisco, and Diego would not want to accompany us. They think we are out studying herbs, and so we shall, but we can also discuss the latest pronouncement of the Inquisition."

Bartolomé was silent as they rode slowly toward a new-growth wood on the edge of a stand of virgin pines. This area was once part of a large estate that had been farmed until about two centuries before when the plague struck the city. The area was hilly and the soil rocky in places, so it wasn't as attractive for farming as the wide plateau lands between the two river valleys to the south. When they arrived, Doctor Ortiz showed Bartolomé how to identify a few of the more common herbs including: Eucalyptus Leaf for coughs, Marjoram for headaches and sore joints, Petitgrain for upset stomachs, and Red Thyme for improving bodily water flow.

They sat on a large rock under a massive pine and unpacked their lunches. Bartolomé had brought a wedge of his favourite cheese made from a blend of cow, goat and sheep's milk mixed with spices; a loaf of wheat bread; and a flask of red wine. Doctor Ortiz preferred oatmeal-based breads and the zest of a pure Manchego sheep's-milk cheese. They were seated contentedly in the shade of the pine eating their lunches when Bartolomé asked, "Why is the Inquisition so against the teachings of Luther?"

"Luther's teachings undermine their authority."

"In what way?"

"Among other things, he wrote against buying indulgences and the immorality of many in the priesthood."

"But how could the Inquisition object to someone pointing out problems of immorality. One of the priests at Santa María la Antigua was caught with a girl from the orphanage. Everyone just laughed at it. I heard a number of people say, 'We cannot fault him, and everyone does it.' How can I go to confessional knowing that he lives in open sin? I lost all respect I had for him!"

"You are right, Bartolomé; there is much of this type of behaviour within the Church. There are many honest and upright priests and monks, but it seems that we hear of more and more who are lascivious."

"How can the Inquisition be against cleaning this up?"

"They agree that there is a problem. They just don't like it being pointed out in the way Martin Luther has done it. They want to deal with it through their own process."

Bartolomé was silent for some time. Then he asked, "Why would they be upset at his speaking against indulgences? Only a superstitious person can believe that by paying a few maravedís he can be excused for robbing someone."

"I can't argue with you on that. How did you come to understand this?"

"My father has always said that indulgences do nothing more than line the cloaks of the bishop."

"He is right, and he has also hit on exactly the reason the Inquisition wants to suppress Luther's teaching."

"It requires large sums of money to finance the curia and their political intrigues. The Pope needs ways to raise money. Kings throughout Europe are also trying to find ways to fund their armies and exploration and are confiscating taxes and revenues that used to be designated for the Church. England is a prime example where the Church has lost many of its sources of funds since King Henry VIII confiscated many of the Church's properties. Indulgences are a way for the Church to raise money that the king cannot have access to."

"But the Church is fooling the people. That is wrong!"

"There are many in the Church who defend indulgences by the good they do for the Church and the individual."

"How could they help someone? They only fleece him!"

"The person who purchases an indulgence obtains a sense of forgiveness."

"But it isn't real."

"Yes, but he *feels* it is real."

"Do you believe that? Are you defending the use of indulgences?"

"No, but I cannot stop being a teacher. I am helping you think from another person's perspective."

Bartolomé didn't ask any more questions. He had heard more than he could absorb all at once, even in this short conversation, and wanted to think through all the new ideas. They continued exploring the woods and found a few additional interesting herbs before returning to their animals that had been enjoying the fresh grass.

On the ride back to the city Bartolomé asked, "How can we decide between what the Inquisition and Luther teach?"

"You have hit upon the key question of the Protestants, those like Martin Luther who are the enemies of the Inquisition."

"What do you mean?"

"They ask the question in a different way, 'What is the final authority for deciding between truth and error?'"

"How do they answer the question?"

"They say that the final authority is the Bible. All teachings and opinions must be judged against the clear teachings of the Bible."

"But doesn't someone have to interpret the Bible? What does the Church teach?"

"The Church holds that there are other equal authorities, including the collective interpretation of the church fathers and the pronouncements of councils."

"Could a church council make a mistake?"

"Do men make mistakes?" They both laughed, even though Doctor Ortiz had not intended his comment to be funny.

Bartolomé was silent again. He needed to think more about the matters of truth and authorities. So, student and teacher rode side-by-side slowly into the city and parted in different directions. Bartolomé took his father's horse to the stable near their house where they rented a stall. He unsaddled the horse and gave her some grain and a brisk rubdown. Before he left the stable he made sure she had some fresh water, and then walked slowly back to his father's goldsmith shop. This had been a far more instructive day than he would have ever imagined.

Chapter 2
(Valladolid, 1554)

The next day, Sunday, October 21st, was dry, but the clouds hung low and thick. Bartolomé looked forward to meeting his friends later in the day, if it didn't start raining again, but he didn't skip Sunday morning mass. He liked going with his father, and looked forward to hearing Father Martinez's homily. He had been preaching a series on the miracles of Jesus. Bartolomé liked the way the priest made the miracles so real. After hearing about the miracle of the loaves and the fish, Bartolomé had almost expected to see his father continue to cut pieces from the loaf of bread they had had for lunch and fill the table full with piles of bread.

Bartolomé's stepmother, Damiana, did not accompany them to mass. She claimed that she had a headache. Bartolomé didn't believe her. She seemed to have little interest in attending services and avoided going as often as she could. He didn't care about her not coming with them. She would have just complained about everything—that the homily was too long, the building too hot or cold, the Sanchez's children too noisy ... Bartolomé liked the peace and calm of the sanctuary. After the final blessing, he would sit quietly and watch all the people leave.

That Sunday, however, Father Martinez did not deliver a homily. Instead, he said that he had been instructed to read a pronouncement. He started to read it. Bartolomé's mouth filled with dust and his stomach began to ache. It was the same pronouncement that had been posted on the church doors the previous Thursday. Since many people could not read, all the priests in the city had been instructed to read it to their congregations. Bartolomé noticed that Father Martinez was reading it in a dry and formal manner. He kept his head down and didn't look up, making his voice almost inaudible. This is not how Father Martinez usually read the Scripture passages. He read from the Latin Bible with great enthusiasm and after he had read a passage, he would always paraphrase it in Spanish so that those who did not know Latin could understand what had been read.

At the end of the service, Bartolomé felt sick. He got up from his seat as quickly as he could. "What is the hurry?" Juan asked, "You are usually the last to leave the church."

"I read that pronouncement when it was posted on Thursday. I don't like it. Hearing it read spoiled the service. Father Martinez didn't want to read it.

Where is Christian charity? It is full of anger and hate."

"I agree with you. I don't like it either. I have read a few tracts written by Martin Luther and I have to admit that I found what he said took me in paths I had never walked before. I have been giving his ideas much thought."

"What in particular did you find interesting?"

"He spoke about man's will being bound to sin and not being able to repent without the work of God's grace. I think that the Church does not like that view because they place considerable emphasis on the merits of works of penance. Penance is tied up with the confessional and indulgences. By these the Church binds us and robs us."

"Father! You should be careful. What you are saying are the very things that the proclamation condemns. Someone might hear you and report you to the Inquisition."

"I know. We have to keep our mouths shut, but they cannot keep our minds in darkness."

"You mentioned tracts by Martin Luther. Do you still have them?"

"No. It is not safe to keep them, even when they are well hidden. You never know who might discover them, including your stepmother. I passed them on to a trusted friend. I won't tell you whom I gave them to. We have to be careful that we don't know too much about who is interested in Protestant teachings. If we know too much, we have more to reveal. One other thing — be careful what you say around your step-mother. When I first encountered Luther's writings, she became very upset with me. She is not sympathetic to questioning the beliefs of the Church."

"What does she care about the teachings of the Church?" replied Bartolomé, almost with a spit.

Juan didn't respond, and they walked together in silence for a few minutes. Bartolomé had, again, been given much to think about. First, his conversation with his tutor on Saturday and now this conversation with his father had begun to open up entirely new ideas he had never considered before. He began to wonder if the Church could be seriously wrong in its condemnation of Protestant teachings.

They had a quiet lunch together. Damiana remained secluded. Bartolomé thought, "I was unfair to her this morning. She may really have a headache. It isn't like her to miss a meal." Under his breath he mumbled, "God, forgive me for judging her. Help me to be kinder to her, like Jesus was kind to those who mistreated him. Amen."

After lunch, Bartolomé took his fishing pole and looked up Francisco, "Do you want to go fishing?"

"For salmon or girls?" Francisco replied with a smile.

"Francisco, all you think about is girls!"

Chuckling he said, "Is there anything else?"

Bartolomé replied, "It is late in the year for catching salmon; we might find a few in the river. What I had in mind was sitting on the bridge over the Rio Pisuerga and watching the *people* go by."

"You mean watching *girls* go by."

"Well — sure we can watch for them, you might even get to see Marina! But what I *really* was thinking was that we might see some of the royal family, maybe even Don Carlos, or other interesting people go out for a ride in the country."

"Sure, sure, you are just pretending that it isn't girls you want to watch. You are hoping that Isabel will be there. I have seen you eating out of her hand. I'll be out shortly. I have to tell my mother where we are going and get my fishing pole. Have you eaten? I'll bring some food."

They sat on the wall of the sturdy bridge, built in 1074 by the Castilian Count Ansúrez, the official founder of Valladolid, and dropped their lines into the water. There was little hope that they would catch anything because of the churning torrent of muddy foam stirred up by the week of rain. In reality, they rarely caught anything. The purpose of coming to the bridge wasn't to catch fish; it was to meet their friends.

It wasn't long before they spied Marina and Isabel coming out of the city.

"Look Bartolomé, the girls are on their own — without a chaperone! What a great chance to talk with them without having to worry about a report going back to their parents."

They pretended to ignore them, and the girls started to walk by on the other side of the road. Of course, that was too much for the boys and Francisco said, "We have to get them to come over."

"Well, think of something quick, or they will walk past!"

Francisco called out, "Look Bartolomé, you have a huge fish on your line." The girls stopped.

"No I don't," said Bartolomé.

"What is — Oh it is caught on that big rock. Hah, Bartolomé has caught a rock!"

Bartolomé's line wasn't caught on anything, but Francisco's ploy had accomplished its purpose. The girls had come across the road to their side of the bridge to see what was happening.

"Hi Marina, hi Isabel," said Francisco. The girls curtsied but didn't say anything immediately. They stood watching Bartolomé bring up his line. Francisco was better at starting a conversation than Bartolomé. Bartolomé tended to shyness, particularly when Isabel was present. Francisco didn't want to lose the opportunity to talk with the girls. They would leave if he didn't start a conversation. He thought quickly and said, "I hear that Prince Felipe was married to Queen Mary of England in July."

"That is old news!" said Marina haughtily. She turned her nose up and looked over her shoulder, "We have known about that for weeks! Trust boys to know nothing about weddings." They all laughed.

"Bartolomé," asked Isabel, "have you decided yet where you are going to go to university?"

"Not yet. I plan to speak to my father this week about it. I am torn between Valladolid and Paris."

"I hope you stay in Valladolid."

"Why? Paris has such a good reputation." He totally missed her point, the blush on her face, and the inflection in her voice.

She recovered quickly, "It would not be a good time to be travelling to Paris with the constant threat of war between France and Spain."

"You are right, but I am not really afraid," he said with masculine bravado. "And it is probably worth the risk to attend the best university in the world."

It had worked; a conversation had been started. Within a minute or two, they were all talking freely as good friends about school and the latest gossip about the nobility. They avoided, not by design but probably from a degree of fear, discussing the recent pronouncement of the Inquisition. However, it was not going to be possible to avoid considering that unpleasant topic.

They had been talking for about a quarter of an hour when they saw a crowd forming at the western edge of the bridge. The crowd started to approach them where they were standing in the middle of the bridge. In the midst of the crowd, they saw two Benedictine monks with serious scowls on their faces and a young man being escorted by two soldiers. By the appearance of his clothes and tonsure, they guessed that the young man was a theology student at the university. He probably lived in the cheap housing just outside the city on the road to Leon.

Bartolomé recognized one of the young men in the crowd and called to him, "Miguel!" He stopped and came over to the four of them. Bartolomé introduced him to his friends, "This is Miguel. His father and mine have travelled to Seville a few times together on business." The young man and boys nodded to each other. The girls curtsied.

"What is going on?" Bartolomé asked.

"The Inquisition has arrested a student for heresy."

"What heresy?"

"I don't know all the details, but I was coming back into the city and was on the road near the house where he was arrested. I saw the monks bring out a number of books. I heard them mention the name Martin Luther. I also heard talk of something they called the *Augsburg Catechism* or *Confession*, or something like that. I don't know what that is, but they told him he had books that were banned by the Church. They are taking him for examination."

Bartolomé said to them all, "It hasn't taken long for people to start reporting heretics."

Miguel responded, "That was what the Inquisition was expecting. We are supposed to report anyone we suspect of heresy to our priest in the confessional or to one of the inquisitors. They have promised that they will keep our names secret if we report anyone."

Bartolomé swallowed hard and went pale. He was thinking of his father, who had told him only that morning that he had read tracts by Luther. "But if someone can report another person and keep it secret, there could be abuses! What if someone didn't like another person and reported him as a heretic out of spite?"

"The inquisitors will examine each case carefully and make sure that the person really is a heretic. There is no need to be concerned. They are only interested in false doctrine polluting the Holy Church. Their examinations will let them know soon enough if the report was false. Don't worry, they will be fair."

Bartolomé wasn't at all sure that that was true. He was filled with a fear worse than what he had felt when he was six years old and had slipped off the bank into the Rio Pisuerga and his father had scooped him out before he could drown. The thought of people being arrested on false charges made him start sweating. He was even more afraid of what would happen to someone who really did have a banned book, or believed a forbidden doctrine. He swallowed hard again, and watched the crowd pass.

Miguel turned to follow the crowd. Bartolomé looked at his friends, "What I have read and seen scares me. I know nothing of what went on in the past with the Inquisition; it is never talked about. I have a sense that we are going to see bad times in this city and in Spain."

They all nodded, and Isabel said, "You may be right, but you had better be careful what you say. We are not permitted to speak against the Inquisition. Both the Pope and the Holy Roman Emperor, Charles, authorized its investigations into heresy."

After what they had just witnessed, they had no more interest in conversing on the bridge, so they headed back into the city. It started to rain heavily again and Bartolomé was soaked to the skin through his cape, before he could reach his house. He burst into his father's workshop and stripped off his outer garments and stood shivering by the fire—but it wasn't just the weather that had made him cold.

After he had changed into dry clothes, Bartolomé and Juan walked over to visit Bartolomé's grandfather. They went together every Sunday evening to spend a few hours with him. Sometimes Damiana accompanied them. She really liked Juan's father. In fact everyone did. He was kind and always interested in what people were doing, and he told the funniest stories.

Today Damiana was not home when Bartolomé returned from the incident on the bridge and he wanted to go as soon as possible to visit his grandfather. They decided not to wait for Damiana, since she was visiting one of her friends and they did not know when she would return.

Andrés Garcia welcomed them into his bedroom with a wide smile. He was comfortably well off. He had been a successful wheat merchant who had become rich through his wide trading network of contacts that covered the Mediterranean world and even extended into Great Britain and the Baltic countries. He was one of the budding capitalists who had made Valladolid into the financial capital of Spain in the early sixteenth century.

In spite of his money, he was not well, and Juan had suggested a few times that he move into their home. However, Andrés would not agree to the move. He always said, "I like living in my own home. Also, I would just be a burden if I lived with you. Here I have servants who can care for me." So Juan had stopped pushing for the move, and visited his father as often as he could.

If someone had asked Bartolomé what his grandfather was like he would have said, "He is a saint." He would not have mentioned that his grandfather was partially paralyzed from apoplexy; he would not have thought to inform the person that his grandfather needed assistance to do the most basic of tasks, including dressing himself. These things faded from the focus of attention within a few minutes. Bartolomé had never met anyone whose presence could make other people feel so comfortable and warm.

Andrés asked Bartolomé about what he was learning in school. He was particularly interested in the field trip to learn about herbs. Bartolomé tried not to bring up the unsettling topic of the arrest on the bridge. Andres looked at Bartolomé and said, "Something is bothering you, Bartolomé. What is it?"

"Am I that easy to read, Grandfather?"

"Like an open book! No, not really, but I have known you like a son for sixteen years, and I can tell when you are troubled."

"I saw a man who possessed Lutheran books being led away by monks and soldiers. It was quite unsettling."

"When I was your age, I saw similar things. Isabella and Ferdinand were strong proponents of cleansing Spain of heresy. I did not like Jews and Moors continuing to practice their false religions, but I did not like the way they were treated. I don't know what the right way is for dealing with falsehood, but I am sure that the Inquisition is not the way."

Bartolomé was relieved that his grandfather felt the same way he did. He started to relax. Andrés saw the tension leaving his face and body and changed the subject to help Bartolomé forget about what he had seen earlier in the day. "So tell me, Bartolomé, have you seen Isabel recently? Are you going to marry her?"

Bartolomé turned a bright red and replied, "Grandfather! No! I did see her today on the bridge, but I haven't asked her to marry me. We had a pleasant talk. I do like her, but — I don't know what it is — something about her just doesn't seem right."

"Is she just a silly girl?"

"No, far from it! If anything, I think she is too serious. I am afraid that if I had a wife like her I would be sad all the time. If — when — I marry, I think I need a wife who will be different from me. I want a wife who — I don't know how to describe it. Isabel is like a donkey. I don't mean her looks; she is very pretty. It is just that she is — boring. What I want is a wife who is like a fine Spanish horse, beautiful, with spirit and a zest for life!"

"Well, you set high goals. I hope you find what you are looking for. I think if you had met your mother you would have felt that she was like that — isn't that true, Juan?"

Juan didn't answer, but at the thought of his first wife, he just smiled.

The discussion turned away from girls and, mercifully, the Inquisition. They spent the rest of the visit discussing international events. Andrés was remarkably well informed for an invalid. Bartolomé wondered how he found out about all that was going on in the rest of Europe, but didn't want to show his ignorance by asking.

Juan and Bartolomé started to leave. However, before they could depart, Andrés called them both over to his bedside and asked them to kneel. With his right hand, he lifted with considerable strain his left hand onto Bartolomé's head, then placed his right hand on Juan's head, and blessed them. He had never done this before. Bartolomé's eyes started to mist over. He thought of Jacob blessing his sons, and hoped, with a pain in his gut, that this didn't mean that his grandfather was going to die soon.

Chapter 3
(Valladolid, 1554)

One evening, later that week, when the other students had left for home, Bartolomé stayed to finish a Greek translation in his workbook. He wanted an opportunity to speak with his tutor in private. "Doctor Ortiz," he asked, "why are the inquisitors accompanied by soldiers when they go to rebuke a heretic? Wouldn't it be better for them to meet with him, discuss his false opinions, and bring him around to their way of thinking? Or, wouldn't it be better for them to pray that he would see the truth? Why do they use the king's soldiers to enforce their beliefs?"

"Bartolomé, you ask difficult questions. I can see that the four years you have studied with me have not been wasted." He smiled and continued, "I have pushed you to think clearly. You don't accept beliefs just because I have pounded them into your thick skull. I am grateful for that. Most good teachers want their students to be able to think, not just repeat by memorization. However, I am also frightened for you. You are asking dangerous questions."

"What can be so dangerous about my questions?"

"I am afraid where they might lead you. You might become curious about Protestant teachings and start to read the writings of Luther or Calvin."

"If I do, I will be very careful not to get caught."

"That is not as easy as you might think. The Inquisition has its spies everywhere. Even parents betray their own children." Bartolomé was silent.

Doctor Ortiz continued, "Should heresy be stopped?"

"I don't think so. Shouldn't a person be allowed to believe and think whatever he wants to?"

"Should a person be allowed to kill another person, rob another, rape another ..."

"Of course not! We shouldn't hurt others. The Ten Commandments speak against those sins."

"But the Ten Commandments also speak against idolatry and blasphemy. If a Turk or a Jew worships a false god shouldn't he be stopped? They are breaking the Ten Commandments just as much as a thief, an adulterer or a murderer."

"What if the person prays privately to his god?"

"What if he teaches others and leads them away from the true God, should he be stopped?"

"I don't know. I'm not sure ..."

"When you consider the Israelites in the Bible, God told them to destroy the pagan idolaters in Canaan lest they led astray the children of Israel. How is it any different today? Spain is God's nation.

The Church must maintain its purity. If a person is not willing to repent of idolatry, shouldn't the king's officers punish him for unbelief?"

"But — I don't know — you are asking harder questions than I asked you!"

Doctor Ortiz smiled, and concluded, "Our country has a tradition of punishing heretics. In the twelfth century, Pope Celestin III sent Cardinal St. Angelo to Alfonso II, king of Aragon, to order the Vaudois to leave our territories. About one hundred and twenty-five years ago musketeers drove followers of Wycliffe from Biscay. Then Isabella and Ferdinand, at the request of Sixtus IV, instituted an inquisition against the Jews and Moors and appointed Thomas Torquemada as their first Inquisitor General. The proclamation of last week against the Protestants is just a continuation of that tradition."

"I understand that, Sir, but what if the beliefs of the Church are wrong? It is possible that the Protestants are right. If they are right, would it be proper for the monks to punish a Protestant? It wouldn't be heresy if what they believe is in fact the truth."

"You have brought us back to the same point we were discussing on Saturday."

"I need to know! How can we tell who is right? What is truth?"

"Pilate, when he was examining Jesus, asked the same question. He asked it out of cynicism. You ask it with a thirst for a real answer. Don't stop looking, don't stop asking — until you are certain of the answer — but be careful. You can never be sure whom you can trust."

Bartolomé collected his schoolbooks and put them in a leather satchel. He wished his tutor a "good evening" and headed home. It was growing dark, and threatening to rain—again!

A gloom hung over the city that week. It certainly was caused by the overcast skies—but it was also the result of the Inquisition. They arrested more people: clergy, students, merchants, nobles, men, women, and even children. It was hard to determine exactly how many were arrested, as everything about the workings of the Inquisition was kept secret. The rumour going around was that they held about twenty-five people in their makeshift jails.

About a week after his evening discussion with Doctor Ortiz, Bartolomé was sitting at the table with his father and stepmother. It had been a pleasant enough meal. Damiana even showed an interest in what Bartolomé was studying and asked, "I heard you speaking the other day to your father about the moon. What has Doctor Ortiz been telling you?"

"He says that he believes that the moon is a globe of solid matter much like earth. He told us that someday men will be able to show that there are mountains and river valleys on the moon."

"What hogwash!" she replied.

"Doctor Ortiz may be wrong," Bartolomé replied, restraining his anger, "but he could also be right. There have been a number of interesting discoveries over the past two hundred years. We should not be closed to new ideas and what might be possible."

"Bartolomé, I am not unwilling to consider new ideas, but I don't think you should be listening to fairy tales. Stick to more important things on this earth — like how to turn lead into gold. Then we can be rich!"

"I don't want to study the transmutation of metals. I want to study law, gain a letrado position, and eventually become an ambassador for the court of Spain."

At this point, Juan interrupted their conversation and asked, "That reminds me, have you thought more about university? From what I can tell, you have mastered your studies well."

"Yes father, I have given it thought. I would like to go to the university in Paris."

"I am not surprised, but what are your reasons for coming to this conclusion?"

"Valladolid is becoming oppressive. Even though the university in Paris is older than our own, it seems it is more open to new ideas. There is no room in this city, or its university, for people who think and ask questions. Also, I want the opportunity to see new places. I am bored of living in Valladolid." What he didn't say, but thought, was that it would also be good to get away from both his stepmother and the Inquisition.

Damiana spoke up, "But it will be so expensive. We could put the money to better use here."

Juan replied, with mild scorn in his voice, "I can afford to send Bartolomé to Paris if he really wants to go. You have enough clothes to outfit a harem, what more could you need?"

"Keeping up with the latest fashions is so difficult and expensive. We have to be respectable!"

Juan glared at her and she said nothing more to express her covetousness. He asked, turning to Bartolomé, "What makes you think that Paris is more accommodating of critical thinking?"

"Doctor Ortiz," replied Bartolomé, "says that any school that can produce a Jean Calvin and Ignatius Loyola has to be open to new ideas. Doctor Ortiz studied in Paris in 1531 when both Calvin and Loyola were students there."

"He has a point. I can arrange for you to start in Paris, in the New Year, if you wish."

"Thank you, Father, I would like that very much."

"I will cover your tuition and give you a reasonable allowance. I will arrange for the transfer of funds. It will be executed through a business associate of mine, Claude Lachy, in Paris."

At the mention of spending money, Damiana whimpered. Both Juan and Bartolomé ignored her.

"Father! That is kind and generous of you."

"I do not think a student should live in luxury, but neither do I think it appropriate for him to have to support himself by 'slave' labour or begging. I want you to be able to study. Promise me that you will use every opportunity to learn and that you will apply yourself to your studies."

"I will, Father. Again, I thank you. I can't wait to tell Doctor Ortiz! He will be so happy for me."

Damiana didn't protest. Even though good money would be wasted on sending Bartolomé to Paris, she would have him out of her sight. She had never liked him from the time she married Juan, when Bartolomé was eight years old. She always felt that Bartolomé begrudged her intrusion into his life with his father. The discussion ended, they left the table, and their maid came in to clear the dishes.

Chapter 4
(Valladolid, 1557)

B artolomé had been in Paris for over two years
when he received a letter from his father asking
him to return home for the summer, if he was able.
His father told him that his grandfather was ill and
might not live much longer. Andrés had asked to see
Bartolomé and had started to cry when Juan told him
again that Bartolomé was away in Paris attending
school and could not come and see him. Juan also
indicated that he had sent a separate letter to Claude
Lachy, who would release additional money to
Bartolomé so that he could come home the fastest
way possible.

Bartolomé was worried about his grandfather.
He quickly collected the travel funds, packed a small
trunk with clothes and books, and rented a private
carriage to take him to the coast. At Le Havre, he was
able to find a ship carrying English woollen cloth,

heading south toward the Mediterranean and Sicily. The captain was willing, for a fee, to drop him in Santander, the principal port of the kings of Castile. From there, he rented another coach that took him through the difficult Carrales Pass to Burgos. They changed horses in Burgos and he was back in Valladolid in just over a week. The trip had cost more than a year's worth of wages for a labourer, but his father's letter had expressed urgency, and he had supplied the funds, so he had felt justified in spending the money.

It was late in the evening, but there was still some light, when Bartolomé arrived in Valladolid on Tuesday, June 22nd, 1557. He had turned nineteen on April 23rd and hadn't seen his father and stepmother during the two and a half years he had been away. When the coach pulled up in front of the goldsmith's shop, Juan and Damiana came rushing out to greet him. After he had given them both a warm hug and the formal kisses of greeting, his father took his travel trunk from the carriage. Bartolomé thanked the driver and paid him the remaining amount he owed.

Bartolomé was relieved to be home. The journey itself had been tiring, but what had made it most stressful was his urgency to arrive. Before he did anything else, Bartolomé asked Juan about his grandfather and was glad to hear that his health had not deteriorated further since his father had sent the letter. Juan warned Bartolomé that he would find his grandfather considerably changed from when he had last seen him. He told him that he was very frail and confused. They agreed that they would visit him the next day.

After he had changed from his travel clothes and had eaten a late supper, Bartolomé sat with Juan and Damiana on their upper patio, with only a single candle as a light, and they talked for many hours. They were particularly interested in how Bartolomé's schooling was going. Bartolomé told them about the classes he had just completed, his teachers, and his fellow students. Bartolomé was pleased to be able to report to his father that he had received top honours in two of his law courses. "I also won a prize," he said, "of twenty gold francs for an essay I wrote, in French, comparing the Roman legal system to that of Charlemagne's."

"In French? When did you learn French?" asked Juan.

"Some of my professors will only lecture in French, so I had to pick up French to understand them. The French like their language. About ten years ago, they declared it the official language of the state. They think that it should replace Latin as the international language of commerce and diplomacy. They try to cultivate its use any chance they get, including funding prizes for essays. Also, I have been living with the family of Nicolas Beranjon. Your friend, Claude Lachy, through whom you send my allowance, recommended him to me. Nicolas' daughter, Symonne, did not know any Latin or Spanish and the only way I could converse with her was to learn French. It has been easy for me to learn new languages, and I became fluent in French without any difficulty."

"Ah, Symonne!" said Damiana, "Have you been developing an interest in a young woman in Paris?"

Colouring slightly, but not noticeable in the low light, he replied, "No, not really — maybe — I am not sure — I have been tutoring her. I really didn't need the extra money I earn from this, but her father asked me if I would tutor her in Latin and history. She is now fourteen. She is pretty, but sometimes acts silly. She often flirts with me and doesn't care an iota about learning. I have been very careful not to encourage her flirtations because of boarding with her family. I would not want to encourage her and end up causing offence. Tutoring her has been a good learning experience for me — if not for her. I have learned patience and how to simplify my presentation of information and how to make my points clearly. This experience helped me to write a clear and simple essay."

"What did you do with the money?" Juan asked with curiosity.

"Nothing. I thought it would be best to save it. I will likely need it to get established when I complete my studies in Paris."

On hearing this Juan said, "I am proud to have you as my son. I thank God every day for your diligence and the sensible head he has put on your shoulders."

Bartolomé blushed and responded with only a quiet, "Thank you."

Bartolomé also told them what it was like living in Paris, and particularly in the *Quartier Latin*. Juan had been to Paris a number of times on business, so Bartolomé did not need to describe the city for him, but Damiana wanted to hear all about it—especially about the latest fashions and the nobility. What impressed Bartolomé most about Paris was its size. He didn't know the exact population but he guessed that it was more than four times larger than Valladolid. This made a real difference in the life of the city. A city of over two hundred thousand people had much more activity, night and day, than did Valladolid.

After a few hours, they were all yawning and Damiana excused herself. As she left, Bartolomé thanked her sincerely for sitting up with him and listening to his stories.

Bartolomé waited a few minutes until he was sure that Damiana had gone to her bed. In a low voice, he asked his father, "Do you remember when you told me that you had read some tracts by Luther?"

"I don't recall the specific instance."

"It was the Sunday after the Inquisition posted their proclamation on the door of all the churches — before I went to Paris — we were walking home after mass."

"Oh yes. Why do you bring that up now?"

"Father, I have become a Protestant."

In the candle light Bartolomé saw a whole range of emotions, from pride to fear, flash across his father's face. "What brought you to that position?"

"In my theology classes I began to consider many things that were different from what we have been taught by the Church. We had to read works by Luther and Calvin as well as some of the recent pronouncements from the Council of Trent, and offer critiques. The discussions were often lively, and even heated. This helped me think more clearly about what is truth and error."

"I, too, have done more reading in this area and a few of us have started to study Protestant teachings together."

"Father! That must be very dangerous. What if the Inquisition were to discover you? You would be arrested."

"We know that, but for the sake of truth we are willing to take the risk. We are careful about keeping the times and locations of our meetings secret. Tell me more about how you became a Protestant."

"Nicolas Beranjon and his family are among the Paris-based Huguenots. They hold a daily time of worship after supper. Since I am living with them, I am expected to join them for worship. Nicolas reads a portion from the Olivetan French translation of the Bible. We sing a Psalm or two in French. We have French Psalm translations prepared by Clément Marot in King Henry II's court. We even use a tune written by King Henry when we sing the one hundred and twenty-eighth Psalm. Nicolas also has copies of a new, incomplete edition of a French Psalter that was printed in Geneva. A person named Louis Bourgeois wrote most of the tunes. Nicolas ends with prayer. Sometimes he asks me, or one of the other students or visitors, who are staying in the house, to pray. After that we sometimes sit for hours discussing theology."

Juan was quite impressed by this account, and said, "I am not surprised that you ended up in the home of Huguenots. My friend, Claude Lachy, is a Protestant and he probably directed you to the Beranjon family for that reason."

"Yes, I know. I have gotten to know Monsieur Lachy quite well. We go to the same Huguenot congregation on Sundays. It was formed two years ago. I was one of the founding members. We meet in a small chapel that was once part of a convent. The building has now been converted into a Latin grammar school for boys, run by Protestants."

"What in particular brought you to the Protestant position?"

"Before I left for Paris I had a number of discussions with Doctor Ortiz about how to determine what is truth and error. I had already started to think that the Bible alone must be our standard for drawing conclusions about truth. I am now convinced that any practice or belief in the area of religion, which is not explicitly endorsed by Scripture, is not approved by God and is idolatry. However, that was not what brought me fully to reject many of the Church's teachings. It was when I considered more particularly the teachings of the Church on indulgences and penance that I changed my views, or as some say, I was converted."

"I also have questioned the merit of these things."

"It was reading Luther that convinced me that salvation is not obtained by belief assisted by works as the Church teaches, and the Council of Trent has reinforced. I have come clearly to believe that salvation is obtained through faith alone. Works are the fruit of salvation, not the root."

"Very well said! You have come to a clear understanding of truth in a short time. It is now late and we must get some sleep so that we can visit your grandfather tomorrow. We can talk more about these things before you return to Paris."

Juan said a brief prayer and they went to their beds, very tired. Bartolomé thought that he would not be able to sleep because of the excitement of returning home and talking with his father. Yet, no sooner had he placed his head on the pillow than he was asleep.

Chapter 5
(Valladolid, 1557)

A narrow ray of light coming through a crack in the shutters and falling on his face awakened Bartolomé. After a quick breakfast, he and Juan walked over to Andrés' large house.

The sun was already blazing hot when they arrived. They were glad to be admitted to the shade of the house. Andrés' bed had been moved from his bedroom to the interior court of the house. Sleeping on the porch was much more comfortable than in an upper room which became too hot in summer. Andrés' servants loved him and took care to make his last days as comfortable as possible.

Juan and Bartolomé were led to the screened-off area under the portico. Chairs were brought so that they could sit by his bed. When they arrived, Andrés was sleeping, so they did not wake him. They were offered cool lemonade mixed with a little sweet red wine. It was brilliantly refreshing after the hot walk. They talked quietly while Andrés slept. Bartolomé kept looking at his grandfather. He had aged 'twenty' years during the time Bartolomé had been away. He looked very frail and he was much smaller than Bartolomé remembered.

When Andrés awakened, Juan said softly, "Father, I, Juan, am here, and I have brought Bartolomé to see you."

Andrés opened his eyes and with difficulty turned his face on his pillow to look at them. They both stood and leaned over him so that he could see them. He tried to move his right arm, the one that had not been paralyzed when he had had the stroke. Bartolomé quickly reached out, grasped his grandfather's hand, and lowered it onto the bed as he held it.

"Grandfather, I have been away at school in Paris. I have come back for the summer to visit you."

Andrés attempted to answer but could not form words. It appeared that he understood what Bartolomé had said, so he continued, "I have been studying law. I want to work for the new king of Spain, Felipe. I would like to become an ambassador and be sent to all the royal courts in Europe." Andrés closed his eyes and Bartolomé continued to tell him about his experiences at school in Paris.

At one point Bartolomé stopped talking. He thought that his grandfather had fallen asleep, but Andrés opened his eyes and looked at him with bright, focused eyes. Bartolomé took this as a sign that his grandfather wanted him to continue talking. He talked for about another hour.

Finally Juan said, "Father, you must be very tired; we will leave you now and return tomorrow to see you."

Bartolomé kissed his grandfather and hugged him gently. He saw that tears had formed in Andrés eyes and started also to cry. He turned away as Juan held his father's hand for a moment. They left. One of the servants who had been sitting outside the screened area came and tended to Andrés.

That night Andrés died.

For the next few days, Juan's household was busy with the matter of the funeral. Many of Bartolomé's friends came to see him when they heard about his grandfather's death. Cambranes and Diego were among the first to come to the house. Bartolomé thanked them for visiting and asked, "How is Francisco? I haven't had time to look him up. I was only back from Paris for one day when my grandfather died."

Cambranes responded, "You won't find Francisco in the city. He did what he always wanted to do; he joined the army. He is now training somewhere down south. I haven't heard from him in over six months."

"What happened to Marina? Did he marry her?"

"No. She is still unmarried, although I hear that her father is trying to make a deal with a nobleman to marry her off." He laughed, "She is not very pleased with that. She says she doesn't like being treated like a cow! She looks like one now."

"What do you mean? Aren't you being unkind?"

"She has gained too much weight in the last few months. I think Francisco broke her heart, and she took up eating to console herself." Cambranes laughed again.

Bartolomé didn't think it was funny, and changed the subject, "What have you been doing?"

"I decided that I had had enough of books! My father has helped me set up as a wine merchant. I have opened a warehouse down by the river. I import French and Italian wines." He boasted, "My business is already doing well and I will be a rich man soon! Then I will marry a princess!"

Bartolomé turned to Diego and asked what he was doing. He replied, "I am working as a bookkeeper for the mint. It has allowed me to put my skills in arithmetic to use. It pays well and I am able to meet all the noblemen in the city, but most importantly I enjoy the work."

Hearing about arithmetic, Bartolomé asked, "Have either of you seen Doctor Ortiz? How is he doing?"

"I haven't seen him in awhile. My parents wanted him to tutor my younger brother. He said that he would consider it after the summer. He has gone to the Pyrenees to get away from the heat."

"That is disappointing. I would have liked to look him up. I may not be able to see him while I am here. I will have to return to Paris in a few weeks to continue my university studies. Will you please tell him I asked for him, and give him my greetings?" Diego nodded. "And, please tell him that I have been enjoying my studies in Paris."

At that Diego said, "Please tell us about Paris and your studies." Bartolomé began to give them a brief account of his experiences in Paris. He didn't want to repeat all that he had told his father and grandfather, so he shortened the account considerably.

As he was telling them about the city, a young woman, accompanied by a maid, entered the house. It took Bartolomé a moment to realize that it was Isabel. He was quite surprised; she had changed considerably. The most visible change was that she was pregnant and, from appearances, due to give birth shortly. "Isabel! I hardly recognized you."

She blushed, "I am sorry to hear about the death of your grandfather."

"I didn't know that you were married."

She blushed again. "Yes, I was married about six months after you left for Paris. It was an arranged marriage. I was unhappy about it at first. Gonzalo was also not pleased about it, as he loved another girl. As it has turned out, we are very happy together and are joyfully looking forward to starting our own family. Gonzalo is a truly caring and considerate husband. I feel that God has been good to me."

Bartolomé smiled broadly and said, "Isabel! I am disappointed; I thought you were going to wait for me." They all laughed. "I am really happy for you. I truly am. I always felt that I would not make a good husband for you. I wanted you to be happy. I am so glad that you are happily married now."

Isabel had been concerned about seeing Bartolomé. She wasn't sure how he would react to her being married and was relieved at his sincere congratulations. She glowed with the warmth of their friendship.

The Garcias' maid brought out some food, and they all began to eat and enjoy being together again.

Chapter 6
(Valladolid, 1557)

O n the evening of the day after they buried
Andrés, Sunday, June 28th, Bartolomé asked
Juan if he could borrow his horse the next day to go
for a ride. He had no particular destination in mind,
he just wanted to get out of the city and clear his
head. He would miss his grandfather.

He awoke early, packed a lunch, and was at
the stables where Juan stabled the horse before the
sun was fully visible over the roof of the cathedral.
He headed southeast from the city and rode through
the farmlands to the open grasslands beyond. He rode
hard for as long as he could push the horse without
hurting it.

When it became too hot to continue, he
stopped and rested under a grove of trees on the bank
of the Rio Duero. He wasn't thinking about anything
in particular. He sat under a tree, leaving the horse

lightly tethered to enjoy the fresh grass at the edge of the water. He read from one of the books he had brought in his satchel and fell asleep with the book on his lap. After awakening, he ate his lunch.

By mid-afternoon he was heading back to the city. He did not push the horse on the return trip and it was early evening by the time they arrived back at the city.

He took the horse to the stables and gave it extra attention as he rubbed it down and fed it. The care and feeding of the horse was included in the boarding fee and was normally done by boys who worked at the stable. However, Bartolomé enjoyed the physical work and the opportunity to keep busy.

Bartolomé knew that he could not spend time talking with his father. A significant amount of work had accumulated for Juan, and he had back-orders to fulfill. He was making a complete set of silver goblets with gold filigree inlay for the new Conde Ansúrez, and he was behind schedule on their delivery. The death of his father had set him even further behind. In addition, his friends from his school days had to attend to their vocations. They were no longer students at leisure on a summer vacation. So Bartolomé was by himself and had to occupy his time until he returned to Paris.

He was getting hungry and decided to head home for supper. It was starting to get dark when he stepped through the postern door into the alley beside the stable. He was lost in thought, on nothing in particular, and walked out of the alley into the street that passed in front of the main doors of the stable.

Just as he stepped into the street, an out-of-control carriage being pulled by two frightened horses came down the street. The carriage was being dragged along the face of the buildings on Bartolomé's side of the street and scraped along the door of the stable. He flexed to jump back into the alley, but before he could move, he was hit hard by the rear edge of the carriage and thrown backward into the alley.

The carriage continued down the street making a loud racket as it bounced off buildings and over door stoops. People from the surrounding houses and shops came running out to see what had happened. One of the stable boys flew out of the postern and stumbled over Bartolomé who was lying in the alley, knocked out cold. The boy turned back to get the owner of the stable who lived upstairs. He met him coming down the stairs to see what had happened outside. The boy said, "A man is lying in the alley, hurt." The owner grabbed a couple of horse blankets as he ran through the stable, and they went to see how Bartolomé was doing. When they arrived, others from the street had started to assemble.

The owner of the stable bent over Bartolomé and said, "He is hurt badly. He is bleeding from his head, and it looks like his leg might be broken; we need a doctor." Turning to the stable boy, he commanded him, "Go fetch Doctor Mendoza, who lives on Calle de la Curraba near the cathedral, across from the apothecary's shop. Run!" The boy took off like a horse being chased by wolves.

The owner of the stable lost his patience with the crowd of gawkers and yelled at them to do something useful or move away. The horses pulling the carriage were long gone, and other than Bartolomé lying in the alley, there was nothing to see. So they started to disperse. By the time the boy returned with the doctor, there were only a handful of people standing around waiting. The owner of the stable had put a blanket under Bartolomé's head so that it was no longer lying directly on the cobblestones, but he had not moved Bartolomé.

The doctor, a man with a beard like one of the Old Testament prophets and wearing a billowing robe, commanded the boy who had called him to get a light. The boy ran into the stable to fetch a lantern. Then the doctor turned to those who were standing around the young man and said, "I am Doctor Mendoza. Step aside and let me see what has happened."

When the boy returned with a light, he held it up while Doctor Mendoza examined Bartolomé. He opened his shirt and felt his ribs. He mumbled, "Nothing broken here, but he is going to be quite sore." He cut off the damaged stockings covering Bartolomé's legs and very carefully felt for breaks. He discovered that one of his lower legs was broken. Even in his unconscious state Bartolomé winced when his leg was moved. The Doctor slowly worked his hands over the rest of Bartolomé's body, checking for other wounds and breaks. He turned to the owner of the stable, "Do you know what happened?"

"I am not sure; I was inside at the time. I didn't see what happened, but from what people said when I came out, it seems a runaway carriage clipped him as it passed. He was on the street and the blow threw him back into the alley."

"Please bring me some staves and strips of cloth we can use to make a splint for his leg."

The owner went immediately to get them.

When he returned, Doctor Mendoza said, "I am going to set his leg now, before I move him. It is good that he is knocked out, so he won't be conscious of the pain." He called one of the other men who was still standing in the mouth of the alley. He instructed him and the owner of the stable to hold Bartolomé firmly by the upper body. He slid a board under his broken leg and pulled the broken tibia into place. Bartolomé groaned. Doctor Mendoza carefully felt around the area to make sure that the pieces of bone were meshed. He then put a board on either side of the leg and bound a number of strips around all three of the boards making sure that Bartolomé's leg wouldn't slip inside of the makeshift brace. He then instructed the owner of the stable to make a stretcher out of horse blankets and longer boards and had the men help him put Bartolomé onto the stretcher.

Doctor Mendoza instructed the men to carry Bartolomé to the clinic at his house. Then he asked, "Do any of you know who this young man is?"

"He is Bartolomé Garcia," replied the owner of the stable. "He is the son of the goldsmith, Juan Garcia, who lives in Plaza del Puente Dorado. The family boards their horse in my stable."

"Are you able to take a message to his father to inform him of the injuries, and that I have taken him to my clinic?"

The man agreed and headed off. The other men took up the stretcher and carried Bartolomé to the doctor's clinic. Doctor Mendoza picked up the satchel that was lying on the ground near Bartolomé and carried it while the men carried the stretcher.

At the clinic, the doctor directed them to put Bartolomé on his examining table. He removed most of Bartolomé's clothes and washed him, paying particular attention to the wound on his temple. He bathed the wound with diluted wine, put a clean linen cloth over it, and bound a strip of linen around Bartolomé's head to hold the cloth in place. Then he asked the men to move Bartolomé to a small bedroom that was off one side of his examination room. It was a simple, clean room with only a bed, a chair, and a stand for a basin of water. There was also a small window, and a candleholder on the wall. The doctor placed a lantern on the stand and pulled back the clean sheet. They placed Bartolomé on the bed, and the doctor covered him. He still had not returned to consciousness.

The doctor thanked the men for their help and dismissed them from his clinic. He filled the basin with water and gently swabbed Bartolomé's face. A few minutes later Juan and Damiana arrived. "We have been told about the accident. How is Bartolomé?" Juan asked.

"He is still unconscious. He must have been hit hard. His head has a wound on it. It is not deep and wasn't bleeding heavily. I have cleaned that. It should heal fine. His leg was broken. I am not sure how that happened. It couldn't have been a blow, as the bone wasn't crushed. Thankfully, it was a clean break, and I have reset it. I think his leg may have buckled under him when he was hit. He was also hit hard in the ribs. None of his ribs appear to be broken, but they are badly bruised. He will find recovering from these bruises to be the most painful part of his ordeal. He will think they will never heal, and at times when he breathes hard or laughs, he will feel pain. This will continue for many weeks, but they will heal. I recommend that you leave him here for a few days. He will be taken good care of here, and it is better to let his wounds heal than to move him unnecessarily."

Juan agreed to the doctor's proposal and asked to see Bartolomé. Bartolomé was still unconscious and there wasn't anything Juan or Damiana could do to help him. Juan held Bartolomé's hand for a minute and then said, "We will return in the morning and see how he is doing."

Before they left, Juan asked, "How much do I owe you for this care?"

"My standard fee schedule is posted on the wall. I am always uncomfortable talking about fees. Of course, I have to charge something, as I make my living as a doctor. But to me, being a doctor is more than a living. I do my work as a service because I care about helping others."

Juan was impressed by his attitude, "If this accident had to happen to my son, I am glad he is in your care."

Both men smiled. It was clear that they were going to be friends. Juan and Damiana departed, and Doctor Mendoza cleaned up the clinic, checked again on Bartolomé and left him to sleep off his injuries.

Chapter 7
(Valladolid, 1557)

The next morning at breakfast in their apartment above the clinic, Doctor Abram Mendoza said to his daughter Catalina, "I brought in a young man last night who was hit by a runaway carriage. His leg was broken, and he took quite a blow to the head. He was unconscious. Can you please look in on him, bathe his head, and see if you can bring him around?"

"Yes, Father. Thank you for giving me a chance to help with another of your patients. It is satisfying to be able to serve in this way. Does that mean I don't have to spend time on my Latin today?" she asked with a bright smile.

"Sorry. No. You can tend to him *before* your tutor arrives."

Catalina went down to the clinic to get a basin. She filled it with fresh water from the well in the courtyard of their house and got some cloths. She quietly entered the room where Bartolomé was lying. She laid the basin on the stand.

Before she sat down, she looked at the patient. What she saw startled her. She had pictured a short, stocky man with the usual Spanish features: dark hair, olive skin and a beard or at least a moustache. Instead, she saw a well-built man with naturally light skin, with a slight coloration from the sun, and light sandy coloured hair. His eyes were shut so she couldn't see what colour they were. He was covered by the sheet but appeared to be taller than most of the men she knew. He lay completely still.

She gently pulled back the cloth from his forehead. She looked closely at his clean, bold face. It was rugged and handsome with only a day's worth of light stubble. She was immobilized looking at it, but she finally recalled herself, wet the cloth, wrung it out, and began gently to wipe Bartolomé's face and forehead. She must have continued this for half an hour. She lost track of time and was going through the motions of cooling his face by rote. She continued the routine: wet the cloth, wring it out, wipe, wet the cloth ...

Somewhere in this process, Bartolomé had awakened. His head ached and he felt like he didn't want to open his eyes. He had no idea where he was and couldn't, at first, recall what had happened to him. He felt a cloth with cool water being placed on his forehead, and his face being wiped. When he finally opened his eyes, his vision was blurry. He could just make out the form of a person sitting beside him. He realized that he was in a bed, but he could tell by the feel that it was not his bed, either at school in Paris or at home in Valladolid. He closed his eyes and tried to think. Slowly he organized his thoughts. He remembered his trip on the horse and went through the rest of the events leading up to his leaving the stable. Then he recalled the wagon coming at him. That is the last he remembered. He tried to reposition himself in the bed and winced in pain. It was the searing pain in his chest that brought back full clarity of mind. This time, when he opened his eyes he saw before him a beautiful sight.

He was looking at an angel—a tall, thin girl of about sixteen. She had long, straight, black hair—shiny like the inside of a hard lump of coal just split in two. She wore a white scarf tied under her hair, and a pale green shift. Her skin was smooth like vellum, and almost the same colour. In his thoughts, he exaggerated the whiteness. She had a small sharp nose, thin pale lips, large dark eyes with full eyelashes, and fine black eyebrows. The contrast between her dark hair and light skin was striking. She was distracted and didn't notice that he was looking at her. He almost held his breath he was so entranced. He could only stare.

Finally, her eyes caught his. She saw light brown eyes staring at her. They shone like the wet skin of a horse that has just run through the river. She realized that he had been watching her for some time. Her bright blush was pronounced. She overcame her embarrassment in a moment and said, "So you have decided to come back to the world of the living?"

He blurted out, "What happened to me? Where am I? Who are you? Does my father know where I am?"

"Please! One question at a time," she laughed, "You are in a doctor's clinic. My father is the doctor. He was called to the scene of an accident, and he brought you here last night. From what he told me, you had a severe bang to your head and your leg was broken. How are you feeling?"

Bartolomé reached up to his head and felt the bandage.

"My head hurts, my side hurts very much — and — ouch — my leg hurts — but other than that, the rest of my body seems to be unhurt."

Catalina smiled and said, "So you hurt all over? My father didn't say anything about your side. You can ask him what happened. He will be down to see you shortly."

"What about my father and stepmother?"

"I don't know anything about them. You can ask my father."

"What is your name?"

"I am Catalina. My father is Doctor Abram Mendoza. Who are you?"

"I am Bartolomé Garcia. My father is Juan Garcia. He is a goldsmith. I am studying law in Paris. I came home for a few weeks this summer because my grandfather was gravely ill. He died last week."

"I am sorry."

"I am too, but it is for the best. He had had a stroke about five years ago, and he was suffering greatly because of it. I will miss him. He was the kindest man you could ever know. He told the funniest stories, and he was always interested in what others were doing and thinking. I know there is no one who is more generous and caring — except of course — Jesus."

At the mention of Jesus, she smiled. Her smile was so radiant that Bartolomé thought someone had brought a light into the room.

"What is Paris like? Have you learned French? Tell me about your studies!" she asked.

He told her a little about what it was like to live near the university, about the school and his studies, about the food, and the interesting things he had done and places he had seen. She asked many questions; her curiosity was insatiable. She asked him what he wanted to do after he completed school in Paris, and he told her of his plans to become an ambassador for the Spanish throne, and travel.

At this, she responded with eagerness, "I would like to travel too. I feel so confined living in this city. I feel like a bird in a cage. I want to get out of here and see what is happening in Pisa and Rome or even Constantinople. I would like to see Jerusalem. I want to travel to London. I want to go to the Americas. In fact, I want to travel to China!"

"How do you know about all these places?" asked Bartolomé.

"Just because I'm a girl doesn't mean I don't know anything!"

Her spirit and energy thrilled him. He smiled with difficulty. "I was not thinking that a girl couldn't know these things, I was wondering how *you* had learned them. I had a tutor for many years who made me consider the many possibilities in this world. It is rare that I meet someone who thinks beyond his or her immediate daily life."

"Oh! I am sorry for jumping to a conclusion. Your tutor sounds something like mine— Master Tomé Diaz de Montalvo. He brings me interesting books. One book I read recently is Marco Polo's *The Description of the World*. I loved reading that book. After I had finished it, I wanted to leave home the next day and retrace his steps. I wanted to go meet the great Kublai Khan. I wanted to sail around India. I wanted to escort a Blue Princess to her marriage with a Persian ruler."

Bartolomé was in awe. He had never met anyone like Catalina.

They continued to talk until Abram interrupted them. He came into the room and seeing Bartolomé awake asked, "How is my patient doing?"

Catalina replied, "He awoke a little while ago, and we have been talking. Father, this is Bartolomé. Do you know he is a law student in Paris? He wants to be an ambassador, he wants to travel ..."

"My dear, slow down!"

"But, Father, he has been to Paris and I have not been farther than Leon in years!"

"Catalina, you need to go upstairs. Your tutor has arrived. I think you will tire out our patient. It is time for him to rest."

"Father?"

"Yes?"

"I don't think Bartolomé has had any breakfast."

At that, Bartolomé realized that he hadn't eaten since lunch the day before. He suddenly felt quite hungry and remembered all his pains.

"I completely forgot," said Abram, "Bartolomé, are you hungry?"

"Yes, Sir, I am. I was heading home for supper when I was hit by the carriage."

Abram turned to Catalina, "Would you please go get him some food before you start your lessons?" He went back into the clinic.

Catalina ran upstairs quickly calling out, "Mother! Bartolomé needs breakfast!"

Susana responded, "Who is Bartolomé, and why does he need breakfast?"

"Bartolomé is the patient whom Father brought in last night. He has just awakened and hasn't eaten since yesterday. He is so handsome, and he's hurt. Father asked me to get something for him. Do we have anything left from our breakfast? What can I take him?"

"Catalina, slow down. We can find him something."

Susana helped her put together a plate of food, and gave her a goblet of fresh goat's milk. This would serve a patient better than wine.

Catalina rushed down with the food as fast as she could go without spilling it, and brought it into the bedroom. She laid it on the stand, flashed Bartolomé a smile, and left.

Bartolomé called out after her, "Thank you, angel of mercy!"

He winced as he leaned over to reach for the plate, but was glad for the food and drink. Abram came back into the room as he was eating and explained to Bartolomé the extent of his injuries and how he had been brought to the clinic. Bartolomé asked about his parents and was relieved to hear that they had been at the clinic the night before.

"I think you will have to stay here for at least a week, before we can safely move you. That will give your leg and ribs time to begin healing. In a few months you will heal completely."

"I have nothing pressing here. I will have to return to Paris by early August to continue my studies, but I have nothing to do right now. I returned to Valladolid to see my grandfather. He died last week." Abram expressed sympathy and asked about his grandfather. As much as Bartolomé loved his grandfather, he was getting tired of telling of the events since he had returned to Valladolid.

After eating breakfast, Bartolomé rested. He dozed until his father and stepmother came to visit him. They were relieved to find him awake and fully alert. Bartolomé explained to them what had happened until he was hit by the wagon, and Doctor Mendoza filled in the remainder of the details for the second time. He then excused himself, as he had patients coming to his clinic and had to make house calls. Juan offered Damiana the chair, and he stood beside the bed.

"How are you feeling this morning?" Juan enquired.

"Sore, but happy that nothing too serious happened. Doctor Mendoza says that I should heal without any problems. He appears to be quite capable and diligent."

"Yes, thank God that he was nearby when you were injured and was able to set your leg while you were still unconscious. I have heard of people whose broken bones were not set correctly and had to have the bones broken and reset. I believe that I heard that this happened to Ignatius Loyola, and he limped with one leg shorter than the other until he died last summer."

At first, the conversation lagged. It was difficult for Juan and Bartolomé to think of anything new to say without getting into the subject of religion. They felt uncomfortable discussing it in front of Damiana. They were particularly cautious about discussing anything to do with Protestantism in her presence. Bartolomé had already told them all about his time in Paris, and they knew all the details of the accident. After a lengthy silence Bartolomé said, "Doctor Mendoza has a daughter who helps him in the clinic. She was wiping my face with cool water when I awoke this morning, and brought me my breakfast."

Damiana perked up with interest, "What is she like?"

"An angel," replied Bartolomé.

"Have you ever seen an angel?" she smiled. "How would you know?"

"She is what I think an angel in human form would look like — at least a female angel. All the angels in the Bible have male form, don't they? If there were female angels they would look like her."

"What is her name?"

"Catalina."

"That is pretty. Do you like her?"

"It is interesting that you should ask. While I was lying here before you came, I was thinking about how much I like her, and I only spoke with her for a few minutes. There is something about her that I find very attractive. It is her spirit — her energy — her love for life. She told me all about her dream to travel. She also seems to be intelligent. She told me that she has read about the adventures of Marco Polo. Now that I think of it, she *must* be intelligent! I have never heard of a Spanish translation of *The Description of the World*. She must have read it in Latin, or she can read the Lombard language."

"So — a pretty girl with spirit and brains," said Juan. "Is that what you have been looking for?"

"I don't know what I have been looking for. I just know what I don't like. I don't like silly girls, and I don't like ones who can see no farther than the window in their bedrooms."

Juan changed the subject, "I have begun to execute the estate of your grandfather. He left you a significant legacy."

"He did? I never expected that!"

Damiana said, "He left the bulk of his estate to your Father, but he gave me a personal legacy also. I didn't expect it any more than you did."

Without any disrespect or rancour, Bartolomé said, "You will be able to buy many nice clothes with that money, won't you?"

"Yes. In fact I was thinking that your father and I could visit you in Paris, and I could buy some new outfits there."

Bartolomé was sure that he would not look forward to that visit, but he said nothing.

"Bartolomé, you will have to decide what should be done with your legacy. For example, do you want to buy a house here? Your grandfather left you enough money to buy one of the finest in Valladolid. Or you could invest it in a ship going to the Americas. I know some merchants who finance ships sailing from Cádiz. Or I could arrange to have Claude Lachy place it with the Anton Fugger in Augsburg."

"Father, I am surprised at you. You know how the Fugger empire has been built on usury and financing the Popes' activities. Let me think about it. I know I have no interest in buying a house in Valladolid. I will not want to live here permanently after I have finished my schooling. If I am working here for King Felipe as a letrado, it will be only temporarily until I can work myself into a position where he will send me to distant lands. I will eventually want the money available if I settle down somewhere else. My inclination, at the moment, is to have you invest it through Monsieur Lachy, but not with the Fuggers!"

Chapter 8
(Valladolid, 1557)

Catalina went to meet her tutor after bringing Bartolomé his breakfast. She found Master Tomé Diaz de Montalvo in her father's library, which she used as her classroom. Master Diaz was sitting at the large table in the middle of the room reading a scribed codex that was from Abram's collection of books. He was a small man and had to put a large book on the chair to sit on, in order to read the book resting on the table. He was not a monk, but he appeared to have a tonsure. His bald head, like a giant egg, poked out of a nest of scruffy hair. His perpetually red face had three prominent features: a nose much too large for his face, bulging eyes, and a growth on the left side of his chin. He always looked like he had just run away from a feral dog or had spent the night under the spout of a barrel of Bordeaux claret.

When Catalina had first met him, when she was about eight years old, she started to cry and told her father that she didn't want him as her teacher. It took gentle cajoling to get her to face the man. Her father even bribed her with a promise of a Venetian-glass mirror. She finally relented and began attending classes with Master Diaz. Six years later, she had nothing but respect for his wide-ranging knowledge and abilities as a teacher. She thought he was superb, although she had nothing to compare him with. She had heard from her friends about their tutors and felt that hers was the best. Not only could he make any subject interesting, but he had also channelled her natural curiosity and given her a discipline to apply herself to learning which was rare among girls and women in her generation, particularly in Valladolid and Castile.

Today she was torn. She would have liked to continue talking with Bartolomé, but she also wanted to study with her tutor. He had told her that they would pursue their studies in anatomy, not Latin as she had pretended earlier. They had been using Andreas Vesalius' *De Fabrica Corporis Humani* that they had borrowed from Abram's library. Today they were actually going to dissect a frog! Master Diaz had already covered a small table along the wall of the library with an oiled cloth, and had set out surgical instruments and two dead frogs. He led her over to the table. He stood on a stool and showed her how to hold down the frog and slice it open. She tried the same thing on her specimen. She was not at all squeamish. This was no different than slicing a chicken. She was glad that they were doing this kind of study that day. She was not sure she could have concentrated on a history lesson with Bartolomé lying in the room below.

After a few minutes Master Diaz said, "Catalina, I sense that you are distracted. Is something bothering you?"

"Nothing is bothering me. Father brought in a patient last night who was hit by a runaway wagon. I cared for him this morning before I came here."

"Is he badly hurt? Will he die? Is that why you are concerned?"

"He has a broken leg, a sore side, and a wound on his head, but he will recover."

"I am glad to hear that, and under your father's care there is little doubt he will get well. So why would you be concerned?"

"I didn't say I was concerned. You have jumped to a conclusion."

"I have taught you too well. Very good! I have made an assumption. Let me recast my question. If he will recover completely, why do you appear to be distracted?"

"Can't you guess?"

"Well, it isn't over his health that you are distracted, so it must be — dare I ask — Do you like him?"

"I don't know if I like him — yet — but I do know that I find him interesting. He is the first boy — young man — I have ever felt comfortable with. We discovered quickly that we have many interests in common. He is a student in Paris who came home for the summer because his grandfather was gravely ill. He died last week."

"Who is he? What is his name?"

"He is Bartolomé Garcia. I believe his father is a goldsmith."

"I know of the family. I think I also know of Bartolomé. A good friend of mine, Doctor Pedro Ortiz de Tendilla, may have been his tutor. If this is the young man I am thinking of, Doctor Ortiz has spoken highly of him and believes that he is one of the best students to come out of Valladolid in many years. He has a bright future ahead of him, whatever he decides to do."

Catalina flushed and felt hot. She didn't realize how much she already liked Bartolomé and to hear this praise of him made her feel almost proud.

They continued their dissection. When Catalina had almost completed taking the frog apart, she suddenly asked, "Can you teach me French?"

"I am not an expert in French, but I can get you started in the rudiments, and we can learn it together. But why? Why would you want to learn French?"

"Bartolomé has learned French while in Paris. It would be fun to speak with him in French."

"Fine. We can work on French. With your grasp of Latin, which I must say is impressive, you shouldn't have too much trouble picking up a third language. I will look in the bookstalls near the cathedral and see if I can find some books that will help. I don't know if any Spanish-French dictionaries exist. Undoubtedly French-Latin ones do, but those are for

French students to learn Latin. I will also see if I can find a basic French grammar."

"No! I want to start today! Now! Teach me French now!"

"But you cannot learn French this morning. It will take time."

"But we can start!"

Master Diaz shook his head. He knew that Catalina would follow through. Her determination was strong. Once she started to learn French she would not stop until she knew it fluently. He was in for a challenge himself just to keep up with her, let alone keep ahead of her. He looked around in the library and was quite surprised to find a French-Latin edition of the *New Testament* printed by Estienne in 1551.

"I cannot imagine how your father would have included this *New Testament* in his library, but it will be a perfect book for you to start learning French."

"I recall that my father bought a number of cases of books from an itinerant bookseller last year. He said it was part of the library of a French nobleman from Languedoc who had died the year before. I heard my father tell my mother that he had looked at a few of the books and that they alone were worth the price of the entire lot. My mother is always gently chiding him for buying so many books. She has pointed out to him that he even buys duplicates and doesn't know it. He probably doesn't even know he has this book on his shelves."

They spent the rest of the day working on French. Susana brought them some lunch and was perplexed when she heard them struggling through French verbs.

At the end of the day, Master Diaz bid farewell and Catalina went to find Susana. She was numb from the hard work. She collapsed into a chair beside her mother.

"I am tired!"

"What were you studying? When I came in at lunch time, I couldn't understand a word you were saying."

"I have decided to learn French. I am learning it from the Latin."

Her mother shook her head, and said, "You are always up to something. Why would you want to learn French?"

"Mother, don't laugh — because Bartolomé knows it."

"This Bartolomé has caught your fancy. I haven't even met him yet; you only met him this morning and now you want to learn French because he knows it? You are so peculiar at times." She smiled and held out her hand to Catalina who held it and stared into the air.

Abram was out. They ate supper without him. They were served by one of their household servants.

"Mother, who took Bartolomé his lunch?"

"María did."

"Has he had supper yet?"

"No. I haven't sent María down with food to him yet."

"I will take it down to him. María, can you please prepare food for the patient downstairs? I will take it to him."

María smiled with understanding and nodded to Susana who returned a wink.

"What are you two agreeing about?" asked Catalina with mock indignation.

"Nothing dear, nothing at all."

Catalina took the food down to the clinic. She gently knocked on the bedroom door. There was no answer. She knocked again a little harder. She heard some rustling, and knocked again.

"Who is it?"

"It is I, Catalina."

"Come in ..."

She entered. "I'm sorry, I had fallen asleep. Your father told me to rest as much as I could. I tried to read one of the books I have in my satchel, but I couldn't concentrate. It is a little hard to read with sore ribs complaining each time you move."

"Are you in pain?"

"A little." He gave her a brave smile. "Your father has assured me that I will heal, but it will take time. I am so glad to see you. Thank you very much for bringing me my supper. Do you have time to stay with me while I eat? Talking with you will help me forget about my injuries."

"Yes, I can stay."

"What did you do today?"

"I dissected a frog."

"You did what?"

"I cut up a frog to learn about the parts of its body. Master Diaz, my tutor, has been teaching me anatomy, and we can see how muscles, organs, and bones are put together inside of a frog. Master Diaz says that there are some similarities to the way humans are put together. Since we don't have access to human cadavers to dissect, we have to use animals to see how a body functions."

Bartolomé was disgusted and swallowed hard, "Would you watch, or participate in, a dissection of a human?"

"I don't know. I have been around my father's clinic since I was a little girl. I have watched him do amputations and clean bad wounds and sew them up. I have also looked at pictures in his anatomy books such as *Fasciculo di Medicinae* and in his *Tabulae Sex* wall charts. I think I could watch a dissection."

Bartolomé frowned and seemed to go a bit green, and said, "Please, let's talk about something else. I have to eat my supper. I didn't realize what I was going to hear when I asked you about your day."

She decided at that moment that she wouldn't tell him about her beginning to learn French. She would wait until she knew more French and surprise him when she could carry on a conversation with him in French, even if it was not perfect.

Catalina smiled and stars twinkled on her teeth and in her eyes. The room brightened and Bartolomé relaxed. He continued to eat his supper, and Catalina asked him if his parents had come by. He nodded. She saw that his mouth was full and said, "I suppose I had better talk and let you eat. If I ask you questions you will die of hunger." She laughed and Bartolomé tried to smile with his mouth full, but it was not easy to smile politely with a mouthful of food.

While Bartolomé ate, Catalina told him about herself. "I was born in 1542. Do you know what is special about that year?"

Bartolomé shook his head, 'no'.

"It is fifty years after Colon sailed to the new world! My birthday is July 7th. I will be fifteen soon!"

"Fifteen, I thought you were at least sixteen!"

"That is flattering. Girls like to be considered older than they are when young, and women like to be thought younger than they are when older. We are never happy with our age as it is." Bartolomé smiled and started to laugh. He had to hide a wince of pain from Catalina. "What about you? How old are you?"

"I was born on April 23rd in 1538. I am nineteen. I don't know of anything special that happened in the year of my birth — except that my mother died."

"So you never knew your mother."

"No, she died giving birth to me."

"What do you know about her?"

"She was a Basque. My father says that I resemble her. That is why I have lighter hair and a lighter complexion than most of the people living in the city. My father used to tell me that she was the most beautiful woman in the city. My grandfather told me that she was full of life."

"When did your father remarry?"

"When I was eight. I have not been able to get along with Damiana. She was never mean to me, but I have always found her to be insincere. All she cares about is having the latest fashions. Please don't misunderstand me, I like it when girls dress up in nice clothes and take care to look pretty. I don't like slovenly, slouchy girls. But they shouldn't be obsessed with outdoing each other."

"Well, I see that you have strong opinions about what you like in girls. How do *I* measure up?" she said with a twinkle.

He grinned and replied, "I am still assessing that. I will let you know!"

"Oh you!" she said, and pretended to hit him.

He told her more about his time in school. She was particularly interested in his time as a *bajan*. He told her how he had learned to avoid the hazing, and having to do cleaning for the older students. He described, without boasting, how he had successfully debated his way into the senior ranks. They both laughed until his side was aching. They continued to talk until Abram came in, sent her upstairs, and helped Bartolomé clean himself and get comfortable for the night.

Catalina's father told her afterwards that he didn't mind her spending time with Bartolomé. Patients recover more quickly when they don't lie around thinking about their aches, but she mustn't tire him too much. She promised she would not tire him, and went to bed. That night she dreamed that she and Bartolomé went together to London to see the new queen, Elizabeth.

Chapter 9
(Valladolid, 1557)

About a week after Bartolomé's accident, Abram and Juan arranged to have him carried on a firm stretcher to the goldsmith's house. Bartolomé was not going to be able to go upstairs for at least a month, so Juan and Damiana had brought a bed down to the workshop and had hung drapes to create a closed-off area beside the window to give Bartolomé a degree of privacy. The bearers placed Bartolomé carefully onto his new bed. Abram told him, with a degree of sternness, "You are not to try to do things on your own. You are not to get out of bed. You do not want to do anything that will disrupt the healing processes, particularly in your leg."

Bartolomé nodded and replied, "I appreciate all your help. I will not do anything to cause damage. Sir, can Catalina continue to visit me, when she is able? I find her company very agreeable."

"Yes, she may visit you, *if* she is willing, has finished her school work, and isn't needed in the clinic. I believe that she finds your company agreeable also, but I leave that decision to her. I will relay your request."

"Thank you, Sir. Again, I thank you for all your assistance."

Juan beckoned to Abram to come to the back of the workshop. They settled the payment for the services rendered.

Bartolomé planned to spend the rest of the day reading one of the books he had brought from Paris. He was feeling much better and thought he could resume studying. He didn't expect that his father would be able to sit with him; he had work to do in the workshop and business to attend to in the city. Bartolomé forced himself to concentrate on what he was studying by reading aloud; but even so, his mind kept wandering, and he saw Catalina's face coming out of the pages of his book and heard her voice on the other side of the drapes.

By mid-afternoon, it was so hot in the workshop that Bartolomé gave up trying to read; he found it too uncomfortable to do anything. The drapes were pulled back and the window was open, but there was no breeze. Wincing, he took off his shirt and lay on the bed in an uncomfortable sweat. Juan had gone out once he had rested after the noon meal. Damiana was upstairs on the patio in the shade, or out visiting. The household maid had been sent to do some shopping. Bartolomé swatted a fly, and just as he began to feel lonely and frustrated with being confined to a bed in an empty house, he heard a knock on the door of the workshop. He couldn't see who was knocking since the door was on another wall, away from his window. He hoped it was Catalina. He yelled, "Come in."

It was Catalina! His heart started to race. He was no longer lonely. Hope revived.

Catalina came over to the bed and stared down at him, "You look really uncomfortable. Where can I find a basin, cold water, and some cloths?" Bartolomé told her where she could locate the items upstairs and indicated that there was a well in the courtyard. She returned in a few minutes and started to wipe the sweat from his face and upper body. He luxuriated in the attention. "You are truly an angel of mercy."

"Well, I can't very well leave you in this uncomfortable position, can I? I would care for a dog if it were hurt. Shouldn't I care for you?" She grinned.

"Well ..."

"Why didn't your parents set up your bed on the back porch? It would be so much more comfortable!"

"They probably weren't thinking about what it would be like to have to spend the entire day in bed. It is generally cool enough at night, so they just didn't consider how hot it would get. Although my father should have realized this, because during the summer he sets up a furnace under a lean-to beside the shed in the courtyard."

"I will tell them what they must do for you when they get back."

"I won't have to worry about anything with you caring for me, will I?"

"You be quiet or I'll stuff this cloth in your mouth." They both laughed.

Later, when his father returned, they discussed moving Bartolomé's bed to the porch. It was a major undertaking without men to carry him. He first moved to a chair while Juan and Catalina struggled to relocate the bed. Then Bartolomé slowly worked his way to the porch on makeshift crutches while they both kept him from falling. They all sat exhausted for a few minutes and then Juan returned into the house to ask that drinks be brought out. Catalina stayed for supper and ate with Juan and Bartolomé on the porch. Juan asked her about her father's training and work as a doctor. He was quite impressed by her knowledge of her father's work. They also learned more about her schooling. Juan had heard of her tutor, Master Tomé Diaz de Montalvo, and was pleased to hear that he and Bartolomé's tutor, Doctor Ortiz, were acquainted.

It was late before they realized it, and Catalina excused herself. Juan said that he would walk her home. She said to Bartolomé, "I will return tomorrow to visit you." They departed.

Bartolomé slept well in the coolness of the porch and had a good day reading. Although as it got near the time for Catalina to arrive, he became anxious with anticipation and had to stop reading. She came as promised.

"Are you more comfortable today?"

"Very much. Thank you for your help yesterday. Could you do me a favour and hand me my satchel?"

She brought it from the table and handed it to him.

"Thank you," he responded. "I have a present for you."

"Why? What for?"

"Don't be so coy. I could say that it was because of the help you have been giving me, but it is really because this is a day that is special to you."

She beamed in excitement, "You remembered! You remembered that it is my birthday." She bent over and kissed him quickly on the forehead. "Thank you!"

He pulled out a new book and gave it to her. She didn't open it immediately. She kept turning it over in her hands and looking at it. She rubbed the leather covers and binding, put the book to her face, and breathed deeply. She traced the gold leaf on the cover.

"Bartolomé! This is amazing! Where did you get it?"

"I ordered it from a printer while I was in Paris. It was printed in Venice."

"A Spanish *New Testament*. I didn't even know that such a thing existed. Thank you, thank you!" She again kissed him politely, this time on the cheek.

She sat on the chair near his bed and leafed through it reading quietly out loud from various passages. Then she started to cry.

"What's wrong?" Bartolomé asked.

"Nothing. I am so happy. It is incredible to hear Jesus speaking Spanish! It is beautiful. You have no idea how much I love this gift. You are so kind. Thank you."

"You are truly welcome. You don't have to thank me again. It pleases me to make you happy."

She read a few more passages aloud and leaned back in her chair, with tears streaming down her face. Bartolomé said nothing.

In a few minutes, she looked at him and smiled. He said to her, "I don't want to spoil your birthday, but I do have to tell you something important."

"What?" She almost yelled, as panic hit her face.

"I don't know what you are thinking. Why are you so concerned?"

"I don't know, I was afraid that you might tell me something about yourself that would make me very unhappy, like you had to go away tomorrow — or worse — you are engaged to a girl in Paris and you have been meaning to tell me."

"Nothing like that! I have to stay in bed for another few weeks. I will try to head back to Paris in early August. And, no, I don't have a fiancée in Paris. I have never yet met a girl whom I truly liked enough to consider marrying — until last Tuesday, of course." They both blushed.

"What is it then that you must warn me of?"

"You are not allowed to have that book."

"But, haven't you given it to me?" Her face was perplexed.

"Yes, it is yours to keep forever. However, you aren't allowed to own it."

"Why not? What do you mean?"

"Because it is illegal in Spain to possess a translation of the Bible. Only approved Latin versions of the Bible are permitted. This *New Testament* is even more hated by the Church of Rome because it was translated by Juan Perez, *charge d'affairs* to Charles V."

"I don't understand what you are saying. How can it be wrong to have a Bible in Spanish?"

"Before I answer that question, take a moment to read the preface."

Catalina read the preface to Bartolomé, and then said, "The translator makes a point of showing that the holy Apostles wrote in the language of the common people."

"Why do you think he emphasized this?"

"I'm not sure, just tell me! I feel like I am in school!"

"The Church, particularly in Spain and the Papal States, has tried to keep people from getting access to the Bible in their native languages. In Saxony, Helvetia, England, and even France, the Bible is becoming quite common in the vernacular. Where the Inquisition is strongest they confiscate and burn translations and lock up people who have Bibles."

"Well, I will hide this book from them and they will never know that I have it."

"That is exactly what I wanted to warn you to do. You must be extra careful that you never let anyone know you have it. It will have to be our secret."

"It will be." She looked with great reverence at the book in her lap. She would guard it carefully like a precious jewel.

She asked Bartolomé, "Why does the Church not want us to have the Bible in the *vernacular*?" She liked that word. It was new to her and it sounded so educated.

"The Church claims that we can't understand it without the help of a priest to interpret it."

"That is stupid! I can read the Bible in Latin. What difference does it make if it is in Spanish?"

"You and I are the exceptions. Most people in Spain cannot read Latin. The Church doesn't want people reading only the Spanish version. They are concerned that each person will form his own opinions and there will be chaos."

"They want to keep the people in ignorance?"

"They don't view it that way. They have seen what has happened in Friesland, where many sects and heresies developed, like the Anabaptists founded by a man named Menno Simons. They attribute this development to allowing even the ploughboy to be his own interpreter."

"You don't agree with this do you? I guess not, or you wouldn't have been carrying around this book."

"No, I don't agree with it. I believe that when we accept the Bible in its clear literal sense, not allegorically, we won't end up with such wide variations in opinion."

She thought for a minute, "You have made me think harder than Master Diaz does. I don't want to think so hard this evening. Let's talk about something else. I promise I will be careful to keep this gift a secret. Thank you again." She wrapped the book in a shawl that she had brought with her in case the evening grew cool.

Catalina started to read her *New Testament* every morning before she appeared for breakfast. She kept it hidden in the bottom of her dowry chest.

Chapter 10
(Valladolid, 1557)

Over the following weeks, a number of Bartolomé's old friends came to visit him. Father Martinez also came at least once a week to see how he was doing and to pray with him. Catalina continued to visit almost daily. She didn't come on a few occasions because her father needed her help or her mother asked her to spend some time at home. Overall, they were indulgent in allowing her to visit him and gave her more liberty than would normally have been permitted between a young man and a young woman. They did not object to her visiting him alone, because of his injuries and because he seemed like a potentially suitable match for their daughter, should anything develop from their friendship. They also had discussed the fact that he would be returning to Paris in a few weeks. They were certain this would cool off their infatuation with each other.

Bartolomé and Catalina often talked of travel. Catalina brought a book she was reading that she had found in her father's library. She had not asked to borrow it, nor had she told him that she had it. They took turns reading to each other out of it. It was entitled *Historia General de las Indias* and was written by Francesco Lopez de Gomara, private secretary to Hernán Cortés. They were both fascinated by the account. What made the reading more interesting was that it was an illegal book. Prince Felipe had ordered all copies of the work confiscated and had imposed a penalty of two hundred thousand maravedís on anyone who reprinted it. They shared this secret just like the secret of the *New Testament*. Their love of books, learning, and dreams of travel bound them closer every day.

At one point in their discussions Catalina said, "I prayed to Mary and Saint Peregrine for you last night so that you would heal more quickly. It would be fun if we could walk by the river or about the city. I like being with you, but I am getting tired of sitting here everyday."

"Catalina, I thank you for your prayers. I don't want to offend you or hurt you, but I don't agree that prayers to Mary or the saints have any value."

She was quite surprised at his comment. "Why not? Some beautiful prayers have been written for the saints and they were so compassionate, especially saints like Martin of Tours and Peregrine Laziosi."

"I know that many of the saints lived godly lives and they were truly helpful to many people, but that doesn't mean that praying to them has any value."

"But don't they ask the Father and Jesus to help us?"

"That is what many in the Church have taught for centuries and was recently reinforced at the Council of Trent, but it is not what the Bible teaches."

"What do you mean?"

Catalina had been keeping Bartolomé apprised of her progress in her reading her *New Testament*, so he asked, "Where are you now in your reading of the *New Testament*?"

"I read from the Acts of the Apostles this morning."

"Have you, so far, found anything in the Gospels or Acts that give you an example of someone praying to a saint or to Mary?"

"I don't recall reading of it."

"You won't find one instance in the New Testament where someone prays to Mary or any of the Apostles. In fact, when the Apostles or an angel get any form of worship they immediately command the person to stop and direct him to Jesus."

"But ..."

"Not only are there no examples, but also there are clear statements to the contrary."

"Such as?"

"Pay close attention when you read the Apostle Paul's letter to Timothy and you will find the following words: 'For there is one God and one mediator between God and men, the man Christ Jesus.' The point is that there is only one person to whom we are to pray and who can act on our behalf, that is Jesus."

"I will look for that."

"I know that it is difficult for us who have grown up in the Church of Rome to see that praying to Mary or one of the saints has no value. As you read your *New Testament* keep asking yourself what other assumptions you need to question. You will be surprised how many of the things we have been taught are not in the Bible at all."

"I had no idea! Isn't the Church telling the truth?"

"In some areas her interpretation is accurate. In other areas the priests teach traditions that may or may not be accurate. And, in some areas, their teachings are just wrong. It has reached the point that the leaders in the Church don't want to admit that they could be wrong. That is one reason why the Inquisition was formed—to protect the Church from being challenged."

"That is terrible!"

"It is, but in this city and country it must never be discussed, except with people you are sure you can trust."

"Does that mean that you believe you can trust me?" She gave him a sly smile.

"Yes!"

"Thank you, you can."

Chapter 11
(Valladolid, 1557)

One Saturday, about a week before Bartolomé was to return to Paris, Catalina planned to spend most of the day with him. She had been unable to visit him for two days.

On the prior Thursday, her father had asked her to help him during a house call to a bedridden elderly and poor widow. He felt that her presence would reassure the woman. The woman also needed some help with her personal hygiene. Susana usually helped her husband with this kind of matter, but Susana was ill and could not go. Since this request came up suddenly, Catalina sent a note excusing herself to Bartolomé via one of the boys who lived on her street. He was disappointed that he wouldn't see her.

On the following day, Friday, Susana was feverish and Catalina felt that she should stay with her mother. So, when Saturday arrived she was feeling a bit guilty for not having visited Bartolomé since Wednesday. She had convinced her tutor on Friday that she should have Saturday free all day, even though she usually had classes on Saturday morning. She told him that Bartolomé was leaving, and she really did need to see him. Master Diaz was indulgent with her and agreed. In fact, he didn't mind having the day off himself.

To make matters more complicated, she had been neglecting her best friend Margarita. Since she had met Bartolomé, she had spent almost every free moment at his house and had not spent much time with her. She decided that she would ask Margarita to go with her to visit Bartolomé.

Margarita was happy to share her time with Catalina by visiting Bartolomé. She was curious about the young man who had caught the fancy of her dearest friend. She had heard much about Bartolomé from Catalina and wanted to meet him. Catalina encouraged her to bring along the musical instruments she could play.

They arrived at Bartolomé's house unannounced. Bartolomé was in the workshop sitting in a chair pulled up to the table. He had his broken leg extended under the table. His new crutches were leaning on the table beside him. He was now able to get around the workshop on his own, but still could not climb the stairs without help. The girls knocked but didn't wait for an answer before entering. Catalina was so familiar with Bartolomé's home by this point, from having visited so often, that she acted as if she were a member of the family. Her exuberant personality let her assume actions without them being considered presumptuous.

The girls entered the workshop and found that Bartolomé had been reading.

"Bartolomé, I have brought along my best friend, Margarita, to meet you. I have been so busy lately that I haven't seen much of her, and I was feeling guilty."

Bartolomé gave Margarita a friendly smile and asked the girls to sit. There was only one chair by the bed. The girls had to drag another, heavy, chair from the other side of the porch. This was followed by an uncomfortable moment of silence. Bartolomé said with a broad smile, "I am sorry I am not much of a gentleman." They all laughed, but then no one spoke for a moment.

Bartolomé looked from one to the other. Catalina was wearing her usual white scarf and a simple dress. Margarita had brown curly hair that surrounded a round olive face. Her nose was flat and wide; she was large-bosomed and looked like she tended to plumpness. She wore an expensive multi-coloured dress with many layers. Bartolomé thought, "She will be fat before she is twenty." He immediately regretted having thought such a thing about a guest in his house.

The silence seemed strange to both Bartolomé and Catalina. They felt so comfortable together and usually fell into talk immediately, but with a third person present, they both felt different. Catalina finally broke the silence, "Bartolomé, I am so sorry I wasn't able to come see you the past two days. You did get the messages, I hope?"

"Yes, I did, and thank you for sending them," he responded gently.

"My mother has been unwell."

"Catalina, you know that I look forward every day to your coming to visit and, truthfully, I missed you very much when you did not come. I am glad, however, that you were able to help your father with the widow, and care for your mother. I would have been disappointed in you if you had let our friendship become so demanding of your time that you could not help your parents."

A huge weight lifted off Catalina's shoulders. She knew that Bartolomé was sincere in what he said, and was so relieved that he hadn't been jealous. She thought he was quite mature in handling this situation. It was at that moment that her strong fondness for Bartolomé turned into a true and deep love. She realized that he was the person she could cherish for the rest of her life. She became flushed and felt like she must have turned bright red. It took all of her will power to say, "Thank you Bartolomé, you are so understanding." What she really wanted to do was hug him, kiss him, and tell him that she would love him forever.

Bartolomé asked, "What do you think is wrong with your mother?"

"We think she has the flu."

Bartolomé had heard about the influenza epidemic that was sweeping through Europe and asked if her mother's illness might be connected. Catalina indicated that it probably was. Then she told Bartolomé about some of the ideas people had about how the flu spread. "My father does not agree with those ideas. He says they are founded on superstitions. He agrees with the belief of someone named Girolamo Fracastoro, that diseases generate something like seeds that can be transferred from one person to another. My father is convinced that someday this will be shown to be correct."

Bartolomé found Doctor Mendoza's views quite interesting. He was not superstitious as many of his contemporaries were, and found Fracastoro's idea intriguing. So he asked, "But how can this be? What do the seeds look like?"

"My father says that the seeds are there, but they are just too small for us to see. I have heard him discussing this with other doctors. They don't agree with him, but he uses two illustrations. He speaks of a person whose eyesight has diminished and can no longer read. He says the letters are still there, but the person just cannot see them. However, when he puts on spectacles, he can see the letters. He says it is the same with things that are far away. Likewise, someone with bad eyesight cannot see distant objects, but the objects are still out there. My father says that someday someone will invent spectacles that will see the seeds of disease."

"That seems reasonable," Bartolomé replied.

Catalina continued to explain, "My father believes that the flu seeds are spread by body fluids when someone coughs or sneezes on someone else. That is why he now tries to keep sick people isolated from others so that the seeds won't be passed along. He also emphasizes washing one's hands regularly as a means of lessening the spread of the seeds."

Bartolomé particularly agreed with that. "I agree with keeping clean. My father always taught me to keep my hands clean."

"Aren't our fathers just so agreeable!" she said. They both laughed.

Bartolomé realized that he and Catalina were doing all the talking. Margarita appeared interested, but Bartolomé made a point of drawing her into their discussion. He was sensitive to Margarita's presence and wanted to make her feel comfortable.

Bartolomé turned to Margarita and said, "Tell me about yourself."

"What do you want to know?"

"Well, the typical questions would include asking about your parents, if you have any brothers or sisters, or about your schooling. Instead, I will ask you some different types of questions. How did you meet Catalina? And what is your favourite book?"

Margarita was intrigued by the questions. "First I will tell you a bit about my family. I have two brothers, one older and one younger. My older brother is a pompous fool. He is set on inheriting all of father's wealth and acts like he is a prince. My younger brother spends all his time figuring out how to torment me."

"Well, you have nice brothers!" They all laughed.

"My father is the alcalde of Valladolid. I don't have a private tutor as Catalina does. Both of my brothers share the same tutor with me. The only thing I have in common with my brothers is that we hate attending classes, and we hate our tutor."

"Well, I see you have had a good school experience." Margarita giggled. "I am sure glad I didn't ask questions about your family or schooling! So how did you meet Catalina?"

"We have been friends since we were little girls. At one time, we were next-door neighbours. Even when Doctor Mendoza took his family to Salerno to do additional medical studies for two years, Catalina and I wrote our childish letters to each other. We keep no secrets from each other. So, you had better be nice to my best friend or I will know all about your bad behaviour!" Bartolomé made a face with mock fear and threw up his hands to protect himself. Margarita broke into an infectious laugh, and it took them a moment to become serious again.

Bartolomé pursued his question about Margarita's favourite book. He found that asking this question helped him learn a considerable amount about a person. This impressed Catalina. She was pleased that he was interested in learning more about Margarita.

Margarita's answer disappointed Bartolomé. She said, "I don't have a favourite book. I'm not much of a reader. I can read Spanish, of course, and know a few words of Latin, but I really don't like to read books. I get bored too easily and can't concentrate. I think what the world needs is more romance. Books are too serious."

Bartolomé was about to contradict her, but she went on, "I like to play and listen to music. I learned to play the recorder when I was only six years old, and the lute before I was ten."

"Margarita can play both of these instruments better than most professional musicians in King Felipe's court," said Catalina.

"That isn't true! I am just competent."

"She will play for you if you would like her to. I asked her to bring her instruments with her."

Bartolomé could not play any instrument, although he had a good, solid tenor singing voice. He encouraged Margarita to play for them. She took her lute out of the bag she had been carrying. It was covered by a second bag of soft velvet. She carefully drew it out of the velvet bag. It was a fine instrument with a white oblong body that extended into the gooseneck. The soundboard on top of the bowl was a polished dark wood with ivory inlay. Bartolomé knew almost nothing about musical instruments, but he guessed that Margarita's lute was of high quality. When he asked her about it, she told him that Georg Gerle of Innsbruck had made it. He didn't need to know anything else to be impressed.

Margarita took out a book of songs. She explained that it was the first book of songs for lute accompaniment published in Spain. She began to play and sing. Bartolomé was stunned. Margarita was not just good, she was outstanding. Her voice was carried on the sound rising from the instrument, which lifted it to heaven. Tears filled his eyes. He had never heard anything that stirred him like her singing.

Margarita sang and played the lute and recorder until the Garcia's maid brought them lunch. After lunch, they went onto the porch leading to the inner courtyard and drank lemonade.

Late in the afternoon, before supper, Catalina and Margarita departed. Catalina was thinking hard about her feelings for Bartolomé. Margarita broke the silence. "My dear, you have found for yourself one especially charming young man! You are so fortunate. If I weren't your best friend, I would be full of envy and would try to steal him! My father, however, would never approve of the son of a craftsman, so I will leave him for you." She giggled. Then she said with seriousness, "I truly am happy for you."

"Oh Margarita, thank you. I love him."

"I know. I can see it in your face."

They hugged tightly when they reached Margarita's house. Catalina went a little farther to her own house. She was elated. She had two great friends, and she loved them both.

Chapter 12
(Valladolid, 1557)

As the coolness of twilight and the quiet of the end of day settled over the city, Juan came out to the back porch and sat with Bartolomé. They talked about his day with Catalina. Bartolomé told his father of Susana's illness and Margarita's music. Then he said, "Father, I think I am in love with Catalina."

"What do you mean *think*? You have been in love with her since the day you met her. It has been obvious to every one of us."

"But Father, I have wanted to be sure that I wasn't just attracted to her as a child is to a puppy and that my feelings for her were sincere. I feel so alive when she is with me. We are so different, she is outgoing and I am reserved; she talks so quickly, I am slow and deliberate. Yet, we also have so much in common. We share similar spiritual thoughts, we love reading, and we both have a broad range of interests and a desire to travel."

"You probably would never have met her if you had not had the accident. Isn't it interesting to see how something that most people would think of as being bad, a broken leg and badly bruised ribs, has turned out for so much good? God's providence has brought you Catalina. I am struck by what the Psalmist says in the 91st Psalm: 'For he will command his angels concerning you to guard you in all your ways.' — Speaking of guarding your ways, come over to the shed with me, quietly. I want to show you something before it gets too dark."

Bartolomé hobbled down the stairs with Juan's help and made his own way on his crutches to the shed. They went inside. There was just enough light left in the fading day for Juan quickly to show Bartolomé a secret.

"Notice how these floorboards are somewhat loose. If you take up these three boards here —" He showed him. "You will see I have a box hidden. — Come, let's go back to the porch and I will explain about what is in the box." They returned to their seats.

In almost a whisper Juan said, "That box contains coins and jewellery. Many of the coins are from your grandfather's estate. I keep the box hidden there for a number of reasons. First, I keep it from your step-mother. She would try to wheedle the money out of me if she knew I had it, and she would spend it on clothing and entertainment. Second, I keep it as an emergency fund. In the event that I ever need to leave the city suddenly, for example, to get away from the Inquisition, I want to have available a ready source of money and transportable value in the jewellery. I also have a third reason, and this is why I am showing it to you. In my will I have left the house and most of my investments to your stepmother. If something were to happen to me, I have an obligation to leave her with support, but I give you what is in the box in the shed. If you ever need it, it is yours."

"Thank you Father. I certainly don't need it. The allowance you give me for school has always been sufficient. With Grandfather's legacy, I have almost enough to live on for the rest of my life, if I live frugally. Or I have enough to buy a fine house if I am working. Speaking of Grandfather's legacy, we have to settle what to do with it. Can you please have it invested with Monsieur Lachy?"

"I will begin the arrangements first thing next week."

"Thank you."

Chapter 13
(Valladolid, 1557)

The following week was Bartolomé's last in Valladolid. He would be starting his journey for Paris on Monday, the 9th of August. Catalina spent as much time as she could with him. Margarita came often as well.

Late on Thursday afternoon, Bartolomé and Catalina were sitting alone on the porch. Bartolomé stopped talking and swallowed hard.

"What is it Bartolomé? What is bothering you?"

"I have to make a confession."

"To me? I am not a priest."

"Catalina, you know I don't make confession to a priest. I believe that this ritual has no value, and deceives souls."

"Ok, I'm listening." Her palms began to feel clammy. She was concerned about what he might say.

"Thank you for bringing Margarita to visit, I have enjoyed her performances. They have been like a cool breeze in this sweltering heat."

"Her playing is beautiful, isn't it? She is so talented. I wish I could play the lute or sing like her. I feel like a child in her presence."

"You aren't envious of her are you?"

"Not really. She is my best friend. We love each other. I am happy for her that she has this skill and I am able to enjoy it. But what does this have to do with confession?"

"I have had bad thoughts."

"About Margarita!" She gulped.

"Yes, but not what you might think. I totally misjudged Margarita when I first met her. I dismissed her based on first impressions. I came to a false conclusion based on appearances."

"I know that she isn't the most attractive girl in the city, but she is the most talented in music. And she is a lovely person when you get to know her. She is also a loyal and faithful friend."

"I know that now. That is where I made a serious mistake at first. I thought her to be less significant than you because she didn't place an importance on reading like you do. I learned an important lesson that I hope will stick with me for the rest of my life. I realized that God gives to all people different gifts and if they use them to the fullest, they are to be honoured. It is not for me to say that one gift is more important than others."

Catalina started to cry.

"Catalina, are you upset with me?"

"No, far from it! I am so glad you shared this experience with me. You have no idea how happy it makes me."

"Why are you crying, then?"

"Oh, Bartolomé, it is hard to explain. What you have told me just now makes me — I *have* to say it — care for you more than I did before, if that were possible. You are a truly considerate person. I didn't tell you this before, but I was proud of you for the way you involved Margarita in our conversation and made her feel welcome the first time I brought her to visit. Your confession has confirmed my faith in you."

Bartolomé blushed and said, "I want to make a promise to you, and I want you to hold me to it. Is that all right?" She nodded.

He continued, "From now on I will always show more respect for people. If I am ever tempted to be haughty because of my intellectual accomplishments and book learning I will remember that I am to respect skills wherever I find them—in painters, carpenters, stonemasons, bakers, mothers caring for children, or farmers."

"And I promise to hold you to your promise," she said with a cheeky smile.

Bartolomé always remembered this moment, and kept his promise.

"Catalina, I have another confession."

"What now? Am I going to cry again?"

"I think you just might."

"What is it?" She wasn't concerned this time.

"I don't want to go back to Paris. I am going to miss you too much."

"I am going to miss you also. I hope you know that by now, but you must go. We are both mature enough to know that you have to finish your schooling. I will be here when you get back. I promise."

Without thinking of the impropriety and the consequences of his next statements, Bartolomé continued, "Catalina?"

"Yes?"

"Can you promise me something else?"

"What?"

"Will you marry me? Will you promise that you will wait for me and marry me when I get back from Paris?"

"Oh Bartolomé! Of course, I will. I love you so much I will wait for you — forever."

"I love you too, Catalina; more than I can ever show you."

He leaned over and gently pulled her face to his. They kissed for the first time.

Bartolomé had been right. Catalina's face was wet with tears of joy.

Chapter 14
(Valladolid, 1557)

It was going to be difficult for Bartolomé to travel by himself with a splinted leg. So Juan arranged for him to travel with business associates of his who were heading into France. They were only going as far as Bordeaux, but they agreed, for a fee, to ensure that Bartolomé was able to find transportation from Bordeaux to Paris.

The day arrived for his departure, and he moved slowly on his crutches to the carriage. With some help, he was able to get into the carriage but was not able to find a comfortable way to sit, since he could not bend his leg. He had to sit with it stretched sideways and wasn't able to sit fully on the seat. Bartolomé was not going to be able to sit like this for the long journey, so Juan set a strong board across the two seats and placed a thin cushion on the board. Bartolomé sat with his back to the side of the carriage, with his leg stretched out in the space between the seats. A box was placed on the floor on which he could rest his leg. They had to hang a thick blanket on the wall of the carriage so Bartolomé could lean back on it.

Only one other passenger was able to sit inside the carriage with Bartolomé. The third person that was to travel with them had to sit up top with the driver. The third passenger was willing to sit outside as long as it didn't rain. Juan gave the two other passengers and the driver some additional money because of the inconvenience they would experience transporting Bartolomé. The money he gave them was more than enough to cover any expenses they might have if they were required to extend their journey because of rain and had a layover at an inn.

Juan gave Bartolomé a strong hug and climbed out of the carriage.

Catalina, who had come to see Bartolomé off, then entered the carriage quickly, and said, "You will write me, won't you?"

"Of course I will, I promise."

"I love you."

"I love you too — more than I can put into words. Thank you for all your help while I have been an invalid and for your company every day. I am actually glad that runaway carriage hit me. If I hadn't been hit, we would never have met and had the opportunity to spend so much time together. I will see you in a year. Promise again you will wait for me."

"Bartolomé! My word has already been given. I don't need to promise again. I will, anyway, because I love you. I promise I will marry you when you return.

Now I have to go, the other passenger is waiting to get into the carriage. Good bye, I will pray for you every day."

"I love you!"

They kissed briefly and Catalina exited the carriage. The other passenger climbed in and the driver gave the command to the horses. Bartolomé could not see Catalina standing on the cobblestones once the door of the carriage was shut, so she went onto the porch of Bartolomé's house and waved to him as the carriage pulled away.

During the journey, Bartolomé sent a letter to Catalina from Bordeaux. He had a longer than expected layover there. Even though he was fluent in French and could pass for a Parisian, it was difficult to find transportation that would take him the rest of the way to Paris. The country was in turmoil because of the recent defeat of the French at St. Quentin at the hands of the Duke of Savoy, who had led an army of Spanish troops accompanied by English, German, and Burgundian troops. Many people were fleeing south. With King Felipe's reputation for cruelty, it seemed no one was willing to travel north to face his army. However, once the news of peace between Spain and France reached the southern areas of the country, people started to return to their normal business.

In the end, the entire journey to Paris was uneventful, but he did not arrive in Paris until well into September and had missed the start of a number of his courses. He had to apply himself diligently to make up for the lost time.

As soon as he arrived in Paris, he sent a second letter to Catalina via a Spanish regiment that was heading home. It was expensive sending letters that distance. He could not afford to send more than one per month from the allowance his father had given him, and then only if he cut back on his regular expenses. He decided, however, that since he had received the legacy from his grandfather that had been invested through Monsieur Lachy, he could use some of the money he had won as a prize from writing the French essay to pay the delivery cost of additional letters. With this money, he could afford to write to Catalina about once a week. On thinking more about it, however, he decided he did not want to put her in a difficult situation where she would feel obliged to send a letter for every one he sent. She would have to ask her father for money to send her letters. So he settled on writing every two weeks. He knew that it would be difficult to discipline himself to write only that often. He ached because he missed Catalina and wanted to write to her every day. He found that it was best to write her a little every day but to send the entire long letter on the schedule he had planned.

His first letter to Catalina from Paris told her mostly of the trip and of his new classes. In his second letter he said:

> *I have had the leg-splint removed and have started to regain the strength in my leg. The doctor told me to walk regularly. He told me to walk to the end of our street and then back*

the first day, and then to increase the walk by
about that much each day. I have now been
walking every day for about a week. It feels
so good to be able to walk without crutches.

The rest of the letter was filled mostly with information about his lectures and the silly behaviour of
some of the new students.

Chapter 15
(Valladolid, 1557-1558)

Catalina loved receiving letters from Bartolomé and shared the news with her mother and Margarita.

In one letter she received many months after Bartolomé had returned to Paris, Bartolomé told her about attending worship at the Huguenot church, and about the sermon that Jean le Maçon Le Rivière, the pastor, had preached. Without thinking about the consequences, Catalina read the letter to her mother, including the account of the worship service Bartolomé had attended.

That evening in their bedroom, Susana innocently told Abram about the news Catalina had heard from Bartolomé, including the account of his having attended the Huguenot service.

Abram became darkly perplexed.

"What is wrong?" asked Susana.

"I am concerned about the news from Bartolomé. I will have to speak to Catalina in the morning."

"What concerns you? His letters reinforce our belief that he is a diligent student and a sincere young man."

"I am somewhat concerned about his being a Protestant. I am more concerned, however, about the fact that he *writes* about it in a letter. The Inquisition often intercepts mail from outside of Spain, particularly from France, and they read the letters. Based on what you have reported that Bartolomé said in his letter, the Inquisition could arrest him for espousing heretical views. I am even more concerned that *we* would be considered guilty because of our association with Bartolomé through Catalina. According to the proclamations of the inquisitors we should report Bartolomé to the Office of the Inquisition."

Susana turned deathly pale and her heart almost stopped. "You wouldn't betray him to the Inquisition would you?"

"No, I would not. I don't care one iota for the Inquisition's wishes, and I would not betray my worst enemy to them. I don't care what Bartolomé believes or does in religious worship. I care what might happen to us. I will talk with Catalina in the morning."

"Please be careful what you say, and how you say it. Catalina is in love with Bartolomé."

"I know that she loves him, but she cannot endanger us with her reckless behaviour."

"She didn't know it was reckless."

"That is exactly what makes it reckless! — Enough for now! I am tired. We will speak more of this in the morning."

Abram fell asleep quickly, but Susana was restless and tossed all night. She got almost no sleep and was not happy when Abram got up and drew back the curtains the next morning.

Catalina had already eaten breakfast, but her tutor had not yet arrived, so Abram called her into his library. Susana entered behind Catalina.

"Catalina, we must talk."

"Why? What about? You seem so serious." She searched her memory to see if she had done anything that could have caused her father to be so serious. She hadn't seen him like this in a long time.

"Catalina, you read a letter from Bartolomé to your mother yesterday. Could you get it please and read it to me?"

"Yes, Father." She went to her bedroom and opened the box where she kept the letters from Bartolomé. She retrieved only the one that she had received the day before, and returned to the library.

"Please read it to me." She did as she was told.

"Catalina, do you realize that Bartolomé is a Protestant?"

"Yes. That doesn't make any difference to me. We have talked about many of the things that Protestants believe and they make sense to me. I might even be a Protestant myself. I would be if I lived where there were Protestants."

Abram's frown grew even heavier. "Catalina, what you say is very serious. Do you realize how serious it is?"

"I must not, because it appears to be really distressing you and I don't understand the reason why."

"Do you not understand that by King Felipe's and the Pope's laws we are supposed to report Protestants to the Inquisition?"

A realization started to grow in Catalina's mind and she felt sick. "Father, you wouldn't report Bartolomé, would you?"

"No. You don't have to worry about me reporting him. I dislike the Inquisition, but I am greatly concerned about our safety. I am concerned that the Inquisition will find out that Bartolomé is a Protestant and then they will connect us with him. If we haven't reported him, we will be arrested as accomplices of a heretic. They will not believe that we were unaware of his beliefs. Nor will they show any leniency. Catalina, I don't think you understand how dangerous it is to be associated with Protestants."

"I had no idea — it never even occurred to me that we might be in danger."

"I realize that, and I am not angry with you. I am just concerned for our safety. I am afraid that I will have to ask you to stop writing to Bartolomé. You may write one final brief letter to him to tell him that you cannot correspond with him any longer. You must not give the reason. If the Inquisition were to discover that letter, we would be guilty."

"Father! I can't stop writing to Bartolomé; I promised that I would write him."

"You must! I forbid you to write to him, ever again."

"But I have promised to marry him," she said without thinking.

"What! You did what?"

"Abram, please be calm," interjected Susana.

"Catalina. You never discussed this with your parents. Bartolomé never came and asked me if he could marry you. You cannot give him this promise. Susana, has she ever talked about marriage with Bartolomé? Are you two in this together? Have you been keeping a secret from me?" Susana remained silent but shook her head to indicate that she had never discussed the matter of marriage with Catalina.

"But I have given him my promise, and I will not retract it. I love him. I will marry Bartolomé!"

"I forbid it!"

Catalina started to cry.

Susana interjected, "Abram, you once said that you were impressed by the young man Bartolomé and that he seemed like a potentially suitable match for Catalina should anything develop from their friendship."

"I did say that, but that was before I knew he was a Protestant and of the danger we are in because of his association with us."

"Catalina, you cannot marry a Protestant! That is final. We will not discuss it any more. You will write to Bartolomé and end the relationship now. Do you understand? — Do you understand?" Catalina finally nodded and left the room in tears.

"Abram, you could have been gentler with her. There must be a better way to deal with this situation."

"Do you want to be arrested by the Inquisition?"

"No. Maybe they wouldn't find out about Bartolomé."

"Susana, you must face reality. There are no 'maybes' with the Inquisition. They have spies everywhere, and they are exceedingly dangerous. We cannot play them for fools. Please, don't take Catalina's side in this matter or we will all end up on the rack! — But I will try to be gentler with her."

Catalina's tutor arrived and, as usual, was expecting to use the library for Catalina's studies. Susana went to fetch Catalina. She knocked and quietly let herself into Catalina's room. "Catalina, your tutor is here. You have to go to your studies."

"I don't want to!"

"Catalina. Having a temper tantrum over the matter of Bartolomé isn't going to change it. You may as well dry your eyes now and go meet your tutor. You know that if not today, then tomorrow, or the next day you will. So, it may as well be now. Your father isn't going to change his mind, and if you display stubbornness over it, you will suffer more than anyone else."

Catalina saw the logic in what Susana said, and even though she wanted to strike out at someone, she wiped her eyes and went to her studies. After her classes, she asked her mother, "May I go visit Margarita?"

"Yes, of course. Please be careful what you tell her about the discussion of this morning. Since her father is the alcalde, if you tell her about Bartolomé's beliefs, she may inadvertently betray him."

"I will be careful. Thank you, Mother, for being concerned for Bartolomé."

When she arrived at Margarita's house, Margarita was surprised to see her. They usually did not get together during the week when Catalina had classes. "Catalina, I can see in your face that something is wrong. What is it? You must tell me!"

"Margarita, will you promise to keep a secret?"

"Yes, of course."

"A really BIG secret?"

"Yes!"

"I never told you this, but not long before Bartolomé left to go back to Paris, he asked me to marry him."

"Oh Catalina! That is great! You agreed of course, didn't you?"

"Of course I did. I love Bartolomé very much and could never marry anyone else."

"Then why are you upset?"

"My father told me this morning that I can no longer write to Bartolomé."

"Why?"

"He is upset that I promised to marry Bartolomé and didn't tell him that Bartolomé had asked to marry me. He also said that Bartolomé should have approached him about it, and didn't. We just forgot all about asking our parents. Things were so different with Bartolomé being an invalid. It isn't like you dream about: a prince comes and proposes on bended knee and you go hand in hand to your parents to ask for their permission. We just simply forgot."

"That is almost unbelievable, but considering the circumstances, I suppose it makes sense. Doesn't your father understand? I always found him to be so reasonable about everything."

"This time he is not being reasonable. Margarita, I have promised Bartolomé that I will marry him. I will keep my promise to him! I don't know how, but somehow I will convince my father that it is the right thing. For now, I don't want to upset him more than he is. So, I have to find another way to get letters from Bartolomé. That is where you come in."

"Me? Why do I think I am about to become a less than innocent participant in some scheme that you have cooked up?"

"No 'scheme' Margarita; I just want you to receive the letters from Bartolomé so that my father won't know about them. My father told me I was to write one final letter to Bartolomé. He told me I was to tell Bartolomé that our marriage is called off. I plan to keep my promise to my father, but I am going to do it on my own terms."

"Catalina, you are being sneaky and could get into big trouble with your father if he finds out."

"But he won't find out, because you are going to keep it a secret like you promised." She flashed Margarita one of her most disarming smiles.

"Can I have some writing paper and an inkwell and quill?"

"Yes, of course."

Catalina wrote the following to Bartolomé:

My dearest. As usual, I read most of what you reported in your letters to my mother. She in turn told my father of the news from Paris. The views that you expressed openly in your most recent letter have caused great concern for my father. I hope you understand what I am speaking of. If I remind you of the caution you expressed when you gave me my birthday gift, it may help you understand what I am speaking about. As a result, my father has said that I cannot marry you. He is also upset at us for not having informed him of our engagement. My father has commanded that I stop writing letters to you. In this, I will obey him. Besides, it will be impractical for me to come up with the money to send you letters without asking my parents. So, I would be found out if I did contrive to send you a letter.

However, I do not want you to think that I have agreed not to marry you. I love you and have promised to marry you, and somehow we will find a way to be married! When you return to Valladolid, we will ask my father to be reconciled to you and gain his approval of our marriage.

My father did not say that I could not receive letters from you. If you still want to send me letters, I would love to receive them. Please send them care of Margarita, but be cautious about what you say. We would not want Margarita to be embarrassed by our love or our secrets.

Please keep me informed of your plans for your return to Valladolid, and I will arrange, through Margarita, for us to meet and discuss our plans for the future. If necessary, I am prepared to run away with you if my father continues to forbid our marriage. So, please do not let this letter cause you distress. I love you now, and forever.

Let me tell you a bit of what else has been happening around here ...

Catalina finished the letter and read selected portions to Margarita, who said, "That is a good letter. You have told him the truth, but you have not allowed him to think that any of this is your doing. If he loves you the way you say he does, he will understand and will continue to care for you. I will be sure to let you know if he sends any letters here. But, of course, I will read them first." She winked at Catalina.

Catalina wrapped the letter and asked one of Margarita's maids to find a runner. When the boy arrived, she kissed the letter and paid the boy a few maravedí to take it to a lawyer who knew her father well. He kept a record of items sent out of Valladolid on behalf of the Mendoza family. Couriers would come by his office on a regular basis to pick up items to be sent to Paris, London, Antwerp, Rome and other cities *en route* to these destinations. A good courier could carry many letters and make a significant profit if he didn't drink away his fees in the inns along his route.

Bartolomé had sent two additional letters before he received Catalina's final letter. Her letter was a shock to him. What concerned him was not, so much, her comments about her father's reaction to their agreement to marry. He knew that he had been remiss. He should have talked to Doctor Mendoza. As Catalina's father, he deserved that courtesy and had the right to consent to, or forbid, his daughter's marriage. He also agreed with Catalina that if he could find an opportunity to speak with Doctor Mendoza, matters would be set right and he would bless their marriage plans.

What concerned Bartolomé the most was the possibility that he might have betrayed himself or her to the Inquisition. He understood Catalina's veiled comments about being careful with what he said. He chided himself for not realizing how dangerous it was to discuss matters of belief with the prying eyes of the Inquisition all about. He thought carefully about what he had said in the most recent letters he had sent. He was thankful that he hadn't said anything more about the Huguenots or his Protestant beliefs since the letter Catalina referred to. He was saddened by the fact that he would not receive any more letters from her, but kept up his regular schedule of writing to her. Even though at first he had pangs of guilt because Doctor Mendoza would not approve, he sent all future letters through Margarita as Catalina had suggested.

Bartolomé was careful to steer far away from discussing religion in all subsequent letters. He decided that he shouldn't even comment on the few theology classes he was taking along with his law course. He told her more about Paris than he had in previous letters.

Catalina was particularly intrigued by the account of his visit to the Hotel de Bourgogne that had opened in 1548 as the first roofed theatre in Paris. He told her that a royal edict prohibited the performance of *mysteres,* or as he translated it, religious dramas, at the theatre even though it was built to house the Confraternity of the Passion. He also told her that Nicolas Beranjon had objected to his going to the theatre to watch the farces and secular plays. He called it 'inappropriate'. Bartolomé did not elaborate on the reason for Monsieur Beranjon's disfavour, but Catalina easily guessed that some people found such visits to be immoral. She laughed at the thought of Bartolomé being scolded by a stern Huguenot.

Bartolomé also started sending her translations of some of Pierre de Ronsard's love poems. She now wished that she had told him that she had been learning French so that he would have sent them in French instead of translating them into Spanish. Reading them would have given her more practice in French and would have allowed her to appreciate the poems in their original form.

She was so excited about the poems that she asked her tutor to find a volume of them. With some difficulty, he was able to obtain two volumes, the *Second Book of Amours* and the *Continuations des Amours* that had been published the previous year. They read many of the sonnets together. Some like *Mignonne* were so sensual that they made her blush when she read them with Master Diaz. She wanted to learn one of the poems by heart and surprise Bartolomé when he arrived back in Valladolid. She had trouble picking an appropriate one, but settled on *The Dove*. Even though it made her cry each time she read it, it expressed her feeling during their time of separation:

What say'st thou and what doest thou, sad Dove,
On this bare tree?
O Traveller, I mourn.
Why mournest thou?
My mate is from me torn,
For whom I die of grief.
Where does he rove?
A cruel fowler with a lime-twig wove
His fate and slew him; night and day forlorn
I chant his dirges here, and death I scorn
That did not kill me with my faithful love.
And would'st thou die and follow thy sweet mate?
In truth, I pine away in this dark wood,
Where I am ever by my grief pursued.
O gentle birds! thrice happy is your fate;
Nature herself appoints you love's own token,
That live and die in faithful love unbroken.

Learning this sonnet made Catalina grow sadder and sadder as she waited for the day Bartolomé would return to Valladolid. She wanted so much to tell him again that she loved him.

Finally the letter came in which Bartolomé announced his planned date of return. He expected to leave Paris mid-August and to arrive in Valladolid in early September. Catalina was so excited that she wanted to tell the whole world, but she couldn't tell anyone other than Margarita. If she mentioned it to her parents, they would realize that she was still hearing from him and would become extremely angry with her. So she held the excitement inside her heart.

Chapter 16
(Paris, 1558)

Bartolomé informed Nicolas Beranjon, "I will be leaving mid-August to return to Valladolid. I will no longer need the room that I have been renting, as I do not plan to return to Paris."

Nicolas replied, "We will all be disappointed to see you go, especially Symonne; she has come to respect you as a tutor, and I believe that she has grown quite fond of you." He actually had been developing secret hopes that Bartolomé might consider marrying Symonne. He thought Bartolomé would make an excellent husband for his daughter, and he would be quite pleased to have him as his son-in-law. Yet, he knew that if he pushed too hard, Bartolomé would likely be turned away, so he was careful how much he said. "I know that Pastor Jean le Maçon Le Rivière will be unhappy to see you leave. You have become such an important part of our congregation."

"I have been quite involved in both your family and in the congregation, but I must return to Valladolid. I have family there that expects me to return, and other obligations that await me."

"You are aware of how dangerous it is in Spain right now with the Inquisition, aren't you? We find it difficult enough in France with King Henry's attitude to the Huguenots, but it is far worse in Spain."

"I know that, but I plan to be extra careful. My father is a Protestant and he has been able to live safely in the city. If we do not draw attention to ourselves, we can continue to live our lives in peace. I do not plan to stay in Valladolid permanently. I would like to obtain a position with the government and take a foreign assignment. I have an ability to learn languages easily, and with my law degree, I should be able to obtain an appointment. I have always wanted to travel and live in different places. I would like to get an assignment to one of the countries in the Lowlands or to England."

Bartolomé did not tell Nicolas that he also had to return for Catalina. That alone was reason enough to enter a lion's den. He had not told the Beranjon family anything about Catalina because he was sensitive to the fact that Symonne liked him, and he did not want to hurt her feelings. He had also been scrupulous never to give her any encouragement toward romantic interests. Even though it was hard to ignore Symonne's advances, and sometimes he dreamed about kissing her, he had always kept his tutoring and relationship with her on a strictly professional level. This, of course, had made Symonne try even harder to attract Bartolomé's attentions. This in turn pushed Bartolomé's restraint to the limit, but he resisted temptation.

Before Bartolomé left, the Beranjon family held a gathering in their home to wish him farewell. They invited the members of the Huguenot congregation, a number of Bartolomé's fellow students and a couple of his professors. Bartolomé was touched by their consideration and affection. They had purchased a gift for him, which he appreciated very much. It was Doctor Jean Calvin's commentary on the *Epistle to the Romans*.

When the crowd had left, Bartolomé spoke with Nicolas, "I really do appreciate the gift of the commentary by Doctor Jean Calvin. However, I must ask a favour of you. I don't think it would be safe to carry it with me into Spain. I would like to leave it with you, and when I have obtained an appointment to a city where Protestants are able openly to meet, I will ask you to send it to me."

"Most certainly, I will keep it for you. Would you mind if I read it while it is in my safekeeping?"

"Of course not. Please make use of it. Also, can I leave most of my other books with you? I will pack them in a crate and I will ask you to ship them to me in the future."

"Yes, that will be no problem. I can understand why you don't want to carry them with you on your trip home. They will only weigh you down."

Bartolomé decided that he would try again to go by the sea route that he had taken when he had had to return quickly to Valladolid before the death of his grandfather. He hoped that he could make more speed than by travelling only over land. He was eager to see Catalina as soon as possible. So he booked a seat in a carriage to Le Havre.

On the day of his departure, the Beranjon family went with him to the place he was to meet the carriage. Symonne clung to his neck and kissed him on the cheek when he said goodbye to her. Tears filled her eyes. Bartolomé felt pangs of guilt on leaving her, but as he entered the carriage, he scolded himself. He said to himself a bit angrily, "I have never given her even a hint that I liked her. I have not led her on or promised her anything. I don't owe her anything. In fact, I have given her a good education. Why then do I feel so guilty?" He was perplexed as to why he felt this way. He wondered if he really did like her and couldn't admit to himself that he didn't want to leave her. He knew how much she liked him and also thought that his feeling of distress could be caused by his concern that he did not want to hurt her; and his leaving caused her pain. He concluded, "She will forget me soon enough!"

Chapter 17
(Valladolid, 1558)

It took a few days for Bartolomé to find a suitable ship in Le Havre, and then it began taking on water off the coast of southern France. His trip ended up taking at least two weeks longer than he had expected. He didn't arrive in Valladolid until Tuesday, Sept 29th, 1558.

His father was especially pleased to see him. Damiana in contrast was colder to him than she usually was. He couldn't understand why, but decided to ply her with honey. He asked her many questions and tried hard to draw her into conversation. At one point Juan said, "I am not sure why she has been so surly lately. I suspect that she knows about my Protestant views, and that is causing her considerable discomfort. Don't worry about her; she can be moody at times. She will come around eventually."

On Wednesday he went to Margarita's house. One of the maids came to fetch Margarita, and with a wink said, "A tall, handsome young man is at the door asking to see you."

Margarita's heart began to beat hard. She felt the pounding in her ears. She went to the door to greet Bartolomé, but she barely recognized him. She had seen him only when he was an invalid who had difficulty getting properly dressed. Here she saw a tall, healthy, well-dressed man who could have stolen her heart. "Bartolomé, you are back!"

"Yes, I have finally returned. Could you please inform Catalina that I am back in the city? I don't know if she will want to see me, or if she will be allowed to."

"I am sure she will want to see you! She can talk of nothing but your return. I will let her know as soon as she gets out of her classes. Her father does not like her being interrupted when her tutor is teaching. He says that it hinders discipline."

"Thank you. If she is able to come over to your house this evening, may I come and meet with her? Or, could you ask her to come by my father's workshop? You may come along also, if she feels that this will be more suitable and appropriate given her father's thinking at the moment."

Margarita had trouble containing her excitement for the rest of the day and went to Catalina's house early, knowing that she would have to wait while Catalina finished with her tutor. The maid was not allowed to interrupt the teaching session unless it was an emergency, and Margarita's coming wasn't an emergency.

When Catalina came from the library, she found Margarita pacing in the sitting room. "Margarita, what are you doing here?"

"I have some news for you," she whispered.

"Come to my bedroom."

As soon as the door was shut, Margarita said quietly, "Bartolomé has returned, and he came by my house and asked me to arrange a meeting for the two of you. He suggested that you could go by his father's workshop or he would come to my house. I think it would draw the least attention if you met at my house. You can just tell your mother you are coming to visit me. Otherwise you will have to make up an excuse for going out."

"Ok, let's meet at your place. Can you invite me to your house for supper?"

"Of course! Catalina, would you like to come to my house for supper?"

They left Catalina's room, and Catalina said to Susana, "Mother, Margarita has invited me to her house for supper. Would you mind if I go this evening?"

"Of course not. Please don't be too late. Margarita, can you have one of your male servants escort Catalina home this evening?"

"I will make sure she gets home safely. Good afternoon, Doña Mendoza."

Catalina practically ran to Margarita's house.

"Catalina, slow down. I can't keep up with you. There is no sense in rushing. Bartolomé is not at my house. We will have to send for him."

"I know, but I am so excited. The sooner we get there, the sooner we can send for him."

Margarita sent for one of the boys in the neighbourhood whom she often used to run errands for her and had him deliver a note to Bartolomé, who went immediately to Margarita's house.

When Bartolomé knocked on the door, both girls were ready for his arrival and opened the door instantly. Catalina was struck speechless by the vision of the young man who stood in the doorway. Her recollection of Bartolomé was, like Margarita's, of an invalid. During the weeks she had seen him he had either been in bed or hobbling around the workshop, or struggling into the carriage. She was not prepared for how tall, striking, and fit he would look. Her mouth dropped open and she just stared.

"Catalina, is something wrong? I have longed to see you every day for a year. May I come in?" he said to Margarita.

"Of course, please come in Bartolomé."

As he entered, the setting sun struck Catalina's face and he saw the angel he remembered. She had matured and any girlishness that she had had previously was gone. He now saw coming to him a woman far more beautiful than he remembered. He set down the burlap bag he was carrying, stretched out his arms and hugged her. She laid her head on his chest, and he held her tight. She started to cry. "Bartolomé, don't let go of me. Please, never let go. I have missed you so much. Everyday I wanted to go north of the city and call in my loudest voice to you. I hoped that the wind would carry my voice. I am sorry I could not write you. — Oh, thank you for writing to me! Thank you for coming back to me."

Bartolomé continued to hold her, and then he bent his head and they kissed. Margarita was not embarrassed in the least. She was so happy for them that she also started to cry.

He finally said, "Two pretty maids crying. This will not do! Let us be happy, we are together at last. Never will we be separated again!"

Margarita directed them to the interior court where they could sit in almost regal comfort. Then they all started to talk at once, and all broke into joyous laughter.

Bartolomé broke in and asked, "Catalina, I have told you all about my classes, but I have heard nothing of yours in many months. So tell me what you have been learning."

This was the perfect opportunity to surprise Bartolomé, so she started to speak in more than adequate French, although with a clear Spanish accent, "Barthélemy, I have been learning more about Pierre de Ronsard's poems. Let me recite one that I have learned."

She recited *The Dove* and then said nothing more as tears rolled down her face.

"Catalina, that was beautiful," Bartolomé responded in French. "I had no idea that you were learning French. I am very impressed. Why didn't you tell me?"

"I wanted to surprise you."

"That you did! But, we need to stop speaking in French, we are excluding Margarita."

Catalina continued in French, "Barthélemy, I love you. You are so kind and considerate. Yes, we will speak in Spanish, but we can use French when we want to share secrets." She leaned over and kissed him. They reverted to Spanish for the rest of the evening.

Bartolomé opened the burlap bag he had brought with him and pulled out two wrapped packages. "I have brought you each a gift. Catalina, this is a belated birthday gift. I didn't forget your birthday. I know it occurred on July 7th, but I didn't want to mention it in a letter without being able to send you a gift. So, I just didn't say anything. Margarita, I don't know when your birthday is, so this is a gift just because you are such a dear friend to Catalina." He handed them each their gift. "Margarita, you can open yours first."

She carefully unwrapped the large package and looked with confusion at the gift. "Thank you. I know it is a musical instrument, but what kind is it?" she asked.

"It is called a *violin*; it comes from Milan. It has become quite the rage in the French court and with the French theatres. It has some similarities to a Mandolin when it is bowed rather than plucked. Here, let me show you how it works."

Bartolomé could not play the musical instrument, but he was able to show Margarita how to hold the bow, place her fingers on the strings, and move the bow to make sounds. "You probably won't be able to find anyone in the city, yet, who can teach you how to play it, but it would not surprise me, with your talent, if you are able to figure it out."

"Thank you Bartolomé, it was so thoughtful of you to bring this to me—and all the way from Paris! I will learn how to play it, and then I will give you and Catalina a private performance." She was so serious and sincere. He knew he could not have chosen a better gift for her.

"We will expect a recital next week," he said with a smile. "Now, my dear Catalina, open your gift."

"Bartolomé, I know it is a book. It is quite large. What could it be?" She gave him one of her dazzling smiles, and his heart melted.

"Catalina, I saw your smile every day, everywhere I went — even when I turned the pages of my books. Seeing it now, is just as I remember it. The sun is no match!" She blushed and smiled again. "Now open your gift. I can't wait to see your reaction."

She opened the gift extra slowly to tease him. "Oh! Bartolomé! This is incredible! I can't believe how well you know me. What a beautiful gift!" She put down the book and kissed him again.

"What is it?" Margarita asked.

"It is a book of maps," replied Catalina.

Bartolomé added, "It is an updated version of Ptolemy's *Geographia* with revised maps added by the German cartographer Sebastian Munster. Let me show you some of the interesting maps." They all sat together on a high-backed bench, with Catalina in the middle with the book on her lap. Bartolomé showed them the map of Europe, with Spain at the top. They also looked at the map of England and the outline map showing the coasts of the Americas. Catalina was so excited that she had difficulty sitting still. She pointed to a number of places on the maps and kept saying, "Someday I will go there."

They ate supper together, and the evening ended. Catalina had to return home. Bartolomé walked her as close to her house as he could without being seen. "We must discuss how I can approach your father and gain his agreement to our marriage, but it is too late this evening. You will get into trouble if you stay out any later. Can we meet again tomorrow?"

"It is not fair for us to keep meeting at Margarita's house. I will find a way to come by your house tomorrow. I agree we have to make plans — tomorrow." They held each other as best they could with Bartolomé holding her big book. After a brief kiss, Catalina quickly went to her house. Bartolomé watched to make sure she was inside safely, and turned for home.

Chapter 18
(Valladolid, 1558)

Catalina went directly to her room and hid her new book under her bed. She did not want her parents asking questions about where she had obtained it. She then went to see her mother. "Mother, I had a pleasant evening at Margarita's. Thank you for letting me go there for supper. I'm tired, so I am going to bed now. Goodnight. Please say goodnight to Father also." She kissed her mother and went back to her room.

She changed into her nightclothes and sat looking at the *Geographia* for a while. The excitement of the day started to catch up with her. Yawning, she put away the book. She climbed into bed and was about to blow out the last candle when she remembered that she hadn't said her prayers. She climbed out of bed again, opened her dowry chest, and took out her Spanish *New Testament* from beneath the clothes and blankets. She began to read a section, but nodded sleepily. She didn't hear her father coming into her room. He came over to kiss her, and she started awake. "Father! Oh, goodnight."

"What were you reading, Catalina? It must not be too interesting if you fell asleep reading it."

"No, it is a good book, but I had a long and busy day. I went to Margarita's for supper."

"So what are you reading?" he said with a sincere interest.

Catalina gulped, "Father, please don't be angry." She held up the book for him to look at.

He perused it. "Catalina, where did you get this book?"

"Bartolomé gave it to me for my birthday last year. He told me that I must keep it a secret, since it would not be wise to let it be known that I have it. So far, I have kept it a secret from everyone. I was just careless this evening."

"Catalina, I am not angry with you, but I am afraid for you. This is a dangerous book. If someone who didn't like us found out that you had this book, you would be arrested by the Inquisition."

"I know that, Father. That is why I have been so careful. I'm glad you are not angry. I have always been fearful of your discovering this book."

"Maybe for your safety you should destroy it."

"Father, please don't make me do that. I know you don't like Bartolomé, but he gave it to me and it is a most precious gift."

"Catalina, it is not that I don't like Bartolomé. In truth, I like him very much. It is rather that your knowing him puts us all in a dangerous situation. Just as your owning this book does."

"Father, you also own a *New Testament* that is not in Latin."

"No I don't!"

"You do! You probably don't even realize what books you own, you have so many." She gave him a sly smile. "You have a French-Latin edition of the *New Testament* in your library. Master Diaz and I used it when I started to learn French. I am now using French poetry books to increase my vocabulary and fluency."

"I didn't realize that I had the book. I suppose that I am in as much danger as you. Well, we had better both be careful."

"May I keep the book then?"

"Yes, but keep it well-hidden. Your mother and I certainly aren't going to tell the Inquisition." He kissed her on the head and went out of her room.

Chapter 19
(Valladolid, 1558)

The next day Catalina begged her tutor to end classes early. She said she had an errand that she must run, and that it could only be done early in the day. Master Diaz could be indulgent with Catalina, and since she was such a good student, he consented. She didn't ask her mother for permission to go out. She went quietly out of the house and almost flew to Bartolomé's house. Juan greeted her when she entered his workshop, and he went to fetch Bartolomé. Bartolomé and Catalina went out to the courtyard and began quietly discussing their plans.

"Catalina, I know that your father is fearful that I will be arrested for being a Protestant. As long as I don't speak publicly about my views, no one will know. How can I convince him to let me call on you? We cannot continue to meet in secret. You know that I believe we must respect our parents' wishes. I feel guilty meeting with you secretly and want your father to bless our engagement."

"I know. I don't like doing this either. I prayed often for forgiveness after I'd read your letters from Paris. I felt that I was being very disobedient. Bartolomé, I love you so much that I couldn't bear to be without a word from you while you were away. I didn't tell my mother I was going out this afternoon. I don't want to continue being deceitful to my parents. We must get this resolved quickly."

"I think the best thing is for us to be honest with your parents. If they disallow our engagement then I will attempt to convince your father. If that doesn't work — well I suppose we could run away together as you suggested in your last letter to me, but I really don't want to do that. We both know that we should be obedient to our parents, *especially* when what they ask of us is reasonable."

"So I should tell my parents that you are back and would like to speak with them?"

"Yes, but how will you know that I am home if you weren't writing to me?"

"I will tell them what happened. You called on Margarita to announce your return and asked her to relay the message. That is the truth."

"That may work. Please let us try to clear up this matter quickly; then we can get married. I cannot go on living without you as my wife."

"I want to marry you as soon as possible also. I will speak with my parents this evening. Let's pray that God wants us married and that he will guide in this."

"Amen!"

They spent the rest of the afternoon talking. Eventually Catalina said, "I must go. I should be home before suppertime to avoid raising suspicion."

Both her parents were at supper with Catalina. Once the meal had been served, Catalina began to broach the subject of Bartolomé meekly. "Father, Mother, can we talk about something that is important?" They both responded with a nod.

"I have heard from Bartolomé. He is back in Valladolid."

"I thought I told you not to write to him!"

"Father, I swear on my *New Testament*, I only wrote him the one time to tell him I could no longer write to him, just as you told me to do."

"Catalina, I am sorry, I should have trusted you." Catalina blushed in shame. "How do you know that he has returned?"

"He called on Margarita, and she relayed the message to me. Father, Bartolomé and I are engaged, and we want to be married. How can he be reconciled to you? How can we obtain your blessing?"

"Catalina, I told you last night. I do not dislike Bartolomé, and I am not upset at him for asking you to marry him. You should however have informed us. Regardless, I cannot now consent to your seeing him, or marrying him. It is not that Bartolomé himself is the problem; it is what he *believes* that causes the problem. As long as he is a Protestant I cannot consent to your marriage."

"Father, Bartolomé is a much better man than many in this city who hold to the teachings of the Church defended by the Inquisition."

"That is probably true. Even so, I am doing this for your own safety. I cannot expect you to understand how seriously dangerous your relationship with him is." He continued in as gentle a voice as he could, "For your safety, I am forbidding you to see Bartolomé."

Catalina started to cry, but did not storm out of the room, and said, "Father, I love Bartolomé. Can't you please reconsider?"

Abram's heart ached, and he went over to Catalina and hugged her. "My dear child, you must forget Bartolomé, please, for your safety and the safety of your mother and me. You must realize that if the Inquisition finds out that Bartolomé is a Protestant he will not be left alive. I know this to be the case for two reasons. First, their enmity against Protestants has been increasing. It is said on the streets that it is as meritorious to strangle a Lutheran as to shoot a Turk. Second, Bartolomé strikes me as a man of character, and if he has accepted Protestant beliefs, he will not recant. The Inquisition will have to deal with him as a heretic if he is discovered. You must see that he is already as good as dead, and there is no sense in being dragged down with him."

Catalina had no energy to argue and just continued to cry quietly.

"May I write a letter to him and tell him that I am not permitted to see him."

"Yes, but you must end your relationship with him."

Catalina wrote, and rewrote, a letter to Bartolomé. She finally said:

Bartolomé, my dearest, and only love.

I discussed the matter of our marriage with my parents this evening. My father will not consent to our marriage. He has forbidden me to see you and has told me to end our relationship. He does not know I saw you yesterday or today. I could see real fear in his eyes when he spoke with me. I know that if I disobey him in this matter he will become angry and I will be in great trouble. It would also make it more difficult for us to reconcile him to the idea of our marriage at some time in the future. So, for the time being, I will obey him and will not see you.

I don't know how long I can go without being with you, my love.

Possibly, you can try to see him and discuss the matter with him. If that will not work, then I am prepared to run away with you. I will go wherever and whenever you wish.

I will try to write you again, if I am able, even though it will cause me much guilt to disobey my father. Please continue to communicate through Margarita.

I promise that I will love only you. I will be your wife, in God's own time.

Thank you again for the beautiful gift of the Geographia. *You are so kind to me.*

With my whole heart and soul, I am eternally yours.

Catalina

The letter devastated Bartolomé, but he was not willing to put Catalina into a difficult situation with her parents by trying to visit her.

He decided to ask Doctor Mendoza directly to bless their marriage, and if that failed, he would begin to arrange for them somehow to leave Valladolid. The week after his return, he drafted a letter to Doctor Mendoza asking for a meeting. He did not send it immediately. He wanted time to think about how best to approach Catalina's father. He wanted to gain Doctor Mendoza's blessing rather than turn him into an enemy.

He wrote a letter every day to Catalina and either dropped it by Margarita's himself if he was passing by or had one of the messenger boys deliver it. He also received a few letters from Catalina that she had passed to Margarita when Margarita visited her. Catalina did not write often. She struggled with her disobedience in her prayers before she went to bed each night and grew more distressed every day about how to bring the whole matter to a happy conclusion.

The Monday following his return, Bartolomé began to visit lawyers in the city seeking a clerk position and asking associates of his father's at the court if there might be an opportunity for him to work there. He had some hope that he might be able to find a position quickly. The city was growing and there seemed to be many opportunities for anyone willing to work hard. One lawyer he approached asked him to check back in a few days. He indicated he would check into Bartolomé's background and give serious thought to how Bartolomé might be able to work with him.

Chapter 20
(Valladolid, 1558)

The first Sunday after his return, Bartolomé attended morning mass with his father and Damiana. He found it difficult to sit through the sacrifice of the mass. Yet, he did listen carefully to Father Martinez's homily. It was just as good as the ones he remembered. The homily this morning was taken from the Gospel of John where Jesus speaks to Nicodemus. Bartolomé noted that Father Martinez presented the necessity of the new birth as clearly as a Protestant preacher from Geneva. He found it quite curious and wondered what exactly Father Martinez believed.

After the service, as they were exiting the church, Father Martinez came around to the front of the building, from the side door of the sacristy, and greeted Juan and Bartolomé. Hugging Bartolomé, he said, "Bartolomé! It is great to see you back from Paris. I heard that you had returned. I haven't seen you since you broke your leg. I am pleased to see you looking so fit and healthy. It looks like the accident has not left any permanent damage."

"I recovered quite well, thank you, Father. The soreness in my ribs lasted the longest, but I found the regular long walks along the Seine and horseback riding, when I was able to find the time, have helped me recover my strength. It is good to see you also. I appreciated your homily. It is good to hear the Gospel presented so clearly."

"Thank you. Yet, I often wonder how many of my congregation really listen. It appears that within two steps of the door of the church they are back to their old practices. It saddens me to see so many people whose only interest in religion is at emergent times such as birth, baptism, marriage, and death. How I wish we would all truly live out our religious professions!"

"I understand entirely what you are saying. I also was very disappointed in how many of the faculty and advanced students at the University of Paris who were teaching or studying theology lived debauched lives. I just cannot understand how they can rationalize the demands of the Bible with their lifestyle. I pray often that I will live a life that is consistent with my profession."

"Bartolomé, I must greet others. Thank you for your words of understanding and encouragement. I will try to get by for a visit this week. Good day."

"Good day, Father."

Bartolomé, together with his father and stepmother, left the church in silence and walked toward their home. Damiana noticed one of her friends and drifted over to talk with her. Juan put his hand on Bartolomé's arm and slowed him down. The distance between them and Damiana increased. Juan waited until there was no one around and asked, "Bartolomé, what did you really think of the service today?"

"I really did appreciate what Father Martinez said in his homily. If I didn't know better, I would have thought I was listening to a Protestant preacher."

"He may just be that!"

"I am greatly confused. If he were a Protestant, how could he continue to celebrate the mass? The claim that Christ's body is sacrificed week after week, and day after day, seems to be contrary to the Bible's teaching that Christ gave himself as a sacrifice *once* for his people."

"We live in perilous times, in a dangerous city. It is not easy to espouse Protestant teachings openly. Those who are Protestants go through the motions of the religious worship of the ceremonies in the church on Sundays and draw off to pure worship elsewhere."

"Isn't that hypocritical?"

"It may be, but if we did not appear in church, we would immediately be suspect and would be arrested by the Inquisition. Then whatever hope we had of being useful as Protestant leaven in this city would be destroyed. Whether right or wrong, we use the example of Naaman as our justification. After he had been healed of leprosy by the prophet Elisha he professed belief in the one true God. Then he asked Jehovah to forgive him for going through the ritual of

Rimmon worship when he supported the king in the temple. I know it sounds like a rationalization, but we hope we will be able to assemble a large enough congregation of Protestants so that we can overrun the Inquisition with our numbers. Unless God intervenes, we will all have to leave the city or eventually be subject to the Inquisition's punishments."

"Father, I cannot be one to judge, I have enough areas where I am inconsistent with my own beliefs and profession — even as I mentioned to Father Martinez after the service today. Let us hope that the evils of the Inquisition are quickly curtailed and the light of the truth shines on our blessed country."

"Amen to that. On another matter, I mentioned other meetings. Would you be interested in joining me at our conventical meeting?"

"What is that?"

"We have a separate worship service that follows the Apostolic form. We are a church within a church."

"When is it? Where does it meet?"

"We never hold a service at the same time at the same location, twice in a row. We vary the time or location so that no one can establish a pattern and betray us to the Inquisition."

"Today's conventical meeting is going to be held shortly. We agreed that we would assemble as soon after mass as possible. We will be meeting today in a barn just outside the city. A meal will be provided. I have brought along some food in my satchel for our contribution. If you are interested we can go now."

"Yes, Father, I would like to go with you."

"Give me one moment to tell Damiana that we are going for a walk outside the city. I will tell her I don't know how long we will be gone or when we will return. She won't mind, and will find one of her friends to visit."

Chapter 21
(Valladolid, 1558)

They headed to the conventical. When they arrived at the wooden barn, Juan looked around to see if anyone was watching, and they quickly went around to the back and knocked with three short taps and a hard rap. The door was opened, and they entered quickly; the door was shut just as quickly. Bartolomé looked around. The barn was decorated in the strangest way. "Father, why are all the blankets and rugs draped across the rafters and hung on the walls of the barn?"

"This barn does not have solid masonry walls like most do, so we had to put up these blankets and rugs to block the sound. We don't want curious passers-by to hear our worship service and report us to the Inquisition. In some of the more solid buildings we only have to stuff the windows with cloths, and the sound is contained."

There were about thirty people of all ages in the barn when Juan and Bartolomé arrived, and every few minutes others arrived. Juan began to introduce Bartolomé to some of them. He was proud of his son and wanted all of the people to hear of his studies at the university and his acceptance of Protestantism. Bartolomé knew none of the people he was introduced to, but he tried hard to remember their names. Among them were Don Christobal de Padilla and his family. His cute daughter, about fourteen, curtsied shyly to Bartolomé. He was also introduced to Doctor Alonso Perez, a former priest of Palencia; Domingo Avila, a grain merchant; Estaban Solera a retired soldier; Tomas Vega and his wife who raised horses; Don Pero Sarmiento de Roxas, the son of the first marquis of Poza, and his wife Doña Mercia de Figueroa, dame of honour to the queen; and Don Luis de Roxas, nephew of Pero Sarmiento. Juan then introduced him to Doña María de Roxas, a nun of St. Catherine. Juan explained to Bartolomé about her excellent work caring for the orphans and poor of Valladolid.

It was while Bartolomé was talking with Doña María de Roxas that the door to the barn was opened and someone Bartolomé recognized came through. It was Father Martinez! Bartolomé excused himself and went over to greet Father Martinez. "I am so pleased to see you here! I suspected from your preaching, that you had been influenced by the writings of Martin Luther and Jean Calvin. I have always loved you as our pastor and am happy that you and I share a common understanding of the truths of Scripture."

"Bartolomé, I also praise God that you are here. Your father had told me of your conversion to Protestantism while in Paris. I was hoping that we would be able to experience the joy of a shared faith when you returned."

With the arrival of Father Martinez, the service was ready to commence. Father Martinez led it, and Doctor Perez preached the sermon. The service was simple, much like what Bartolomé had experienced in Paris. After an opening Psalm, sung in Latin, and an extemporaneous prayer, the Scripture lesson was read in Spanish. This was followed by a recitation of the Lord's Prayer and the singing of two Psalms and the sermon. Doctor Perez preached from the Gospel of John: 'Jesus said, "If you hold to my teaching, you are really my disciples. Then you will know the truth, and the truth will set you free."' The service concluded with the singing of a few more Psalms, prayer, an offering collection, the singing of the doxology and a benediction by Father Martinez.

After the service Bartolomé asked Father Martinez, "Why was there no Eucharistic celebration during the service?"

"There is debate among us," replied Father Martinez, "whether or not we should observe the Eucharist at every service. Some argue that the weekly celebration of the Eucharist reminds them of the mass and that we should distance ourselves from it as much as possible. They also say that the Apostle Paul says only that 'as often as you observe it ...' but does not say how frequently it should be observed. Others point to the example of what appears to be a weekly observance of the Lord's Supper by the disciples in Jerusalem. For the sake of peace we try to satisfy both groups, so we observe the Eucharist twice a month — with both the wine and the bread being served to the congregation."

Bartolomé, as usual, had to think about what he had heard. His introduction to Protestant worship and teaching had been strongly influenced by his experiences in the Beranjon family, and among the Huguenots. He had not yet experienced differences among Protestants in a congregation. He had incorrectly concluded that there was a wrong way, that of the Church of Rome, and a right way, that of the Reformers. He now had to deal with the new idea that it was necessary for a congregation of Protestants to work out together the application of the principles they believed in.

During the afternoon meal, Bartolomé talked with many of the people in the congregation. He learned how Reformed books and translations of the Bible in Spanish that had been printed in Antwerp were brought into Spain. The books were wrapped in thin sheets of lead and placed inside casks of champagne and burgundy that were then shipped into the country. He also listened with great interest to the friendly, although passionate, debates about whether or not the conventical services should be made public. There seemed to be two equally valid positions. On the one hand, the Protestants should be ready to stand firm for the Faith in the face of opposition from the Church of Rome and the Inquisition. On the other hand, experiences in Seville and other parts of Spain indicated that the Inquisition would crush any visible expression of Protestantism, harshly and quickly.

Late in the afternoon Bartolomé and Juan began to walk back into the city. "What did you think of the service today?"

"The worship service is almost the same as we have in Paris, although we have the advantage of being able to sing the Psalms in French. It would be good if we had the Psalms available in a Spanish translation for singing. I have thought about trying my hand at translating some of them. Although I can sing well, I have never had any training in music and am not very good at writing poetry. I am afraid my fledgling attempts have produced stilted translations. I pray that someone will come along who is good at music and can translate the Psalms for singing. I was so glad to see Father Martinez at the service. Being able to get together in fellowship is a real blessing. Thank you for inviting me. I am glad to know that there are so many like-minded believers in this city."

"Yes, we are blessed to have such good friends of like mind. May God bless this country with freedom so that all the people can worship together in spirit and in truth."

When they arrived home, Damiana was seething with anger and demanded to know where they had been for so long. Juan replied, "As I told you, Bartolomé and I walked out to the country. We ate lunch there together. We have now just returned."

"You are always out on Sundays. You are up to something! I don't know what it is, but I intend to find out!"

"I am sorry, dear, that you cannot share our walks and talks. It would be good for your soul."

"Phah!! A pox on your walks and talks!" She stormed out of the room.

Chapter 22
(Valladolid, 1558)

The following week the conventical service was in the evening and held in an inner room in a casita in the city. The service was much like that of the week before.

It was on the third Sunday after Bartolomé had returned to Valladolid that events transpired that changed the course of all of their lives—forever.

The conventical was scheduled for early Sunday morning. On Saturday night, Juan had told Bartolomé that they would sneak out of the house quietly and be careful not to wake Damiana. On Sunday morning while it was still dark, Juan gently awoke Bartolomé. He dressed quickly and they left the house.

What they did not know was that Damiana had heard Juan get up. She wrapped a cloak over her nightclothes and followed in slippers as they left the house. In the dark, she was able to follow them and not be seen. She saw them enter the same casita that they had been at the week before—although then the service had been in the evening.

Damiana went quickly to the convent of the Cistercian nuns, named Santa María de las Huelgas de Valladolid that had been taken over by the Inquisition. She banged on the door. The porter came yawning to the door and enquired, "What is all the commotion? It's Sunday morning. The sun isn't even up. What can be so important?"

"I demand to see the chief Inquisitor! Now!"

"He won't take kindly to being awakened. He had a busy night examining heretics. Go away and come back at a better time."

"Now! Or I will report you as being a co-conspirator with the heretics!"

That frightened the porter, and he opened the door to let her in. He motioned to a seat and went to arouse someone. He returned quickly with a Dominican monk.

"How may I help you?"

"I wish to report a den of heretics. Please take me to the chief Inquisitor."

"I cannot take you to him. Give me the details."

"I shall not! I demand to see someone in authority!"

The monk paused for a minute and then said, "I shall return shortly." He wasn't long. He returned with a more senior cleric who was dressed in white silk with a matching skullcap. It appeared from his neat composure that he must have already been dressing when the monk called on him.

"How may I help you?"

"Are you the chief Inquisitor?"

"No, I am one of his deputies. I can speak for Francisco Baca, presiding inquisitor of the Holy Office. How may I help you?"

"I would like to report a den of heretics who are meeting right now."

"Please give me the details, and we will enquire."

"Not so quickly! I know that information of this kind is worth something to you. What are you willing to offer me for exposing them?"

"Doña, you should be willing to expose heretics for the sake of truth and the furtherance of the Church. We do not pay for this kind of information. Now please tell me what you know."

"I know that you will pay, and pay well, for this information. Don't give me your pious trifle! Bring me someone who will take me seriously. Do it now or you will miss the opportunity to catch a large number in an illicit assembly. Now!"

The cleric was not someone who was intimidated easily, but he found Damiana to be quite a force. "If what you say is true — if there are a number meeting — it might be worth a little token of consideration."

"Bah! Speak to me seriously. I bring you a catch that will warm you hotter than the fires of Hell—and you speak of a 'token'!" She spat. "Speak to me seriously or I will leave."

"Doña, the Church is in the service of Christ. We espouse poverty and discipline. We are not blessed with riches like the court of Spain. I can offer you five coronas for the information."

"You are not taking me seriously! I know that the Pope has allocated tens of thousands, maybe even hundreds of thousands, of ducats for the Inquisition. I will give you one last chance. Offer me something worthwhile, or I will depart!"

"What do you think is reasonable?"

"My husband is among the heretics. I demand his estate, and I want an annuity of 50 ducats for life."

" Doña! What you ask is ..." Damiana started to leave. "... but we may be able to arrange it."

"In writing. Now!"

The cleric wrote out an official record of the transaction.

"I want it witnessed!"

The cleric called the monk and he countersigned.

"Thank you! Now hurry or you will miss the opportunity! You will need a number of soldiers."

The cleric sent the monk to rouse an arresting party. Within minutes, there was an assembly of about twenty soldiers and monks in the courtyard outside the porter's room.

Damiana led them to the casita where she hoped the meeting was still in progress. She pointed to the casita and went into a side street to watch the outcome.

Without knocking, the party sent by the Inquisition went into the house. With the door open, they could faintly hear singing. Following the sound they came upon an inner room in which were gathered about fifty worshipers. They burst into the room and the captain of the guard yelled, "You are under arrest for heresy and subversion, and for holding a secret conventical." The children started to scream and cry. The mothers tried to protect them. There was no way of escape for anyone. Without another word, the soldiers and monks roughly tied the hands of all the worshipers in the room and marched them out of the building.

They did not consider young or old, male or female. All were treated alike. A guard dragged one of the children along like a pile of brushwood. Two of the monks dragged an elderly gentleman who could not walk. A number of the men and women were hit with whips and prodded with the butt-end of spears.

Damiana watched as the congregation of Protestants was led from the casita to the convent. She saw among them Juan and Bartolomé. As they passed, Bartolomé looked across the street and in the dawn light noticed Damiana in her gown standing in the entrance to a side street. He knew that she had betrayed them. She saw the loathing in his eyes, chuckled, and said under her breath, "A pox be on your walks and talks! I have what is good for my soul!" She turned, went down the side street, and headed home.

Chapter 23
(Valladolid, 1558)

The Protestants who were arrested were taken to the Santa María de las Huelgas de Valladolid convent where they were placed in cellar storage rooms that had been converted into prison cells. The cells were crowded. The Inquisition preferred to keep each of its prisoners in isolation so that they could not pollute one another with their heretical teachings or encourage one another with friendship. They also found it easier to convince a person who had been kept in isolation for a long time to betray others and to recant of his sins of imbibing false teachings. The guards also liked to keep the women separate so that they could use them for their pleasure until they were too broken to be of interest to them. For now, the prisoners would have to share cells, since so many Protestants had been arrested.

Bartolomé was placed in a cell with about twenty other men. A few of them he knew from the conventical. The rest were new to him. His father was not in the same cell as he was. Some of the men appeared, from the length of their beards, to have been in the cell for quite some time. A few of them seemed to be in great pain. One was lying on his side, moaning.

Manacles were placed around his arms, but not on his feet. The manacles were attached to the wall with chains. The chains were long enough to allow him to move about. The floor of the cell was covered with mouldy straw. A gutter in the middle of the floor led to a drain. This gutter was used for defecation and urination. Water for drinking was available in pails near the door. Other than that, the room appeared to be empty. There were no tables or chairs.

Bartolomé sat stunned for a number of hours. He had no idea of what time it was. Eventually a guard opened the door and brought pails with food. He also refilled the water pails. He learned that food and fresh water were brought twice a day. The main food at every meal was a stew-like mixture of beans, lentils or another grain, and carrots, with a hint of some meat. Usually there was also bread and a fresh vegetable; sometimes some fruit. The Inquisition didn't want the prisoners dying of starvation. They preferred to torture them to death. There were a few bowls and spoons in the cell that the men shared when they ate.

After eating the food, the prisoners who were in the cell when Bartolomé arrived became sociable with Bartolomé. After finding out who the new prisoners were, they asked what day of the week it was, and the date. They were told that it was Sunday, October 9th, 1558. At first Bartolomé didn't understand why they were so concerned about this, but after he had been in the cell for a few weeks he understood the reason. There was a small window in the door. The hallway outside the cell was lighted during the day with more torches than at night. This, along with the mealtimes, gave them some indication of what time of day it was. However, with essentially no contact from the outside, it was hard to distinguish one day from another. Bartolomé quickly lost track of what day of the week it was, and the date.

Within the cell a community had developed. Someone had a Bible. Bartolomé could not imagine how he had gotten it, or how he kept it hidden. Others had blankets, knives, candles and other personal objects. Over time, Bartolomé discovered that the men had secret hiding places in alcoves and behind stones that had been carefully removed from the wall. Within the community, there was a sharing of Bible knowledge, times for prayer and singing the Psalms in Latin. Some of the men were former monks, so they tended, by habit, to follow the liturgy of the hours. Bartolomé joined them in their discussions, prayers, and singing. These sessions were conducted quietly, almost in a whisper. They kept their voices low so as not to attract attention from the guards, and abstained from all communication around the times the guards were delivering food and water or were heard in the cellar retrieving or delivering prisoners to the cells.

Occasionally one of the prisoners was removed from the cell for examination and returned a few hours later; sometimes in pain from the tortures associated with his examinations. This was usually the only interruption in their routine—other than hearing screaming from the torture cells at various times throughout the day and even in the night.

One day, Don Christobal de Padilla was taken out and carried in later by the guards about the time they normally slept. His body was bleeding in many places, and he was in great pain. It appeared that his legs had been broken or crushed. Two of the men in the cell used a piece of torn shirt dipped in water to cleanse his wounds and wipe his brow. Other than that, there was little they could do to help him.

Bartolomé felt sick and sat quietly praying. His prayer at first was that God would protect him from that kind of torture. As his spirit calmed, he prayed for all the men in his cell by name, and then for all the other prisoners. He also prayed for Catalina. He didn't know why she came into his thoughts at this time, but he had a sense of great urgency to pray for her.

Chapter 24
(Valladolid, 1558)

Bartolomé's turn finally came to appear before the Inquisition. He had no idea what day it was. When the guards came for him, he felt a rush of weakness and a hollowness in his stomach. His manacles were removed, and he was led between two guards to another former storage room in the cellar.

They entered the room. At a table sat three inquisitors. None of them, as Bartolomé discovered later, were the supreme inquisitor or even one of his immediate deputies. His initial examination was entrusted to subordinates. He was left standing, facing the men sitting at the table. At first, the inquisitors said nothing, continuing to consult pages in the pile of records in front of them on the table.

He looked around the room. He saw a priest sitting at a small portable confessional. Other than the three inquisitors, two guards, and the priest there was no one else in the room. Bartolomé also noticed that there were tables and chairs with various metal contrivances. Similar objects hung on the walls. From what little he knew of the methods of the Inquisition he was able to make out the tools of torture. He saw pulleys and racks, and a wooden contraption that looked something like the body of a horse or donkey, which he assumed was used to pull apart a victim's legs until the hips were disjointed. He noticed, laid out on table, many metal instruments that looked like they were taken from a surgical theatre he had seen in Paris or Doctor Mendoza's clinic.

He also saw a table on which a person would be strapped. Above the table hung a gigantic metal ball on a chain that ran over a pulley. In the ball was embedded a sharp blade. He could see that once the ball was set swinging it would be lowered onto the prone victim on the table. It would cut at his nose and face first and would gradually be lowered until it cut the person into two parts. He shuddered and breathed a prayer asking God to give him courage and wisdom. Words from the Gospel of Luke came into his head, about Jesus comforting his disciples: "When you are brought before synagogues, rulers and authorities, do not worry about how you will defend yourselves or what you will say, for the Holy Spirit will teach you at that time what you should say."

One of the nameless inquisitors spoke, "By the power vested in me by the Holy Office of the Inquisition, and in the name of Christ, we will now begin your examination. You appear at this examination because you have been charged with heresy. You have been charged with being a Lutheran. You are not here to defend your views. You are here to admit your guilt and repent. I exhort you to be humble and tell the complete truth. What is your name?"

Bartolomé's mouth went dry, but finally he stuttered out the words, "I am Bartolomé Garcia, son of Juan Garcia, the goldsmith."

"Where do you live?"

"I have just recently returned from studying in Paris. I have been living in the home of my father. Our home is in Plaza del Puente Dorado."

"Are you a Lutheran?"

"No, I am not!"

"Liar! I told you to tell the truth! Do you not espouse Lutheran beliefs?"

"I agree with many of Luther's teachings."

"Are you a Lutheran?"

"No, I am not!"

"Liar! How can you say you agree with Luther's teachings and not be a Lutheran?"

"Luther taught about salvation by faith, through grace. However, he continued to hold views about the bodily presence of Christ in the elements of the Eucharist, and continued to follow the liturgy of the Church of Rome. I do not accept his understanding of these matters."

The examiner turned red in anger, "Even while you despise the teachings of the Church you claim you are not a Lutheran! What are you, if not a Lutheran?"

"I hold to the teachings of Geneva. I have been attending a Huguenot congregation while in Paris."

If it were possible, the examiner became even redder, "Do you accept the wicked teachings of Calvin?"

"I agree with his teachings, but they are not wicked. They are consistent with the Bible's clear teaching."

"What do you know about the Bible's teachings? Are you a priest? Are you trained in theology? Are you able to interpret the Bible accurately?"

"I studied law. I attended some theology courses while at the University in Paris. I am not a priest. I can interpret the Bible, because I can read it, and its teachings are clear."

The examiner was so furious that he could not continue for a few minutes. Breathing deeply he continued, "You admit you read the Bible and can interpret it without a priest?"

"Most certainly. The Bible does not require a priest to be understood. When the Bible is made accessible to the people in their common language, they can read it and understand it."

The examiner almost leaped over the table he was so enraged. "You are clearly a heretic. From your own words, you have condemned yourself. We have no need to continue this examination of your beliefs. You will be given time to repent of your sins. If you repent and deny your heretical views, you may be spared death. If you do not repent, you will die. Whom in the city of Valladolid do you know who holds the same teaching that you do?"

Bartolomé was frightened by the thought of being sentenced to death, but he put on a bold face and spoke, "I have just returned from studying in Paris. I know only a few people in this city. I was introduced to Protestants in this city the Sunday after I returned. We were all arrested the third Sunday after I had returned. Every Protestant I know in the city was arrested that day. I do not know any others in the city who hold to Protestant teachings."

"Liar! You know of others! You are protecting them."

"On the Word of God, I do not know any others."

Yelling, the inquisitor said, "Don't speak of the Word of God, you heretic, you befoul it with your putrid dung! We will teach you a lesson for spouting lies and blasphemies. We are done with him. Give him the screws! Next time we meet you will tell no lies — you will be humble — you will repent!"

The three inquisitors and the priest left the room and a large man wearing a black hood came into the room. Bartolomé was strapped into a rough wooden chair, and his hands were placed into a machine where his fingers and thumbs were spread apart. He could not move any of the digits of his hands. The large man began to tighten the screws of a clamp over each of his thumbs, working back and forth between the two screws. Within a few turns, Bartolomé was wincing from the pain. With each additional turn, the pain increased. Sweat poured down his face, and his clothes were soaked. He could not contain the scream. His thumbs started to bleed. He became faint. He vomited and choked on the vomit—spitting it out. Then he passed out.

Bartolomé awoke in his cell, manacled to the wall. His thumbs were throbbing sorely. He was shaking. His friends in the cell tried to comfort him as best they could. They offered him a bowl with water and suggested he soak his thumbs in the water. When he dipped his thumbs into the bowl, he flinched from the sting. Nevertheless, the cooling effect of the water did help. He looked at his thumbs. His nails had turned black. He could still move his thumbs, although it hurt when he flexed them. Yet, as he thought about his ordeal he reflected that he had spoken the truth and was still whole. He would heal. What had happened to him was not anything like what had happened to Don Christobal. Nor was it as bad as what he had heard had happened to others, but what would they do to him next time?

Chapter 25
(Valladolid, 1558)

Catalina sent a letter to Bartolomé during the week of October 10th.

Margarita was not able to come to visit her until the following Saturday. When she came to Catalina's house, Catalina pulled her into her bedroom and shut the door. Whispering she said, "Have you received any letters for me from Bartolomé?"

"No, not a single one."

"That is peculiar. I wrote to him again this week. I don't understand why he hasn't written. Do you suppose my letter didn't get to him?"

"That is possible, but why?"

"Can you find a reason to go by his house and find out what is going on?"

"Catalina! I can't do that. You know my father will find out somehow and will tell your father, and we will both be in trouble. It is much safer to use small boys to act as messengers to deliver the letters. So far I don't think anyone suspects you of still having correspondence with him."

"Oh, but something has happened to Bartolomé. I just know it has! I have to find out. Please help me!"

It was then that Margarita recalled the news that she had heard from her father earlier in the week. "Catalina, I don't know if I should tell you what I heard ..."

"What?" Catalina responded with fear filling her like bile.

"It may be nothing; it may not have any connection to your letters not being answered ..."

"What is it?" Catalina barely rasped out the words, since her mouth felt as if it were filled with sand.

"My father heard a rumour that there was a dawn raid by soldiers of the Inquisition on a nest of Protestant heretics meeting in a house in the city last Sunday."

Catalina went paler than her usual light complexion, and she became dizzy. Collapsing on the bed, she finally stammered out, "Do you think Bartolomé was in that house?"

"I don't know. The Inquisition is so secretive. They never report whom they have arrested. One day a person can be going about his business, the next day he is just gone. Catalina, I didn't know Bartolomé was a Protestant. Is he?"

"Margarita, I have not been totally honest with you. Yes, he is a Protestant. That is the main reason why my father won't let me see him. Margarita, you have to find out if he is in prison!"

"How can I do that? I have no way of finding out whom they have arrested. My father can't even find out that kind of information. I suspect that even King Felipe couldn't find out!"

Catalina was quite worried; she wrinkled her brow and frowned as she thought about what to do. "I know. You have to go by Bartolomé's house and find out if he is there."

"Catalina, I told you, I couldn't do that. We will both get into so much trouble."

"Please, you have to!"

"Catalina, you know I love you and would do just about anything for you, but it is for your own good that I refuse. You are in enough trouble now with your father. You cannot afford to get into more trouble. I also think you had better stop sending letters to Bartolomé. If the Inquisition has arrested him, they may be watching for who corresponds with him as an opportunity to arrest more people."

Catalina went cold. "Oh dear, you are right. What did I say in those letters? Did I say anything that could get any of us into trouble with the Inquisition?"

Margarita smiled, "I don't know, you haven't let me read your letters to Bartolomé, or his to you. They are too romantic, aren't they?"

Catalina blushed, "Bartolomé does say nice things to me. But I am more concerned if I said anything about religion. I hope that the fact that the letters were in French does not attract more attention to them. Oh dear what did I say?" She sat silent for a while. "No, I didn't say anything about religion in any of them. It was in an earlier letter that I told him about father's reaction. I know he got that because he replied. And I burned his reply. My letter this week said really nothing more than I love him and miss him. I also told him about what I had been reading and studying. I don't think the content of the letters will get me into trouble, but the Inquisition might connect me to him, and through me, to my parents. I don't know why, but my father is deathly afraid of the Inquisition. He has never shown any interest in Protestant teachings, but his anger over Bartolomé's beliefs was not so much a reaction against the beliefs themselves but out of fear. I could see the fear in his eyes when he was rebuking me. I should never have written to Bartolomé. I should have obeyed my father! I hope, and pray, that nothing happens because of the letters."

Weeks went by and there was no news from, or about, Bartolomé. Finally, Margarita relented and agreed to go by Bartolomé's house to see if she could find out anything.

She brought the bad news to Catalina, "I went to the house. The maid who answered the door recognized me. She was the same one who served us the lemonade the first time I visited with you when Bartolomé had the broken leg."

"She remembered you? Oh dear, so much for our idea that you would be unknown to them. What did she say?"

"She was really quite nice. She remembered my singing."

"That is not surprising, your singing is truly memorable. But what did she say about Bartolomé?"

"She told me that Bartolomé and his father had been arrested by the Inquisition. I didn't see Bartolomé's stepmother, but she seems to be doing quite well. She obviously has not suffered at the hands of the Inquisition. The goldsmith shop is no longer in the lower portion of the house. The room has been turned into a fancy sitting area for entertaining guests. There is a harpsichord and stuffed cushions for the seats ..."

"I don't want to hear about it! What I know of Doña Garcia from Bartolomé, is that she hated him. She probably was paid-off by the Inquisition. What an evil thought! To think that someone would betray her own husband and stepson to the Inquisition."

"You don't know if she did that. You must be careful what you say."

"I know in my heart that she is evil. Even if she didn't betray Bartolomé, she would have if she had had the chance. Margarita, thank you for finding out what happened. Even though it is as we feared, it is better to know for sure rather than always being in doubt. Do you know where they keep the prisoners?"

"Oh dear, are you going to ask me to find out more information?"

"Can you just see if there is some way to find out where the Inquisition takes its prisoners? Please."

"I will. Yet, what difference will it make? You won't be able to visit him."

"I know, but at least knowing where he might be, will help me to pray better for him."

Chapter 26
(Valladolid, 1558)

Margarita was able to find out where the Inquisition took their prisoners. It was easier than she had thought it would be. When she reported to Catalina she said, "Since my father is alcalde he has access to all kinds of information about what is happening in the city. I had seen soldiers going in and out of the convent of the Cistercian nuns, called Santa María de las Huelgas de Valladolid. So, I used an indirect approach and asked my father why soldiers were going there. He told me that the convent has been converted into a temporary prison for the Inquisition. I then asked him if they had any others. He said that they were building a new prison. It is currently under construction but won't be complete until next summer at the earliest."

"Wow! Margarita, you have found out everything we need to know. And, you did it without raising any suspicions. Thank you."

"I am glad I could help," she said, feeling pleased with what she had been able to discover.

"Now we must find a way to see Bartolomé!"

"Catalina, you can't be serious! We must not go see him in that prison!"

"Why not?"

"There are soldiers and guards. The Inquisition will not allow anyone to visit a prisoner."

"I must see Bartolomé! We will find a way to get in that prison."

"What if we get in but never get out? And why is it 'we'? *You* want to see Bartolomé. It is too dangerous. I don't want to have anything to do with it!" She began to cry she was so frightened.

"Margarita, you aren't going to abandon me now, are you? I need your help. Anyway, it wouldn't be safe for me to go there alone. The guards could molest me, but if we go together they will be much less likely to touch one of us."

"Catalina, I can't believe what you are thinking of doing. If your father knew — if mine knew — we would get into so much trouble."

"I don't care. We have to see Bartolomé!"

Catalina prevailed, and they started to talk about a strategy for getting into the prison. It was agreed that they would go at night when there would be fewer people around. They would take money in case they had to bribe the guards, and they would dress in their best outfits to look like members of the aristocracy.

They would also take many blankets, soap, eating utensils and other things that the prisoners would find useful.

The evening arrived when they were going to execute their plan. Abram was not at home. Catalina told her mother that she was going to bed. Susana replied, "So early, do you have a headache?"

"I am not feeling myself."

"I hope you feel better in the morning. Sleep well. I will be going to bed soon also. Your father has been called away to the delivery of a baby. The midwife was unable to deliver it because it was a breach-birth. I don't know how late he will be. Goodnight."

As soon as Catalina heard her mother shut her bedroom door she tiptoed through the apartment and down through her father's clinic, locking the outer door behind her. She put on her shoes outside and worked her way in the shadows through the few streets to Margarita's house. Margarita was waiting for her as she promised she would. They both were wearing long black shawls over their gowns, as it was quite cool—almost cold. The black helped them become almost invisible in the shadows.

When anyone approached them, they would stop and hide in a doorway or quietly slip down a side street. They arrived at the porter's door of the convent and knocked. The porter opened the door roughly, but on seeing the two attractive ladies, he changed his demeanour. "What can I do for you?"

Catalina replied, "We would like to visit the prisoners. We have blankets and other supplies to deliver to them."

"I am sorry; we are not allowed to admit visitors. This is not like a debtors' prison, nor a criminals' prison. All of the people in the cells here are jailed because they are Protestant heretics. If you want to see them, you might be viewed as sympathizers to their position. You would not want the Inquisition to think that, would you?"

"We do not have to agree with their beliefs to care for them. Jesus told the story of the Good Samaritan who took care of a Jew. They didn't agree with one another's beliefs, but they could at least show mercy in a time of need. Are you not willing to show mercy?"

"I am — but we aren't allowed to admit anyone..."

"My father is the alcalde of Valladolid." interjected Margarita, "He would not be happy if he heard that you would not let his daughter provide mercy to those who are suffering."

"But I — wait a minute and I will find one of the guards."

In a few minutes he returned with a guard. Margarita was surprised and pleased to see that she recognized the guard. "Alvaro! It is good to see you; we have come to visit the prisoners. We have brought blankets, soap, and other items for the prisoners. Can you let us in please?"

"Well, you know that we aren't allowed to do this, but because you are the daughter of the alcalde and I know you, we will make an exception." He winked at her. Margarita was pleased that he repeated the statement about her father. It made the porter realize that she had been telling the truth and that they were women of standing.

The porter opened the door and Alvaro signalled to them to be quiet. He led them across the convent courtyard to the steps leading down to the cellar. In a small room at the top of the steps, there were two other guards playing cards. He said to them, "These are friends of mine who have come to visit the prisoners on a mission of mercy." They shrugged their shoulders and continued playing cards. As he went through the room, he picked up a bundle of papers that contained a roster of the prisoners. He led them to the bottom of the stairs.

Margarita said, "We would like to go to the room where Bartolomé Garcia is being held."

The guard looked up his name in the roster in the torchlight and led them to the cell. He said, "I will give you five minutes, no more. Be quick!"

He opened the door to the cell. They stepped in. The smell of excrement, urine, and body odour almost knocked them over, but they made their way into the cell. The guard did not shut the door, but stood in the entranceway. Their eyes didn't take long to become accustomed to the low level of light because they had been in the dark on the way to the convent and the porter's vestibule and the sentry's room had only candles burning. Catalina looked around and didn't recognize anyone. She called quietly, "Bartolomé!"

"Here. Who is it? Catalina, is that you? What are you doing here?"

"I have brought you a blanket and some other items." She went over to him.

Margarita took the rest of the items they had brought and began to hand them out to the other prisoners.

"Bartolomé, I didn't recognize you with a beard!"

"I know, I am sorry, there is nothing to shave with in this cell. Thank you for bringing these items. It has been getting numbingly cold. The blanket will help. The soap will be such a luxury. Thank you."

She noticed his thumbs. "What happened to your thumbs?"

"I was examined by the inquisitors. They tried to squeeze falsehoods out of me." He smiled.

In spite of his appearance and smell, she hugged him and said quietly, "I love you. I pray that you will get out soon."

"I don't know what will happen. I trust God. He will take care of me — and you."

"I will wait for you."

"Thank you. You are again my angel of mercy. I love you so dearly I ache when I think of you."

"What do they want of you?"

"They want a confession that I am a heretic and they want me to repent of my Protestant beliefs?"

"Why don't you do that and they will let you out."

"Because, Catalina, truth is more important than life. I cannot deny what I believe with my heart to save my body. God will save my soul even if the Inquisition destroys my body. Jesus said, 'Do not be afraid of those who kill the body but cannot kill the soul. Rather, be afraid of the One who can destroy both soul and body in hell.' Besides, the Inquisition already knows that I am a Protestant. They arrested me at a conventical."

"I know, we heard about it."

"I have already been caught in their web of intrigue. If I were to recant, they would still accuse me for having been a Protestant. I have already done all the things they condemn including reading banned books and giving the banned books to others, including you—don't worry they don't know. I have also listened to Protestant preachers, lodged in the house of a Protestant, failed to attend confession, eaten meat on fast days, shown disapproval of the work of the Inquisition, and denied assertions made by an inquisitor. In their eyes, I am guilty many times over. The Inquisition operates on the maxim that it never makes a mistake. The most lenient sentence I could possibly receive would be imprisonment for life. Even if I recant, they will likely still torture me and probably condemn me to death as an example. The only possible hope I have is that God will stop the evils of the Inquisition or remove me from these evils through death."

"Bartolomé! Don't say that. You have to get out of this place. I can't live the rest of my life without you."

"Pray for me!"

"I have been, every day. I will, I promise."

The guard called to them, "Time is up and you must leave. I have given you more than five minutes. Come on out. Now!"

Catalina kissed Bartolomé on the forehead, and he held her hand as she turned to go out of the cell.

"Thank you, my angel of mercy. I love you."

The girls left and the door of the cell was slammed shut and locked. They were led quickly out of the prison the same way they had come in.

They walked along in silence from the prison. Finally, Margarita said, "It is awful how they treat the prisoners, isn't it?"

"Yes, especially since they are not criminals. They have done nothing wrong except believe something different from what the Church teaches."

"I wish there was more we could do for them."

"I fear that there is not. I have heard that the Inquisition does not allow anyone to act as a positive witness on behalf of a prisoner. If we were to speak on behalf of the prisoners, we would be viewed as sympathetic to their beliefs and would be imprisoned as heretics."

"Catalina, if what you say is true, there is no mercy! There is no hope for Spain."

"Let us pray that God will spare Spain. Thank you for coming with me. God will bless you for your kindness to me and to those prisoners."

"After seeing their plight, I am thankful I came with you, and knowing what I know now, I should not have been so against going. I am just glad that we got out of there safely. It is a good thing that I knew Alvaro. His being there made it possible for us to get in — and out."

Chapter 27
(Valladolid, 1558)

The next day Abram received a caller. It was Margarita's father. After he had departed, Abram went upstairs to the apartment and asked Catalina, in a serious voice, to come into his library. She knew something was amiss and entered meekly. Susana followed. Abram asked, "Catalina, what did you do last night?"

"I went out with Margarita."

"What?" said Susana, "I thought you said you had a headache."

"No, Mother, I didn't say I had a headache. I said, 'I am not feeling myself.' You inferred that I had a headache." Susana frowned at the correction, and was about ready to rebuke Catalina.

Before she could speak, Abram asked again sternly, "What did you do last night?"

With her head bowed, she said meekly, "I went with Margarita to the convent of the Cistercian nuns called Santa María de las Huelgas de Valladolid."

"Catalina, you are being evasive. What did you do last night?" Abram's voice grew louder.

Proudly she replied, "I went and visited Bartolomé in prison! There, I have told you!"

Susana collapsed into a chair.

"I know what you did! Do you have any idea the troubles you have caused?"

"No, how could that cause trouble?"

"The guards talked about your visit and it came into the ears of the officers of the Inquisition. Changes were made. I am afraid that some guards lost their jobs." Catalina turned pale and hung her head. Every ounce of pride she had a moment before was gone.

Abram continued, "It is surprising that they weren't accused of being sympathizers with the Protestant heretics. Margarita's father was called to appear before Francisco Baca, presiding inquisitor of the Holy Office. It took many denials on his part to ensure him that he had no idea you had planned this, and assurances that it would never happen again. Catalina, you have put us in grave danger with the Inquisition. You have no idea how close you are walking to the precipice of the fires of Hell! Do you realize that visiting a prisoner of the Inquisition is considered assisting a heretic and chargeable as an offence against the Church? You could be thrown in prison yourself for this brash and stupid action. You have not only disobeyed me, you have brought your- self and your mother and me close to death!"

Catalina began to tremble in fear as her father spoke, and said, "Father, I am sorry. I had no idea what the consequences would be. I was just concerned for Bartolomé and had to see him."

"Catalina, I do not want to hear that name in this house again, ever! Do you understand?" She nodded. "You are confined to the house. You will not leave this house for two months. No reason at all will be acceptable. You also will not be allowed to see Margarita, although I understand that she also is confined to her room, so she won't be coming over."

Susana said nothing, but the look in her face indicated that she thought this was too harsh a punishment.

"Father, I am truly sorry. I beg your forgiveness."

"Catalina, you know I love you. I forgive you, but you are still punished. You disobeyed my express command about seeing B — that person — and you endangered our lives greatly. You must learn that the Inquisition is not something to be trifled with. The Pope issued another decree that just arrived in the city. It charges Francisco Valdes, the Inquisitor General for Spain, to be severe in his purging of heretics from Spain. These are dangerous times."

"Father, may I write to Margarita? I at least owe her an apology for getting her involved in my schemes. It was not her fault. I planned it all."

"Yes, you may write her, but you are not to leave this house — for any reason. Do I have your word on that?"

"Yes, Father."

Catalina spent that evening writing her letter of apology to Margarita, and in penance before God. She asked God to forgive her for disobeying her father. However, she did not ask God to forgive her for visiting Bartolomé. Although she was truly afraid of the Inquisition, she was convinced in her heart, regardless of the consequences, that she had done right and that since Bartolomé had done nothing wrong, she couldn't be at fault for caring for him. She also prayed earnestly that Bartolomé would be protected. She then took out her *New Testament* from its hiding place, and as she started to read it, she thumbed her nose at the Inquisition.

Chapter 28
(Valladolid, 1559)

Late one afternoon, after Epiphany, a court servant appeared at Abram's clinic and asked, "Are you Doctor Abram Mendoza?"

"I am," he replied.

"I have a letter from His Majesty King Felipe II for you."

Doctor Mendoza was surprised and took the rolled sheet of paper into his workshop. He untied the royal ribbon that was around the scroll and read the letter. It said:

> *To Abram Mendoza, Doctor of Medicine*
> *You are asked to present yourself at ten o'clock at the palace of the Pimentel family on February 1, in year of our Lord, 1559 to meet with the marqués de Villena, the chancellor of the Court of Spain.*

The court seal was attached to the letter. After reading it, he tied it closed again with the ribbon. He was curious why he would be called to the court, but he continued his work receiving patients, prescribing treatments, and preparing his supplies of medicines and bandages.

He was first to the supper table and placed the rolled-up letter beside his plate. When Catalina and Susana arrived for supper, they were so intensely engaged in conversation that they didn't notice the letter. While he was serving himself from the platter of meat, he deliberately pushed the rolled-up letter to draw attention to it.

"Father, what is that letter?" asked Catalina.

"Oh, nothing, nothing at all."

"Can I see it, please?"

"If you wish." He handed it to her as casually as he could.

She read it and with excitement asked, "Father! Why are you being invited to the palace? What would King Felipe want with you? — Sorry, Father, that didn't come out right. For what reason would he want you to come to the palace?"

"I really have no idea. I didn't know that he even knew I existed. Maybe he wants to try my latest herbal recipe for curing the common cold."

"Father! Don't make fun of this. This is serious! Being invited to the palace! I can't wait to tell Margarita!"

A few weeks later Abram made a rare appearance at lunch. The eyes of both Catalina and Susana nearly popped out of their heads.

"Abram, what have you done with your beard? And your hair?" asked Susana.

"I have had them trimmed."

"Yes, we can see that," said Catalina, "but why?"

"Have you forgotten? I have to go to the palace on Wednesday."

"So? What does that have to do with trimming your beard?"

"I want to make a good impression when I am there."

"But your long beard made an impression! It was distinctive and made you look like a prophet or a wizard."

"That may be so, but in King Felipe's court it is better not to stand out. He doesn't look kindly on people being different, or oddities. Besides, King Felipe himself keeps his beard cleanly trimmed, and I felt that I should conform."

"Conform! Father, I have never known you to be a conformist. What is happening? You have always told me that I shouldn't just follow the crowd. You have always said that I should be myself and not what other people want me to be. Why are you doing it now?"

Abram sat quietly for a minute and then replied in a low voice, "The truth is, Catalina, I am a coward. I haven't the courage of my convictions to practice what I preach. I am not sure why I have been called to the palace, but I suspect they may want to offer me a position in the court, and I want to make a good impression."

"Father, it would be exciting for you to be able to serve in the court, but I am disappointed to hear that you would bend in your principles to receive a position."

"I am not sure that trimming my beard defies any principles. I admit that I have not been consistent with my statements about being your own person. I think you are going to be even more disappointed," he said with a smile.

"Why?" she said warily.

"I have had a new suit made for the occasion. I won't be wearing my robes."

"Father! New clothes. I can hardly believe it! This I have got to see!"

"You will, but I am not going to parade around in the latest fashions just to satisfy your curiosity. You will have to wait."

On Wednesday, Susana and Catalina inspected Abram in his new outfit and were quite impressed with how regal he looked. Catalina had never seen her father look so splendid and realized how handsome and sophisticated he could look if he wanted to.

"Father, you said that your long beard and robe would stand out too much. I think you were wrong! You are going to make a much greater impression in the court dressed as you are today. Be careful how you bow and doff your hat. All the courtiers will be wondering who the new visconde is."

Abram blushed. He had never had Catalina make any fuss over his clothing. As long as she had lived, he had dressed in more or less the same fashion—in clean durable, but well worn, gowns like those used by university professors. He liked giving the air of academic authority to his medical practice. It was new for him, and secretly he had to admit that it was pleasing to have his beautiful daughter compliment him on his appearance.

Around two o'clock Abram returned home. Susana and Catalina were waiting for him and excitedly asked about the meeting.

"As I suspected, I have been asked to serve as a doctor in the court. One of my colleagues from my student days at the University of Valladolid, who now serves King Felipe, recommended me for consideration. I had interviews with a number of the advisors to King Felipe and finally with King Felipe himself."

"You actually spoke with King Felipe?" cried Catalina. "Won't Margarita be impressed!"

"Yes. I spoke with him. Don't get too excited. He is a man just like me. He needs doctors just like anyone else. It is not as if he is taking me as a friend. He just needs a doctor. As far as he is concerned a doctor is just another servant."

"You mean that you are going to be King Felipe's doctor?"

"*One* of his doctors. He has been experiencing gout and needs advice about diet to control the gout, and advice on how to treat it when he has a case of it. It's not exactly a glamorous reason for going to the court."

"What do you mean, by 'going to the court'?"

"Well there is more — I hesitate to mention it, because it might upset you."

Catalina gave a sly smirk and said, "Father, you are obviously going to have to tell us at some point, so it might as well be now."

"I warn you, it might not be something you will want to hear. King Felipe is going to move his court to Madrid and he wants me — us — to move to Madrid with him."

"Madrid? But, why? What is wrong with Valladolid? It has been the capital of Castile for hundreds of years. Why would he want to move to a — village?"

"He has a number of reasons. His main reason is he wants to get out of Valladolid. He has become distressed over the number of Lutheran sympathizers who have been arrested in this city. He has said that Valladolid has become a nest of heretics. Beside, Madrid isn't a village. It is smaller than Valladolid, but once the court settles there it will grow quickly and surpass Valladolid."

It dawned on Catalina how serious this was going to be, "But that means I will be separated from Margarita — and Bartolomé."

"Catalina! You must forget about Bartolomé. He is not for you. He is one of the Protestant heretics whom King Felipe detests. I told you that you were not to mention him again."

At that, Catalina started to cry quietly, turned away, and left the room.

"Abram," Susana said, "it really wasn't necessary to hurt Catalina that way. She can't help it if she likes — loves — Bartolomé so much."

"She may not be able to control it, but I can! I am tired of hearing about Bartolomé. It is extremely dangerous for us when Catalina expresses any interest in a prisoner of the Inquisition. She could get us betrayed into their hands."

"You are right, but you need to handle Catalina much more gently. She is a most sensitive and caring young woman. She doesn't understand fully your worries. Can you try, again, to explain them to her — gently?"

"I will explain my concern to her. It really is for the best if we move away from here. Maybe in time she will forget about Bartolomé and begin to show an interest in another young man. There are many suitable young men in the court who will be attracted to her when I join King Felipe's staff."

Chapter 29
(Valladolid, 1559)

Abram went to Catalina's bedroom and asked through the door if he could speak with her. Through her tears, she agreed. Susana followed him into her room.

"I am sorry I hurt you. I should not have spoken that way about Bartolomé. I realize that you love him, but we cannot do anything for him. In fact if we tried, we would endanger his life more and also bring ourselves under suspicion of the Inquisition."

"I know that, Father, but I miss him so much and I worry about him. I pray for him every day."

Susana went over to Catalina, sat on her bed, and held her.

Abram continued, "Catalina, there is one other matter that I have never discussed with you about the Inquisition and feel I should now."

"What?" she said as fear filled her face.

"How much do you know about our family background?"

"What do you mean? I know the names of my grandparents. I vaguely recall meeting my grandmother on Mama's side. I know that none of my grandparents are alive. I know that I was born here and lived in Italy for a few years. What else is there to know?"

"Your grandparents on both your mother's and my side were Jews."

"What? You never told me that!"

"We know that. It is not something that one discusses openly. They converted as young adults to Christianity under the Inquisition at the time of Ferdinand and Isabella. If they had not converted, they would have been killed. Both your mother and I were brought up in the Church of Rome, but on the whole our parents were not devout believers. Their conversions were for convenience, not out of conviction. I admit that I am not a believer either. I go through the motions of religion, but I don't really believe. I do not speak for your mother on this matter."

Catalina was shocked beyond anything she had heard or seen in her life. She sat silent for quite awhile as tears continued to trickle down her face. Finally, Abram broke the silence, "I have never wanted to tell you this. I know that you really do believe. When you were a little girl you used to love to hear the stories of Jesus your nanny told you, and now I know that you love to read your Latin Bible and — yes even the *New Testament* that Bartolomé gave you, which we are never to speak about."

Catalina couldn't help smiling thorough her tears. She knew that even though her father had disapproved of her having the *New Testament* because of the Inquisition, he showed that he really loved her by never taking it away from her and by agreeing to let her keep it a secret.

"There is a truly important reason why I must accept the request of King Felipe to move to Madrid with his court. If I don't, I will become a suspect. Someone might think that I must have a reason for turning down a request of the most powerful king in Europe. He would then start to investigate. He certainly would not find that I am a Protestant. However, it wouldn't take long to discover our Jewish background. We would then be accused of being Jews and be handed over to the Inquisition. I am sure that you can understand the danger we are in if we don't go along with King Felipe's request. The best thing we can do is to be obedient servants and stay as inconspicuous as possible. This is the reason why I changed my clothing and trimmed my hair and beard before going to the court. I know that I have given you a great deal to think about, but I was not jesting when I told you earlier this week, 'I am not a brave man'. I have no religious convictions and I certainly don't want to be called up before the Inquisition. I have probably disappointed you greatly. I am sorry."

When he had stopped speaking, Susana, wiping away Catalina's tears, said, "Catalina, I do believe what the Church teaches — at least most of it — but that does not change what your father has said about the danger to us if we are suspected of being Jews. We must go to Madrid."

Catalina could not respond. So, after a few minutes both Susana and Abram kissed her and left her to be alone to absorb these revelations.

Later Susana came to Catalina's room and brought her some food, and they talked.

"I know that you are very unhappy about the move and about what your father told you about our Jewish background," Susana said.

Catalina replied, "I ache all over. I don't want to leave Valladolid. What bothers me the most, however, is not our Jewish background. I could care less about that. I am most unhappy about Father's attitude to Christianity."

"I know, dear, but he has to come to understand in his own time and way. We don't like the tactics used by the Inquisition. In the same way, you cannot force a person to believe. Pray for him."

"I will. I don't understand why God is doing all this to me. I try so hard to please him. I read my *New Testament*, and I pray every morning and evening; but now I am so unhappy. Bartolomé is in prison, Father doesn't believe, and I am going to miss Margarita."

"Catalina, you must not distress yourself with things you don't understand. I cannot explain the way of God's working, but we must trust him. I am afraid that I cannot even help you by suggesting passages of comfort you could read. I am so ignorant of the Bible. You know so much more of it, being able to read Latin. Maybe you can share some passages with me, translating them into Spanish please. That will help us both understand. Will you do that?" Susana made this suggestion for two reasons. First, she thought it might help Catalina overcome her disappointments, and second she really did believe that the Bible had answers for precisely this kind of situation.

Catalina thought for a minute then said, "Job had many bad experiences, and it all worked out well in the end. Let me read some of that story to you." She read the opening sections through Job's first statements of distress, and a few short portions from the dialogue with his associates. After she read a few sentences in Latin, she translated them into Spanish for her mother. She then turned to the place where God addresses Job directly. She picked up the reading again at that point and read to the end of the book.

They enjoyed sitting together reading. Susana was so proud of Catalina's abilities. After she had completed reading, Catalina began to weep silently, and her mother held her and then kissed her good night and covered her with the blankets.

Chapter 30
(Valladolid, 1559)

The following Saturday afternoon Margarita called to visit Catalina. Susana invited her in, "Catalina has been greatly distressed over the past few days."

"Why?"

"She will want to tell you herself, so I won't give you the details. Please see if you can comfort her."

"I will. May I go to her room?"

"Yes, of course."

Margarita knocked on the door of Catalina's room. "Who's there?" came the answer.

"Margarita. Will you let me visit you?"

"Yes, please come in." Catalina started to cry again. Margarita didn't say anything. She sat on the bed, held her hand, and let her cry. Through deep sobs Catalina said, "Margarita, we are moving to Madrid."

"What? Why?"

"My father has been asked to be a doctor on King Felipe's staff."

"That is exciting! So, why all this unhappiness? I know that we are good friends and realize that we will be separated, but we have been separated before when you went to Italy. We can write. We will see each other again. Days of tears cannot be over our separation. What else is going on?"

"Margarita, Bartolomé is still in prison. I cannot leave him here alone!"

"Catalina, you know that there is nothing we can do to help him. When we tried to, we got into so much trouble. I thought I was going to be confined to the house forever!" They both giggled.

"But this is no laughing matter," said Catalina.

"I know. But we aren't laughing at Bartolomé's plight. That is truly sad. We are laughing at the episode of our visiting him."

"At least we got to see him!"

"Catalina, what have you told me many times?"

"I don't know. I probably bore you with my pearls of wisdom, don't I?" She smiled through the remnants of her tears.

"You never bore me. You are so wise. I always listen to you. You tell me that we shouldn't worry because God will take care of the situation. You have to believe what you tell me. God is watching over Bartolomé. He will take care of him."

"Margarita, you are right! I have been such a beast. Thank you for coming to visit."

"Tell me about your father's new position. I had heard from my father that King Felipe was moving the court to Madrid. Are you going to be part of the court?"

"My father is joining the medical staff as one of the doctors to King Felipe's household. I believe we will be directly associated with the court."

"I am so envious!"

"Don't be. I would give it up in an instant to be here with you — and near Bartolomé."

"When do you leave?"

"We have to go almost immediately. As soon as my father can close down his practice here and we can pack our belongings, we are going. Father even plans to sell the house right away."

The girls talked for the rest of the afternoon, until Susana came to call them for supper.

Catalina washed her face, combed her hair thoroughly, and put on a clean outfit and white scarf. Her eyes were still a bit puffy, but she smiled as she came to the table.

"Father, Mother, I'm sorry I've been so unpleasant the past few days. I realize that it is necessary for us to move to Madrid. I won't be any bother now, I promise. Margarita promises she will write. Can she visit us also?"

"Of course you may come to visit us, Margarita," said Susana, "We love you as if you were our own daughter. We are so thankful that you have been a sister to Catalina. It has been lonely for her being an only child."

Catalina said, "It would be fun having Margarita as my sister, but I wouldn't want brothers like hers." They both giggled. "When you come, you must bring your musical instruments. I will find a way to introduce you to the court, and maybe you will be able to play for the king!"

Margarita blushed, "That would be fun!"

Abram and Susana were relieved that Catalina was almost her cheerful, considerate self again.

Serious efforts were applied to completing the packing, and Abram was able to transfer all of his patients to other doctors. He also made a trip to Madrid and found lodging for them just off Plaza de la Paja not far from the alcázar where he would be working. It would be temporary, as it was not suitable for a long-term clinical practice. Abram also purchased a vacant lot, where he would have a new house built once they were living in the town and he could supervise the construction.

Catalina was surprised at how difficult it was when her father explained to Master Tomé Diaz, her tutor, that his services would no longer be needed. The family had discussed whether they should ask Master Diaz to move to Madrid, but concluded that Catalina would not need a tutor any longer and could just as well continue her education on her own. There was no possibility of her getting advanced education unless she went into a convent, since no university would permit female students to attend.

Catalina recalled her first reaction to the arrival of Master Diaz as her tutor and had to admit to herself how wrong she had been. She told him on their last day together, "I have been honoured and privileged to be your student. I have not deserved your patient instruction and wise guidance. I thank you very much for opening up the whole world to me and encouraging me to see the possibilities in it."

"Catalina, I in turn have been honoured and privileged. You have been my best student. You have made teaching a joy. Your natural intelligence, excitement for learning, and love of life have brought out all that is best in me. I am prouder to send you into the world than an eagle when its fledglings make their first flight. You will be among the few truly educated women in the court of Spain. You could hold your own with any scholar." Catalina blushed crimson.

"Thank you."

"But I have one final instruction for you, one piece of advice to give you."

"Please. What one lesson do you consider most important?"

"Catalina, do not misunderstand me when I give you this advice. You are a caring and generous person. This advice is not given, in any way, to correct you. It is given to prevent you from changing from what you are now. I am concerned that you will find people in the court to be simpletons compared with you. Among the men, you will find many who have risen to position and power only because of inheriting titles, and others only because they are sycophants. Among the women, you will find many who are silly, superstitious, and ignorant. My fear is that you will start to think of yourself as being superior to them. This would be unwise and would make you unhappy.

You must be considerate to all of them, whether or not they seem to be your intellectual equal. Don't be afraid to become their true friends. You will be surprised that there are other qualities of importance beside intellectual gifts. Consider Margarita, for example. She is not your equal in some areas, but she excels you in others—like music. I have written in my best monkish script a portion of the Apostle Paul's letter to the Romans as my final parting word to you."

He handed her a piece of parchment. On it she found written, in Latin, the following words, "For by the grace given me I say to every one of you: Do not think of yourself more highly than you ought, but rather think of yourself with sober judgment, in accordance with the measure of faith God has given you." Later that evening she slipped the piece of paper into the front of her New Testament and promised God in her evening prayer that she would try to live by this standard.

Margarita came as often as she could during the last few days before the Mendoza family moved. She helped Catalina with her packing, but also helped Susana and the two household maids. The Mendozas were taking only one of their maids with them. The other was married and would have to stay with her husband. The younger one, María, who was coming with them, was excited about the prospects of being associated with the court.

Abram packed most of his books and medical supplies himself. He didn't trust anyone else to help, except Catalina. She helped when she could. Abram ended up packing almost twenty crates of different sizes. Most of them were too heavy for him to lift, but when the men came to move their household effects, two of the strong young labourers were able to lift them without any problem. The movers loaded all of the crates and furniture onto three large carts. Abram was amazed at how many possessions they had accumulated in the twenty years since they moved into the house in Valladolid. He hoped he would never have to make a move like this again.

After a final evening of saying good-bye, they set out early on March 7th for Madrid. The move took three days.

They did not unload the wagons on the evening that they arrived, as it was too late. The next day they organized and stacked the crates and barrels in a storage room. It would take many months for them to unpack and find a place for all their furnishings in their rented house.

The construction on their new house could not begin until autumn at the earliest, and possibly not for a year. There was a shortage of workers in Madrid since it was a town of only twenty thousand inhabitants—about one third the population of Valladolid—and King Felipe had already contracted for a large number of renovations to the alcázar. This made it difficult to find skilled workers for any other construction work. Additional tradesmen were soon to be brought in from the surrounding cities.

Chapter 31
(Madrid, 1559)

Catalina, Susana, and their maid were left with most of the unpacking, as Abram had to start work as soon as possible in the royal household. They unpacked only the crates and barrels with goods that they would need immediately. They left all of Abram's books and much of his medical equipment for later. Catalina grew tired of cleaning sawdust off everything. It had been used as packing material to prevent damage.

Part way through their second week of endless unpacking and sorting, Catalina asked her mother if they could take a rest and go for a walk around the town. Susana agreed. Although the town was raw and not as developed as Valladolid, they enjoyed the outing. They crossed the river Manzanares west of the town and walked along a trail in a pleasant wooded area beside the bank. They rested there, had a picnic, and headed back into the town. On their return, they passed through the area where the nobles and wealthy merchants lived. They nodded to a number of the people as they passed them.

At one point, Susana stopped to ask for directions from another woman who was also walking with her daughter. Very quickly, they fell into a friendly conversation. The other couple was pleased when they heard that Abram was working as a doctor in the court. Catalina and the daughter of the woman began to talk on their own. Catalina quickly discovered that Luisa had turned seventeen in January, which made her about six months older than Catalina. Luisa was a friendly girl and quite curious about Valladolid and anything Catalina knew about King Felipe, who had just moved to their town. Catalina was thrilled to have met someone she could talk with, and shared with her as much as she knew about the court.

As Catalina and Susana were preparing to return to their house, Luisa offered to come and help Catalina with unpacking the next day. Catalina accepted the offer gladly.

Luisa arrived early. Catalina wasn't even out of her nightgown, since she had started to unpack a box without bothering to get dressed. Luisa waited while Catalina got dressed and then they started to unpack a large crate together. It took a long time to unpack this crate, as there was a story associated with each object that they discovered in the sawdust.

Luisa was interested in Catalina's books. Luisa asked with her eyes wide in surprise, "Are all of these books yours?"

"Yes. Why?"

"I have never seen so many books. I don't have any books."

"But you can read?"

"Yes, I can read and write Castilian reasonably well. But these books are almost all in Latin. Can you really read Latin?"

"Yes, and I can speak it." Catalina spoke humbly. She remembered the piece of paper inside her *New Testament* given to her by Master Tomé Diaz.

Luisa was impressed, but said, "Latin is not used much in Madrid, except by those in the Church."

"That will change. It used to be that way in Valladolid also. Only recently, has there been an acceptance of Latin by the court as the language of diplomacy and commerce. Many in Madrid will have to learn Latin to communicate with the many foreigners who will start coming into this town — from England, Germany, The Lowlands, France, Italy ..."

"Oh, it will be exciting to see all these foreigners. Do you think we will ever get to meet any of them?"

"I don't know, but your father has an important job overseeing the roads and waterworks. King Felipe and his staff will likely have to work closely with him when they undertake their construction projects. I think your father will have an opportunity to meet these foreigners at times. Maybe he will let you meet them also."

"That would be fun."

"But if you ever get invited to meet any of them, you have to invite me also!"

"I will, if you promise you will invite me if you get to meet them first. Maybe we will meet foreign princes who will want to marry us!" They both giggled.

From that moment, they became the best of friends. Catalina told Luisa about her good friend Margarita and about meeting Bartolomé, her promise to marry him, and his being arrested by the Inquisition. She did not, however, tell her about the Spanish *New Testament*. That might prove to be dangerous, and other than her parents who had found out by mistake, this was her secret with Bartolomé.

One evening, Abram came home very late. Catalina had already prepared for bed, but she went to meet him. She went to give him a kiss of greeting and paused, "Father! What is that awful smell? You smell like you have been sitting beside a chimney that has a broken flue, but this smell is even worse!"

"I know. I don't like the smell either. I'm going to have these clothes thoroughly cleaned. Even then, I am not sure that will get the smell out."

"What caused the smell? Why would you have been near a fire? It is too hot now during the day to need a fire for warming. Were you in the kitchen at the alcázar?"

"No, I was not in the kitchen. A new fashion is sweeping the court. A few years ago, returning conquistadors brought back with them the leaves of a dried plant called *tobacco*. The leaves are rolled into little sticks about the size of my index finger and the sticks are set on fire at one end with a candle. The tobacco burns slowly, and a person holds the unlit end to his lips and sucks smoke through the dried leaves into his mouth."

"Whatever for?"

"I asked exactly the same question."

"I understand that the natives of the Spanish Americas use this as a form of medicine. They claim that the smoke makes them think more clearly and has magical qualities."

"What is it supposed to do?"

"Among other things they claim it cures colds, protects against diseases, enhances manliness, and gives a general sense of well-being."

"Can this — *tobacco*, is that what you called it — really do all this?"

"I don't believe it. I can't imagine how something that causes people to cough and gives me a headache can have any real medicinal value."

"Does King Felipe use this stuff?"

"I haven't seen him do so. He well might. He has some strange views about the maintenance of his health."

"Like what?"

"King Felipe's father, Emperor Charles, had significant difficulty with gout, and King Felipe himself is showing increasing tendencies to it. His favourite medicine right now is also from the Spanish Americas. It is called *cacao*. The beans are baked and ground to a powder. A hot drink is made with the powder and mixed with honey. Spices are then added. They use cinnamon, vanilla, or cayenne pepper brought over in the ships with the *cacao*. I don't know if there is any medicinal value in this drink. I am, however, concerned that King Felipe is dealing with his gout in the wrong way. He has become convinced that he shouldn't eat fish and fresh fruit and vegetables. I think he is doing the opposite of what is good for him."

"You are his doctor, won't he listen to you?"

"I am not his only doctor. There are differences of opinion on how to treat gout. And besides, King Felipe is a stubborn man. When he was in England and was married to Queen Mary, the daughter of King Henry VIII, he was instructed from the *Boke of Kervynge*, which speaks of preparing food. He quotes this book as saying: 'Beware of green salads and raw fruits for they will make your sovereign sick.'"

"How can fresh fruit and vegetables make anyone sick? When God created man he placed him in a garden and all he had to eat was fresh fruit and vegetables. God said what he had made was very good."

"Catalina, I wonder if we can really use the example of the Garden of Eden for our dietary guidance? Nevertheless, I agree with you, eating fruit and vegetables makes a person healthy, not sick. We have to overcome many superstitions. This is why I don't think people really understand what they are doing with *tobacco*. Someday we may learn otherwise."

Chapter 32
(Madrid, 1559)

The next day a messenger arrived from Abram at the court requesting that Catalina send a particular book to him. She decided that she would use this as an opportunity to gain access to the alcázar. So she sent the messenger away and told him that she would find the book, which could take awhile, and would have it brought to the court. She found the book and took it herself.

Upon arriving at the court, she explained to the guards that her father had requested the book and asked to be directed to where she could find him. One of the guards was apprehensive about letting her in and was ready to take the book from her and deliver it himself. She said in a firm voice to the one who seemed to be in charge, "My father, Doctor Mendoza, is doctor to the king. He specifically requested that this book be brought to him. I am his assistant. I insist that you take me to him. My father will be most upset with you if I do not bring him this book."

The guard did not want to get into an argument with a lady, so he relented and led her to the office of her father.

"Catalina! What are you doing here?"

"I have brought you the book you requested."

"Thank you dear." Turning to the guard he said, "You may go now. I will keep my daughter with me."

"Yes, Sir!"

Turning back to Catalina he said, "You devil, you connived a way to get into the alcázar, didn't you?"

With a beaming smile she replied, "Yes, Father, I am too transparent, aren't I?"

"Well, since you are here, you can assist me. In fact you can read to me from the book while I prepare the mixture."

He found the place in the book, and she started reading slowly to him, "Mix one portion of dried ..."

When they were done, she left her father to make her way out of the alcázar. She had paid careful attention when she was being led in and thought she knew the way out. However, she got lost and came into a hallway she didn't recognize. It had a wooden parquet floor and was lined with portraits. She came upon two elderly courtiers standing near a tapestry and talking quietly outside a door. She guessed that King Felipe might be on the other side of that door. She greeted the two men and asked them for directions to the door by which she had entered the alcázar. They gave her directions in muffled voices. She thanked them and turned to leave.

As she walked away, one of the courtiers said to the other in Latin, "Whose strumpet is that?"

Before the other could answer, Catalina turned around, her nostrils flaring, and replied in loud, flawless Latin, "I am no strumpet! I take offence at your suggesting such! My father is Doctor Mendoza. I have been assisting him with his work. I demand an apology!"

The jaws of both men dropped. They could hardly believe their ears. They rarely encountered a woman who could speak Latin, and so well, and one demanding an apology too. They stuttered without knowing what to say.

Just then, the door of the room opened. It was King Felipe. He said firmly, "I told you to be quiet! What is all this noise about?"

Before the men could answer, Catalina quickly curtsied and then boldly replied to the king, continuing to speak in Latin, "Your Majesty, I am Catalina Mendoza, my father is part of your medical staff. I have just come from assisting him with his work. These men here made a disparaging comment about me. One of them called me a strumpet. I asked them to apologize"

King Felipe was stunned. He had never been addressed in this way before by anyone—let alone by a young lady speaking Latin. He said in return, in Spanish, "I am sorry señorita, I do not understand Latin very well. Please repeat what you said, but in Spanish." Catalina did as he asked.

King Felipe found it somewhat amusing and turned to the men, "Well then, apologize to her!"

They mumbled out an apology. Catalina curtsied and made her way from the alcázar. As she exited the alcázar, she began to shake uncontrollably and her arms broke out with goose bumps.

She stopped by Luisa's house on the way home and told her all about her experience. They both had a good laugh at the expense of the courtiers. Luisa was most impressed by the fact that Catalina had seen the king and spoken with him personally. "It must have been quite a shock for him to have been addressed by you in that way."

"Yes, I think I had the advantage of surprise over them all. I hope it doesn't get my father into trouble. I seem to have a way of doing that."

"Tell me!"

"One time Margarita and I convinced a guard to let us visit Bartolomé in his cell. Both our fathers were quite angry with us. My father was also told by the alcalde of Valladolid, Margarita's father, that he should have better control over his daughter. I was confined to the house for two months and, until we moved here, was only allowed to go to the market or to Margarita's house, if I was accompanied by one of our maids. It was like being under house arrest. It was terrible!"

"But this time it wasn't the same. Your father was pleased that you had brought him the book and worked with him, wasn't he? So he won't get angry with you if he even hears about your encounter with King Felipe. I bet the courtiers will keep it quiet; they will be quite embarrassed. I would have loved to have seen the faces of those men when you told them off."

That evening, Abram couldn't keep the smile from his face, "So, Catalina, I hear you created quite a stir in the alcázar today."

"How did you find out?" she said with mock exasperation.

"King Felipe himself told me — and many other people."

"Father, I hope I haven't gotten you into trouble."

"No, you haven't, although it could have caused trouble. In fact, on the contrary, King Felipe was so impressed by your spirit that he has told me that you may come to the alcázar any time you wish. In other words, you are now granted direct access to the court."

"Really, Father?"

"Yes. You made quite an impression. However, I suggest you avoid the two men you met in the hallway today. Their pride has been wounded. They did not take kindly to the rebuke you gave them, nor to the one they received from King Felipe."

"Father, I did not mean to offend anyone, let alone a courtier to the king of Spain. I was only objecting to their calling me by a most inappropriate name."

"They had no right to speak as they did; you did the right thing, but do try to be genteel next time you come to the court." He had difficulty disguising his pride.

"I will Father," she replied with mock humility and a big smile.

The next time Catalina went to the alcázar, the guards immediately let her in. Her reputation had preceded her and they treated her with respect, and almost awe. She visited the alcázar regularly to see her father.

She became known to more of King Felipe's staff and the nobles, and their wives, and she started to receive invitations to events in the alcázar, including afternoon music recitals and other forms of entertainment. Though she found the music entertaining, she was convinced that Margarita was a better performer. Catalina also liked hearing the jesters' biting satire. She had a reasonable grasp of international and Church politics, so the jokes of the jesters meant something to her, even when most of the people being entertained didn't understand why the jokes were funny.

Luisa was excited to hear about Catalina's access to the court and asked her to find a way of getting her access also. Catalina promised she would. Faithful to her word, Catalina was soon able to include Luisa in her company when she attended events at the court. They especially enjoyed attending the juggling and gymnastic displays, but they did not like it when dwarfs and cripples were used as part of the entertainment. They found this repulsive, and would leave. It was when they first walked out in the middle of one of these performances that the young men of the court noticed the presence of these two new, pretty, and available, young women in the court.

Chapter 33
(Valladolid, 1559)

On Saturday, May 20th after the evening stew had been delivered, Doctor Alonso Perez, a former priest of Palencia, called the prisoners together for prayer. Following the prayer, a monk from the San Isidro del Campo monastery near Seville led the singing of the Psalms for Vespers. Bartolomé always participated in the singing. The cadence of the chants caused the pain of the physical to fade. He also believed that God had a special ear for their singing from prison. He often felt that the Apostle Paul and his travelling companion, Silas, were sitting on either side of him when he sang. Sometimes as he sang, his thoughts would drift, and he could hear their voices from heaven. This encouraged him, and he always sang with a deep confidence.

There was something special about the singing of the Office that evening. It seemed as if the prisoners knew that for many of them this would be their last night on earth. They were truly joyful that their trials were ending. Tomorrow they would be in glory.

As Bartolomé attempted to settle for the night, words from the Psalms they had just sung kept creeping into his mind. From Psalm 144 he repeated the words, "Deliver me and rescue me ... from the hands of foreigners whose mouths are full of lies, whose right hands are deceitful." Psalm 146 filled him with hope, "Blessed is he whose help is the God of Jacob, whose hope is in the LORD his God, the Maker of heaven and earth, the sea, and everything in them—the LORD, who remains faithful forever. He upholds the cause of the oppressed and gives food to the hungry. The LORD sets prisoners free ..."

Bartolomé loved the Psalms. No matter what happened to him tomorrow, even if he had to be tortured in ways far worse than the thumbscrews, he had eternal hope.

As he was drifting into a semi-sleep, he dreamed that suddenly a violent earthquake shook the foundations of the prison, all the prison doors flew open, and everybody's chains came loose. In his dream, he also saw one of the jail guards, who had had a change of heart like the Philippian jailer, washing his father's wounds from his torture.

But the violent awakening was no dream! The doors of the prison flew open and the guards yanked them all to their feet. Their clamp-irons were unlocked and they were all roughly herded out of the prison cell. Don Christobal de Padilla couldn't walk, and he lay motionless. One of the guards struck him in the ribs with the butt end of a spear. Bartolomé and another prisoner, named Hernán, took Christobal by an arm and helped him to his feet. Christobal put his arms around their necks, they put their arms around his waist, and the three of them followed the rest of the prisoners from the cell. No one knew what was happening or where they were going. The cells had never been emptied like this before, but no one dared to hope that they were being freed.

They filed into a large, vaulted room with upper grated windows that looked into the courtyard. It was once used as a wine cellar. In the room, a portable confessional had been set up. Guards stood on either side. A table was to the right. It was covered with dried blood. It had probably been used in one of the torture halls that were adjacent to the room they were now in. Seated at the table was Francisco Baca, presiding inquisitor of the Holy Office. He was dressed in royal-purple silk with a pink sash. He wore a skullcap of the same silk.

The male and female adult prisoners from all the cells, a total of fifty-five, were lined up against the left wall, facing the confessional and the table. There were guards blocking the door and others spaced along the wall.

Behind Baca was a row of lesser inquisitors standing shoulder-to-shoulder, dressed entirely in white. Each was clean-shaven and wore a white skullcap. In the flickering light of the lamps and candles, their faces floated like disembodied spectres above the bank of white robes. If it hadn't been for the belt of jet-black beads that each wore around his waist, it would have been impossible to tell where one body ended and another began. Polished silver crucifixes, floating at the ends of their black tethers, glittered as they moved. The effect was mesmerizing to the exhausted and emaciated prisoners.

They heard the bell of a church faintly from a distance. It was midnight.

In a nasally sing-song, Baca began to read charges against many of the prisoners, "In the name of God, and in accordance with the will of the most Holy and Reverend Sixtus IV, God be praised, and their venerable majesties Ferdinand the Catholic, King of Aragon, and Isabella Queen of Castilla, Christ Jesus have mercy on their souls, the founders of this tribunal, you are charged with ..." At this point a prisoner was called forward.

Juan Garcia was one of the first to be called. When his name was read out, one of the guards pushed him into a prostrate position before the table. The specific charges against him ranged from heresy to blasphemy and witchcraft, and included every form of malignancy between. The list of crimes went on and on, including all the Lutheran doctrines that Juan espoused and had propagated.

"How do you plead?" said Baca. Juan attempted to lift his head to reply. He was slapped down by one of the guards who smashed his face on the floor with a booted foot. Baca lifted his left fist, folded his eyebrows, and with clenched teeth spat out the words, "You dare lift your head before God and his holy ministers!" It is strange what a person thinks about in the middle of such a serious affair. For the rest of his life Bartolomé remembered that Baca raised his *left* fist. He recalled thinking that that was odd and wondering if Baca was left-handed or had a deformed right hand.

Juan said nothing. Again, Baca asked, "How do you plead?" Juan, with a bloody nose and his cheek crushed to the floor, started to repeat the *Creed*, "I believe in God, the Father Almighty, the Creator of heaven and earth, and in Jesus Christ, His only Son, our Lord: who was conceived of the Holy Spirit, born ..."

Baca in a frenzy bellowed, "Guilty! You, Juan Garcia, are found guilty of treason against God Most High. You are condemned to die of strangulation, and to have your body burned. The world, this blessed country of Spain, and our mother, the most holy Church, will be rid of you forever. Confess your sins!" Baca pointed to the confessional.

Juan didn't move. The guards dragged him back to stand with the other prisoners; they heard him say, "Thank you, God!"

The nauseating voice of Baca continued hour upon hour. In total, thirty of the prisoners were sentenced. Fourteen of them were given 'light' sentences that ranged from a severe whipping to life imprisonment. Some would be sent to row on the galleys as slaves until they died, poisoned by their own filth, and of exhaustion. Sixteen were condemned to die at the hand of the civil authority the next day. Every one who was sentenced had property confiscated. At minimum, half of their property and wealth was taken. The families of most of the prisoners would be left destitute. After all, the Holy Office needed funds to carry out its work of protecting the Faith from heretics and infidels.

Bartolomé was among the twenty-five who were not called before Baca that night. The inquisitors obviously had not finished his purification yet.

A number of the prisoners fainted during the proceedings. When one of them collapsed, a guard would throw water from a pail in his face and slap him. The guards appeared to treat the women with the most contempt and harshness. Bartolomé's stomach tightened in anger when he saw them abuse the saintly Doña María de Roxas, a nun of St. Catherine. She was about forty, but had aged twenty years since her arrest at the conventical. He had heard of her work among the orphans and poor children of Valladolid when he attended the conventical for the first time. He wondered how these men could be so cruel to someone who had cared for many of them, and their friends, as a mother when they were children. He remembered how Jesus had prayed for his tormentors, "Father, forgive them, for they do not know what they are doing." And he tried to do the same.

It was after five o'clock in the morning when the sentencing ceased. It might have continued if it were not that other events of the day began to press on their time. The Dominicans had a busy schedule ahead of them. All the prisoners were directed quickly out of the examination hall. They were not, however, returned to their cells.

Chapter 34
(Valladolid, 1559)

The bells of St. Francis began to ring, and then all the bells of all the churches in Valladolid joined in to signal the beginning of this special day of celebration.

All the prisoners were led upstairs and to a courtyard in the midst of the convent that had been turned into the prison. Mercifully, it was still dark and their eyes would gradually become reacquainted with the light of the sun, but it was cold. They had nothing to keep them warm but their tattered clothing. They all stood huddled together, shivering.

One of the monks among the prisoners began to sing the Sunday Psalms for Prime. They all joined together singing Psalm 118, "Give thanks to the LORD, for he is good; his love endures forever. ... In my anguish I cried to the LORD, and he answered by setting me free. The LORD is with me; I will not be afraid. What can man do to me? The LORD is with me; he is my helper. I will look in triumph on my enemies. ... I will not die but live, and will proclaim what the LORD has done. The LORD has chastened me severely, but he has not given me over to death. Open for me the gates of righteousness; I will enter and give thanks to the LORD. ... You are my God, and I will give you thanks; you are my God, and I will exalt you."

It was Trinity Sunday, the first Sunday after Pentecost. As they sang in the courtyard, most of the churches were following the early hours of the Office ordered by Pope John XXII and composed by the Franciscan John Peckham, Canon of Lyons. However, a few of the ancient churches in the city were following the Office composed by Bishop Stephen almost a century earlier.

It took some time to sort the prisoners into groups. The inquisitors had to be fair in their allocation of punishments. Bartolomé, along with the others who had not been sentenced during the night, was directed to stand in the cloister near the chapel where guards were posted. Their future had not yet been decided. That would change as their examinations continued.

Some Dominicans entered the courtyard. They carried bundles of clothes. Black robes were handed to those who had been given lighter sentences. They were commanded to put them on, and to help others who could not clothe themselves because of their injuries or weakness. Bartolomé realized that these robes symbolized the sins that had been confessed.

They had, in the eyes of the Inquisition, only erred to a slight degree.

The prisoners who were to die that day were given a *zamarra* to put on. This was a loose-fitting, sleeveless vest that slipped over the head. Most of the yellow vests had red flames burning downwards. This indicated that the wearers were to be spared a death by burning. They were to be strangled or drowned and then their bodies would be burned.

Two of the prisoners had been sentenced to burning alive. These were Francisco de Vibero Cazalla a parish priest and former chaplain to Charles V, and Antonio Herezuelo. Their vests had been painted with flames burning upwards. Around the flames were caricatures of devils carrying bundles of wood and fanning the flames. In addition, they wore 'dunce' caps made of thick paper, also painted with the same symbols.

Before the prisoners were led from the square, tables were set up. Servants brought out platters and goblets and laid out a full breakfast. The sixteen prisoners in the yellow vests were led to the tables and offered the food. They all refused to eat. The monks and other menials of the Inquisition greedily consumed the feast.

Bartolomé and the others were taken back to the cellar, as a large crowd began to assemble in the courtyard and form into a procession.

Forty soldiers, in ten ranks of four abreast, led the procession. They wore identical new uniforms. Their billowing breeches were of alternating blue and yellow pleats, as were their shirts. Their breastplates, codpieces, and morion helmets had been polished like silver. They wore knee-high leather boots with shiny buckles, and they carried flintlocks.

Behind the soldiers was a group of priests in their surplices accompanied by a boys' choir from the church of St. Francis which chanted the liturgy. The prisoners came next, arranged according to the severity of their crimes, with Cazalla and Herezuelo last. Each prisoner carried a cross about the size of his forearm or an unlit torch, and was accompanied by two soldiers wearing the same uniforms as the leaders of the procession and two Dominican friars dressed in black gowns. The city magistrates, judges, and officials followed the prisoners. Following them were the nobility and gentry on horseback.

At a distance, a large group of secular and monastic clergy followed. Then after a space, moving with slow and solemn pomp came the members of the Holy Office. They wore serious expressions, but the glint in their eyes spoke loudly of their triumph that day. At the front of this group, two of their officials carried the standard of the Inquisition bearing the insignia of their founders, Ferdinand and Isabella, on red silk damask, and a massive crucifix of silver on wood overlaid with gold. A rear bodyguard of mounted soldiers closed the procession.

The procession did not go by a direct route from the prison to the church. It wound its way through the narrow streets of the city. As it passed along each street, large crowds who had assembled to watch the passing spectacle cheered. These crowds would fall in behind the passing procession. In this way, the procession grew longer as it proceeded toward the grand plaza between the Church of St. Francis and the house of the consistory. This is what the organizers had planned. They had chosen a feast day so that there would be as many people as possible present to witness the punishment and atonement of the criminals. They hoped that others would be dissuaded from consorting with the Lutheran heresy by what they saw.

Among those in the crowd who watched the procession was Margarita. She felt compelled to find out who the prisoners were, so she could report the outcome to Catalina. She hoped that she would be able to relay good news and was relieved when the last of the prisoners passed with no sign of Bartolomé. However, it was only a momentary relief, for she recognized, with some difficulty because of the length of his hair and his unkempt beard, Juan Garcia, Bartolomé's father. Fear pounced on her, and her legs became so heavy that she couldn't move. It was only when she heard a child scream that she shook herself into motion. She turned to the sound and saw that a little boy about four years old had been knocked into the gutter by a carpenter who had come down a side street too quickly. She went to pick up the boy, but a woman, probably his mother, had already pulled him out of the rushing stream of feet. She joined the crowd and followed it into the square.

As the choir arrived in the square, it began singing the *Kyrie*. Most of the soldiers stepped aside and the inquisitors marched slowly up a wide stair onto a platform that was level with the top of an average man's head. It had been erected for the *auto-de-fe* (act of faith). Everyone watching the spectacle would have to look up to see God's ambassadors. As Baca mounted the stairs, the choir burst into the *Gloria*. The prisoners were led to another, but lower, platform facing the one on which Baca and his assistants sat. In the centre of this platform, a large green cross, the symbol of the Inquisition, had been erected. It was covered on the day of the *auto* in a black veil, a token of the Church's mourning for its lost ones.

A priest invited the people to pray, and, together with him, they observed a brief silence calling to mind their sins before God. He then read a prayer composed by the elderly Fernando Valdes, the supreme Inquisitor General, sent from Seville for the occasion.

After the Scripture readings and the *Alleluia*, the homily was delivered. The guest preacher that day was the celebrated Melchior Cano. He was the leading theologian among the Dominicans. He was known for his severity and had crushed many of his rivals by condemning them to torture at the hands of the Inquisition. He had been appointed by the Council of Trent in 1552 as the bishop of the Canary Islands, but never took up residence there. He endeared himself to King Felipe through the best known of his works, *Theological Consultations*, in which he advised the king to resist the attempts of the Pope to become involved in the political affairs of Spain. He encouraged King Felipe, as absolute monarch, to defend his right to the administration of church revenues, and made Spain less dependent on Rome. Later, when

Margarita wrote to Catalina to recount the events of the day, she told her that Cano looked sickly and would not likely live another year.

Cano preached from Sirach, where the prophet said, "Do not delay your return to the Lord, do not put it off day after day; for suddenly the Lord's wrath will blaze out, and on the day of punishment you will be utterly destroyed." It was a long dreary sermon. Margarita found it impossible to follow what Cano was saying. Yet, she didn't want his sermon to end, because when it did, subsequent events of the *auto* would be far worse. The liturgy proceeded through the profession of faith and the intercessions, and ended with the celebration of the Eucharist by those on the platform. The laity was not invited to participate.

By the time the celebrant had kissed the altar, it was late morning, and the crowd should have been ready to dissipate, but no one moved. They all watched Baca. It was as if each person's eyes were attached to him with invisible silk threads. As he moved, every eye moved with him. Baca could sense the expectancy, and revelled in the attention. Never had he commanded such an audience. It had been worth spending what seemed like excessive amounts of money to outfit the *auto*. The extravagance of the ceremony would stick with everyone. It would be talked of throughout Spain and Europe, and news of it would even reach the Americas. It would tell the world that Spain was zealous about protecting the true religion from the incursions of the heresy of Lutheranism.

The prisoners had been on their knees throughout the entire service. Now the clerk of the tribunal read, in turn, the sentence of each one. As his sentence was read, each prisoner was handed the missal and charged to confess his sins. Nevertheless, none of them could have said anything because their mouths were bound tightly with cloth, and most refused to put their hands on the missal. It was the symbol of the mass that they had come to despise. After the last sentence was read out, Baca rose from his throne, advanced to the altar, and absolved them, leaving them to face the punishments to which they had been sentenced: penances, banishment, whipping, hard labour, imprisonment, or death by strangulation, drowning, or fire.

Beside the platform, a box had been built for the royal family. King Felipe was not in Valladolid on that day, but the young prince and his aunt were seated in the box. Baca addressed those in the box and placed them under an oath to support the Holy Office. This was the first time such an oath had been demanded of Spanish royalty. Don Carlos, who was then only fourteen, vowed to himself from that moment that he would forever hate the Inquisition.

Baca then turned to face the crowd in the square and administered an oath to all present at the spectacle. They were bound to live and die in the communion of the Holy Roman Church and to uphold and defend it against all its adversaries.

Margarita slipped behind a large man, a blacksmith by the appearance of his hands, and refused to repeat the oath. When the crowd concluded with the words *"In nomine Patris et Filii et Spiritus Sancti,"* she held her hands at her side and did not make the sign of the cross to acknowledge agreement with the oath. In her letter to Catalina, she reported what the people did but was careful not to speak of her own refusal to take the oath. The Inquisition had spies everywhere. They might read her letter before it reached Catalina's hands.

Those sentenced to die were degraded by having their clothing stripped from them, piece by piece. The objective was to expose their skeletal and bruised bodies to ignominy and to stir a loathing in the superstitious crowd. Then they were handed over to the soldiers to suffer the punishment awarded to heretics by the civil law.

At this point, Baca turned to the civil authorities and with total seriousness begged them to treat the condemned with clemency and compassion. By this, he believed that he cleared himself and the other members of the Inquisition of any irregularity. For, after all, canon law denounced clerics inflicting physical injury on anyone.

However, the secular authorities would show no leniency. They had been informed of the sentences in advance and had prepared a site outside the city wall where the executions would take place. They had built a scaffold, set up sixteen stakes, supplied piles of kindling and logs, and filled four large half-barrels with water. At about two o'clock, the penitents in black robes were led away to the prison. The doomed, naked and chained together, were taken to the place of execution.

Chapter 35
(Valladolid, 1559)

The mob followed the soldiers to the execution site. They had come to see the spectacle, and a spectacle they would see! The nobles also went outside the city. They were required to act as witnesses to ensure that the city administrators carried out their duties.

Margarita was torn. Should she go to the place of execution? She decided that it was not morbid curiosity leading her. Rather, she really was concerned for those being led away. She offered up a prayer for their souls as the crowd pushed her along. She prayed especially for Juan, being led outside the city, and for Bartolomé who she hoped was still alive in the prison.

Later when Margarita was writing to Catalina about the executions, she said she couldn't remember much. She claimed that she had kept her eyes closed through much of the affair and prayed intensely. She did, however, report how Doctor Augustin Cazalla, while on the scaffold, begged for mercy for his sister. He said, speaking to the princess Juana, "I beg your highness, have mercy on this unfortunate woman, who has thirteen children!" But Juana, a secret member of the Jesuits, had no ear for the request. She had encouraged her brother's request to the Pope which resulted in the declaration of February 4th authorizing the council of the Supreme Inquisition to deliver to the secular authorities any convicted of adhering to Lutheran opinions. With disgust, she turned to one of her companions and began talking with her about King Felipe's plans to build the greatest monastery in Christendom.

Margarita cried bitterly when Juan was led to the scaffold and strangled, and then his body was tied to one of the stakes nearby and the fagots were set ablaze with a torch. She cried out, "Please God, have mercy on his soul!" Then, quietly, she cursed Damiana Garcia for betraying her husband and stepson to the Inquisition.

Vibero Cazalla and Antonio Herezuelo were tied to two stakes beside each other. Cazalla's resolve weakened and he begged to be released, but Herezuelo stayed courageous to the end. The only thing that had moved him during the entire proceedings of the day was the sight of his wife in a black robe, the garb of a penitent. When he had passed her leaving the site of the *auto*, he had glared at her. This bit into her soul, and from that moment she swore to herself, and God, that she would no longer be weak before the tortures of the inquisitors.

Herezuelo didn't even blink when the flames were applied to the fagots. For many of those who watched, it was frightful to think that he expressed no fear and no repentance when in a few moments he would be in Hell with his associate and master—Luther! One of the guards was so enraged at Herezuelo's fortitude that he plunged a spear into his side even as the flames were consuming his body. The blood dried on the tip of the spear before it could be removed from the flames.

There was one final event at the site of the execution. The bones of the mother of the Cazalla brothers had been dug up the day before the *auto*. Her bones were placed among the kindling, and she was burned in effigy at the stake. Then a declaration was read out that required the house in which she had lived and reared her sons be razed, and the ground sown with salt. The declaration also required that a pillar be erected with an inscription declaring the site to be the den of a brood of heretics.

The crowd of witnesses returned to the plaza in front of the Church of St. Francis where they were invited to partake of a great feast. It could not be presumed that the spectacle of fellow humans being executed would impair either their appetite or their thirst, or that the sound of hissing flesh in the fire of execution would prevent them from eating and drinking lustily.

Margarita returned to the city, with an aching chest from weeping, and went to her room to cry herself to sleep. She had seen men usurp God's authority over the Last Judgment.

Chapter 36
(Valladolid, 1559)

After the early morning events in the courtyard, Bartolomé and the other remaining prisoners were led back to the cells in the cellar of the convent. The guards began to distribute them among the cells. Over the past few weeks, they had been crowded in the cells. The inquisitors much preferred keeping the prisoners isolated, so they could not encourage one another in their heresies. In particular, they did not like them sharing Bible teachings and worshiping together.

Bartolomé was thrust into an empty cell. It was not his former cell. He was left standing alone. The guard had shut the door of the cell, but had not yet put the manacles on him. He thought quickly and then put the manacles on his own arms and closed the padlocks, but did not shut them tight. He hoped that this contrivance might escape notice. A different guard than the one who had shut him in the cell opened the door and led in another prisoner. The second prisoner stood there somewhat witless. A moment later, the door opened again and another prisoner was added to their number. After about ten minutes, there were four prisoners in the cell. Eventually two guards came to put on their manacles.

The guards put the manacles on those standing in the middle of the room, spacing them as far apart as possible. Bartolomé had chosen a spot in a dark corner. One of the guards looked at him huddled in the corner with his manacled wrists on his knees and assumed, as Bartolomé had hoped, that the manacles had been put on earlier and were locked in place. At first, Bartolomé sat quietly and didn't talk with any of the other prisoners for fear a crack in his voice might give him away. He eventually gained control of his emotions and shaking body.

The day dragged on. In their cell, they could not hear any noises from the street or convent, so they had no idea what time it was or what was happening in the city. It was Sunday, and even though they had little strength, they carried out a makeshift service of worship. Bartolomé prayed earnestly for the prisoners who had been led away to execution, particularly for his father. His prayer was not so much that they would be delivered from the executioner's hand, although he did pray that, but rather that even in the midst of evil, God's will would be done and his name given all the glory. He asked God to strengthen his servants and cause them to persevere to the end. He thanked God that his father and friends would soon be talking with Jesus.

After their service of worship, they sat for hours in silence and most fell into a restless sleep. They were exceptionally hungry. They had not eaten anything since the night before. There wasn't even any water in the pails.

It seemed like more than a day passed, but finally a servant of the inquisitors along with two guards came to fill the pails with water. They took the pails out and brought them back a few minutes later while the guards stood at the door. Then one of the servants brought in a basket filled with bread, purple carrots, one small cheese, and a peculiar, large, root they had never seen before. One of the guards said, "Baca is feasting us tonight, eat heartily, you may not see the likes again!" The other said, "He's just fattening them for the slaughter." The two grunted an ugly laugh and roughly pushed the servant out of the cell.

At that moment, there was a loud scream, a woman's scream, from one of the nearby cells. The two guards ran out. One slammed the door shut. All went silent again. They were left in near darkness.

The four prisoners offered a prayer of thanks and shared the food. Only one could reach it, but he passed pieces to the others. Domingo Avila knew where a knife was hidden in the cell and they were able to use it to cut up the heavy root vegetable. Another prisoner, Estaban Solera, could not bite into the vegetable because of his sore mouth from his most recent examinations at the hands of the inquisitors. His closest neighbour chewed the root into smaller chunks and helped him eat it. Bartolomé later learned that these roots were turnips that had been introduced into Spain for cattle feed, from the Low Countries during the reign of Charles V. They shared the cheese with great care, making sure that everyone got an equal portion. Someone said aloud, "The carrots are particularly crisp for this time of year. They must have been stored in sand in a cool cellar through the winter." This was a strange thing to notice when they were on the edge of starvation.

They all ate a considerable amount of food—far more than they had had in weeks. They washed it down with water. If it was possible, they were almost content. It was amazing how quickly their spirits recovered when they had a bit of solid food in their stomachs.

They then encouraged one another from the Scriptures—praying and singing. Bartolomé never forgot the words that Tomas Vega quoted from memory that night. They were taken from Saint Paul's *Epistle to the Romans*: 'I consider that our present sufferings are not worth comparing with the glory that will be revealed in us. The creation waits in eager expectation for the sons of God to be revealed. ... in hope that the creation itself will be liberated from its bondage to decay and brought into the glorious freedom of the children of God. ... In the same way, the Spirit helps us in our weakness. ... And we know that in all things God works for the good of those who love him, who have been called according to his purpose. For those God foreknew he also predestined to be conformed to the likeness of his Son, that he might be the firstborn among many brothers. And those he predestined, he also called;

those he called, he also justified; those he justified, he also glorified. What, then, shall we say in response to this? If God is for us, who can be against us? He who did not spare his own Son, but gave him up for us all—how will he not also, along with him, graciously give us all things? Who will bring any charge against those whom God has chosen? It is God who justifies. Who is he that condemns? Christ Jesus, who died— more than that, who was raised to life—is at the right hand of God and is also interceding for us. Who shall separate us from the love of Christ? Shall trouble or hardship or persecution or famine or nakedness or danger or sword? As it is written: "For your sake we face death all day long; we are considered as sheep to be slaughtered." No, in all these things we are more than conquerors through him who loved us. For I am convinced that neither death nor life, neither angels nor demons, neither the present nor the future, nor any powers, neither height nor depth, nor anything else in all creation, will be able to separate us from the love of God that is in Christ Jesus our Lord.'

They blessed God for providing them with this feast and settled for the night.

Chapter 37
(Valladolid, 1559)

For hours, or so it seemed, Bartolomé sat with expectation. He was sure that when the commotion occurred around the time their food was brought in, the guards who had shut the door had not locked it. He was so excited it was hard to sit still, but he didn't want to move too soon. He might waken his fellow prisoners or, if the door was unlocked and he was able to get out of the cell, he might stumble into the guards. Finally, he felt he could wait no longer and slipped off the manacles. The room was in near darkness, but there was enough light coming through the window grill in the door so that he was able to make his way to the door without stumbling over anyone.

As he moved toward the door, he wondered why he was so concerned about not waking anyone. Was he afraid that one of his fellow prisoners might make a noise wishing him well as he tried to escape? Or even worse, betray him by calling for the guards? Was it because he felt guilty about the possibility of his escaping when the rest were left locked up? What could he do to free them? Even if he could remove their manacles, how could they all get away without being caught? They were all doomed, unless God intervened miraculously. Was it his responsibility to achieve freedom if it was offered to him? He struggled with thoughts about God's ways of dealing with his people. Why does he provide good things for some, while others have to suffer? He would have to think this through, and, if he ever had the opportunity, talk it through with someone who had studied more theology than he—at that moment he had to stay focused.

He was right! The door wasn't locked. "Praise God!" It opened easily and almost without a sound. The cell had been used until quite recently as a storage room by the nuns of the convent, and the door was oiled and in good repair. He quietly closed the door and walked toward the steps. He was thankful that he had been led directly from the courtyard to the cellar, so knew what direction to head to find the stairs.

There was a lantern burning at the foot of the stairs. He peered carefully around the corner and could see that there wasn't anyone on the landing at the top of the stairs, so he started up with great care not to be heard. This was one time he was glad to be barefoot. His progress was silent except for his breathing, which to him sounded as loud as a winter wind coming off the north Atlantic.

As he mounted the stairs, he heard a faint noise from the room beyond the landing. He paused, and after a short time continued his slow and silent progress toward the landing. At the top of the stairs, he carefully peeked into the room and saw two guards sleeping in chairs. The head of one was resting on his chest; the other was leaning over the table resting his head on his arms. He was thankful that neither was snoring. They could have awakened each other, or made it more difficult for him to hear sounds from outside.

Crawling, Bartolomé began to work his way around the room toward the door leading to the courtyard. He hoped it wasn't locked. He didn't relish the idea of getting the keys from one of the guards. He was about halfway between the stairs and the door when a clock near the convent struck the hour. His heart ended up in his mouth, and the guards stirred. He froze, but they settled back into their dreams about the feast they were digesting. That was a scare! At least he knew what time it was. It was one o'clock. He had a few hours to find a hiding place before the changing of the city watch.

He reached the door and opened it slowly. It squeaked a bit, but not enough to awaken the sleepers. He wondered, "Should I shut the door?" There was a lantern on the wall outside the door; he didn't like standing in the open where he could be seen if anyone was looking. Nevertheless, he took the time to shut the door carefully, just in case a cool breeze should awaken the guards and cause them to wonder why the door was open. Keeping low and in the shadows, he duck-walked in a squat along the cloister heading toward the porter's entrance. There was a lamp burning in the room. He lifted his head so he could see through the window. What he saw was a major disappointment. The porter and a guard were sitting at a table, wide-awake and talking. There was no exit that way. He sat down under the window, discouraged, and wondered how he was going to get out of the convent.

He moved back into the shadows of the cloister and paused to think. What other way could he get out? Could he climb over a wall? Not too likely. He had lost much of his strength during his months in prison. Where would other doors be? Could he use the entrance to the kitchen and workshops? This is where the lay workers would enter and exit the building for their workday, but where was it? He didn't know the layout of the convent, and in the darkness he could wander around for quite awhile and not find the entrance. He looked around. It was a clear night, and he saw the bell tower of the chapel standing black against the full moon shining in the background. Then a solution started to form in his thoughts. He could go out through the chapel.

He started to head toward the chapel. Then he realized that it was nearing Matins. He must find a place to hide and wait until the monks had completed the Office. He found an alcove between two buildings and tried to make himself as small as possible. As he sat there waiting, he realized that he was cold. How long would he have to wait? He started to drift into sleep. He bit his tongue until it hurt; he had to stay awake, even though he hadn't slept for almost two days. Then he heard the shuffle of dozens of feet, and the clock struck again.

He didn't have to wait too long before he heard the return of the monks. Thankfully, they had observed the breviary. He couldn't see them, but the padding of their bare feet and the muffled swish of their robes spoke of their passing on the way to their chambers. He waited a few more minutes and quickly went around the outside of the courtyard to the chapel.

Finding the door open, he paused. He could see the flickering light of the candles on the altar. He knew that he should enter carefully in case someone was still there. This chapel was of the new design and had pews. He crouched down, crawled into the chapel, and quickly slid along the wall hidden from the altar by the pews. He peeked over the back of one of the pews in the last row and saw a monk kneeling at the altar.

He sat behind the pews near the main doors of the chapel and waited. What would he do if the monk decided to pray all night? Eventually the monk moved, and after much genuflection walked backward out the side door of the chapel, the same one that Bartolomé had entered a few minutes before. Bartolomé waited until the monk would be well away from the chapel, and then went over to the main door of the chapel. Standing up was difficult. He had been crouching and kneeling for so long. He removed the plank from the brackets and opened the door, stepped out onto the pavement, and quietly closed the door. He was free!

It was extremely difficult to resist the temptation to run, and he had to use every ounce of will to discipline himself to move slowly and carefully.

Where should he go? He could not return home. His stepmother, the traitor, would call the alcalde, and he would be back in prison faster than a cat can jump away from a dog. He thought about going to Catalina's house; he did not know that her family had moved from the city. Catalina would receive him with joy, but her father would probably turn him out, or like his stepmother, hand him over to the Inquisition. He needed to decide quickly to avoid going in the wrong direction. He considered going to one of the houses of Francisco or Diego, his former school friends, but it had been a few years since he had been close to either of them. It was difficult to know how they might react if an escapee from the Inquisition showed up at their door. He wasn't sure that they would even be in the city. He concluded that the only person in the entire city who offered any hope of being considerate of his situation was his former tutor, Doctor Pedro Ortiz de Tendilla. He prayed that he was still alive and living in the same house.

He knew the city well, so it took only a moment to plan a route that would be reasonably direct and yet would keep him off the streets most likely to be travelled in the middle of the night. He had to be careful to avoid the wardens and the night watch. He moved with stealth and stayed in the shadows. He didn't even stir a dog. It took him over an hour to make the trip that he would have walked in a quarter of an hour in the past.

When he arrived at his tutor's house, he approached it from the alleyway to the rear. There was a small stable, more like a shed, behind the house where the donkey was housed. This is where he planned to hide out until he could figure out his next step. The door of the stable facing the alley was locked, as he knew it would be, but climbing over the wall into the small courtyard was not difficult. He landed softly on the other side and went into the stable. He talked quietly to the donkey, which acted as if it recognized his voice. It was probably the same poor creature he had known four years before. Even, if not, it seemed to appreciate the presence of human company and stirred gently in its stall.

Above the donkey's stall was a shelf on which sheaves of straw, bundles of hay, and baskets of grain were stored. A short ladder went to the shelf. Bartolomé climbed this ladder and pushed the supplies forward to give himself room against the wall. He lay down on a bundle of hay. He desperately wanted to sleep. His body was tired. Even though his mind was overactive because of the escape, it really didn't take long to fall asleep. He slept deeply, as if he hadn't slept in months, even years.

Chapter 38
(Valladolid, 1559)

The city came awake. The shed was isolated from much of the noise of the merchants and craftsmen, carts and wagons, buyers and sellers, children and scholars. Bartolomé slept and slept.

Eventually Doctor Ortiz came to the stable to tend to the donkey. He was kind to the animal and called it pet names like 'Tickles'. He led it out to the courtyard where it could munch its feed in a trough, enjoy the spring sunshine, and flick its ears to annoy the flies. Doctor Ortiz puttered around in the stable, cleaning out the old straw and manure, putting it into a wheelbarrow and carting it to the far corner of his small vegetable plot. The noise eventually awakened Bartolomé.

Bartolomé peered over the supplies and quietly called, "Doctor Ortiz." The old man was startled. He wasn't sure where the voice came from. He looked outside the stable, but saw no one. Again, Bartolomé called his tutor's name. Doctor Ortiz looked up, saw Bartolomé on the shelf, and asked, "Who's there?"

Bartolomé wasn't sure if he should give his name or how best to reveal himself. He moved forward a bit, so that Doctor Ortiz could see his face, now bearded and unrecognizable to Doctor Ortiz, and said, "Sir, could you close the door please, I must ask you to keep this meeting private." Doctor Ortiz hesitated, but the young hairy face peering over the bundles of straw did not look particularly dangerous, and it had called to him by name.

After the door was shut, Bartolomé climbed down the ladder and approached the older man. Doctor Ortiz looked Bartolomé over in the limited light entering through the small window and saw standing before him a thin young man wearing tattered clothes and no shoes, with an untrimmed beard, and lengthening hair. "Who are you?" he asked.

"I am Bartolomé, Sir, your former student, the son of Juan Garcia the goldsmith. I went to the university in Paris to study law a few years ago. I hope, Sir, that you remember me."

"Bartolomé? I remember the name, but you do not look anything like the young man who used to tease me and my donkey."

"I, Sir, am he."

"What are you doing here? Why are you dressed like that? Why have you grown such a scruffy beard and not cut your hair? Have you fallen on hard times? Your father, God rest his soul, was so prosperous.

Oh, dear me, you do know about what happened to your father. Don't you?"

"I don't know exactly what happened, but I presume that he was executed yesterday. Is that correct?"

"Yes. I am so sorry. I did respect your father. He was a gentleman among gentlemen. Oh, the harshness of the Inquisition. Oh, I must not say such things! Dear me, what times we live in. — You have not answered my questions. How did you end up here, in this state? Are you hiding? Here, sit down, tell me what is going on."

At this, Bartolomé turned over a wooden feed pail and sat down. Doctor Ortiz rested his lean body on a trestle. Bartolomé then recounted for him the events of his story, beginning with his return to Valladolid from Paris until his escape from the prison. At this point, he said, "It seems so long ago, yet it has been less than twelve hours since I walked out of that cellar. I understand how Saint Peter must have felt when the angel led him out of Herod's prison. No visible angel led me out, but my escape is just as much a miracle. That, Sir, is how I ended up here in your stable. I didn't know where else to go, or to whom else to turn. I hope, Sir, that by coming here I have not put you into a difficult situation. If the Inquisition discovers me here, you will be considered a co-conspirator for harbouring a heretic. I am sorry for putting you in this position — for putting your life at risk. I should not have come. I am sorry."

"Don't fret yourself over the Inquisition. I have evaded them for over fifty years. If they catch me now, so be it. I am an old man. The worst they can do to me is hurry-up my departure for Heaven. I have no one on earth to worry about, except poor Flor, and I am sure she could find a new friend soon enough, gentle soul—anyone who would feed her. And, in case you have any worries at all, don't have them! We shall find a way to get you out of this city and away from the Inquisition. I am no friend of theirs and will not see you recaptured!"

"Thank you. I really don't know how to thank you. I praise God that I turned to you for help. Thank you!"

Waving his hand, Doctor Ortiz said, "Now let us start to think of the future. Are you hungry, should I get you some food?"

"I could do with some food, thank you."

"Why don't you come into the house? Let me go out first and make sure that no one is around or watching. I will open the door to the house. When I return, you go quickly into the house. I will put Flor back into her stall, and come in shortly."

Bartolomé went into the house and sat at the table. Doctor Ortiz followed a moment later. "As long as you sit in the middle of the room here, no one can see you from the alley or from the street." He placed in front of Bartolomé bread and cheese, some winter greens, and a piece of mutton that had been cooked on Saturday. The meat had been stored in a jar set in a basin of water and covered with a cloth, so that the evaporation kept the meat cool. Then Doctor Ortiz poured some wine into a wooden goblet. Bartolomé gave a short prayer of thanks and sipped the wine first. He hadn't had a drop since his arrest. This meal was a feast.

As he ate, they talked. "I need to get out of Spain," said Bartolomé. "I should go to France, I know people there who could provide me with a refuge. I met a number of Huguenots when I was at law school in Paris. Can you help me get there? Could you get me a horse?"

"Of course I will help you get to France. Yet, even if I could afford to buy you a horse, you cannot go by horse."

"Why not?"

"It is too obvious. By now, the guards will have discovered your escape and may have reported it to the alcalde. They may hide the fact that you are gone for awhile, but word will soon get out. It will not go well for the guards who were on duty when you escaped—if they can determine who it was. The alcalde has a reputation for harshness. He will probably hand those guards over to the Inquisition, charging them with complicity with a heretic. They will end up on the gallows. As soon as the alcalde knows of your escape, he will alert the captain, and all the soldiers at the city gates and along all the roads to the Pyrenees will have your description. You would be stopped."

Bartolomé, on hearing Doctor Ortiz speak of the alcalde, thought about how different he sounded from what he had heard about him from Margarita.

Doctor Ortiz continued, "Also, you cannot ride a horse into France."

"Why not? You know I can ride."

"For almost two hundred years, Spain has been trying to stop the exporting of horses to France. King Felipe has again outlawed their export into France. He is upset at how many horses from Spanish lines seem to be in the hands of the French. The recent wars with France have reinforced his concern. Even nobles cannot ride their own horses into France. I hear that he is even thinking of using the Inquisition's spy network to stop the smuggling of horses."

"What do you suggest I do?"

"We have time, you are safe. Even if they begin a search of the city, it will take a long time, and they will do it discreetly. The last thing the Inquisition wants is to let it be known that they let a 'heretic' escape. Their reputation for invincibility would be questioned. Let's plan your departure carefully. Come, eat! Then let's get you cleaned up. I will go out and buy you some new clothes. I will return shortly. There is shaving equipment in the cupboard there, and a small mirror of polished brass on top."

Bartolomé finished eating and then shaved off his beard. He thought he would look more like a Frenchman if he shaved completely. Frenchmen did not wear moustaches and groomed beards as often as the Spanish. It wasn't long before Doctor Ortiz returned. He came in with some readymade clothing. They were previously worn but were clean and sturdy, the type of clothing rustics wore from Holstein to the Algarve: a linen undergarment, a heavy cotton shirt, a wool jerkin with a leather belt, sturdy stockings, low leather shoes that were almost sandals, and a felt hat with a new goose feather.

Doctor Ortiz cut Bartolomé's hair and heated some water so he could bathe. Once he had put on the new clothing, he felt like he was ready to take on the world. It was less than a day since he had been a prisoner.

Bartolomé said, "How were you able to pay for this clothing? I wish I could repay you. Do you have any income?"

"I still do a bit of tutoring, mostly in languages, but I have no regular students now. I am too old to keep up the pace, and the young people today are so disrespectful. I find that the youth of today don't really care about learning. They are only interested in flirtatious encounters and entertainment. It was very different when I was a youth. We took our schooling seriously! Don't worry about me, however. I live frugally and have put away a small sum of money over the years. It is good to have some money set aside in case of a sudden need. What better way is there to spend it than helping you? Now let us think about your plan of escape."

They talked for a while and finally came up with a strategy. Bartolomé would pose as a French merchant returning to France with wares purchased in Spain. Since he was fluent in French and had light coloured hair, this would be quite easy to accomplish. Yet, when they thought about the goods that would have to be purchased, Doctor Ortiz said, "I haven't got enough money to outfit a merchant."

"If only," Bartolomé mused, "I could get at the money I received from my grandfather and have invested with Monsieur Lachy in Paris —" At that point Bartolomé remembered something very important. "Oh! Am I ever forgetful! Almost two years ago—it seems like many more—my father showed me a place where he had hidden money from my stepmother. He told me that the money was mine should I ever need it. He was putting it away for his own safety, but it was also a legacy for me. I don't know how much money is there or if it is even still there. But if it is, it could help us execute this plan."

"How can we get it?" said Doctor Ortiz.

"Can you find a reason to go to my former house? If so, it may be possible to get it without attracting too much attention."

Bartolomé explained to Doctor Ortiz how the money was hidden under the floor of the shed in which his father stored the charcoal for his furnace. It was kept in a wooden box. If the box was still there, it should contain some money to help defray the cost of getting him out of Spain.

They discussed a plan for getting at the box, and spent the rest of the day thinking about how to put the steps of Bartolomé's escape plan into action. After the evening meal, they slept.

Chapter 39
(Valladolid, 1559)

The next day, after breakfast, Doctor Ortiz attached a small cart to Flor's harness and headed to the former home of Juan Garcia. When he arrived, he found that Damiana Garcia still lived there, and in considerable luxury.

The maid who answered the door, showed him into a sitting area. He realized that a renovation of Juan's workshop had created it. While he waited, he recalled what Bartolomé had told him about his stepmother and thought, "It is hard to understand how anyone could work with the inquisitors, and harder to understand how a lady could spy on her friends and family. I am especially appalled that this woman betrayed her husband and stepson. She must be very wicked. Besides inheriting her husband's estate, she has obviously been well paid by the Inquisition. May she receive her reward! God spare me from such greed." He loathed meeting her.

A painted Damiana swished into the room. Doctor Ortiz was convinced that he was looking at Jezebel, the Devil in female form, walking among the graves of Gadera. He was tempted to apply the sign of the cross. She in turn, didn't recognize Doctor Ortiz. She had met him when he was Bartolomé's tutor, but she was so caught up with her own appearance and position that she hardly considered anyone else. All she saw was, as she thought, a dirty, old day-labourer. "What do you want?" she asked harshly.

"I understand that your late husband used to be a goldsmith."

"Yes," she said, warily. She didn't want the subject of her deceased husband discussed, "What is that to you?"

"I was wondering if you might want to sell his charcoal. I could use it, and since it is probably of little use to you, you might be willing to provide it to me at a reasonable price."

Damiana, seeing the opportunity to make some money, said, "But we use it for cooking." This was a lie, but she hoped it might increase the price she could get for it.

"What do you want for it?" he said.

She had no idea what the price of charcoal was, so she said, "You may have it for fifty real."

"That is absurd, that is more than a labourer earns in many months! I can get excellent charcoal from the oak forests of the Cantabrian Mountains for a fraction of that! I am just offering to take it off your hands. As far as I am concerned, the charcoal can rot. Good day, Doña."

Seeing an opportunity to make a little money evaporating, she asked, "What do you offer for it? After all, it is a full shed of charcoal."

"I will give you two hundred maravedís for it," he said, knowing that he was quoting a figure below what the charcoal was worth.

She replied, "Five hundred and nothing less!"

"Three hundred is my final offer."

"You take advantage of a widow! Fine, you may take it."

He paid over the money, went outside to fetch his donkey, and led her around back.

In the shed, he found more charcoal than the little wagon could carry. He worked slowly at loading the wagon, so that if the woman was watching from the house she would get bored and return to her own business. He found the box, about the size of a goose, where Bartolomé had indicated it would be; and surrounding it with a bundle of charcoal sticks, carried it, with some difficulty as it was heavy, to the wagon. He finished filling the wagon as full as he could, making sure the box was well covered with large and small pieces of charcoal, and headed home.

He had left the gate to his garden unlocked. He opened it and led the donkey with the wagon into the little courtyard between the garden and the shed. He slowly unhitched Flor and led her into her stall. After he was sure that she had some hay, he began to unpack the wagon. Bartolomé watched from the middle of the house and was tempted to go out and help, but Doctor Ortiz had warned him to stay hidden until they figured out a way to explain his presence. Doctor Ortiz stacked as much of the charcoal as he could in the shed but had to store some of the larger pieces beside the house. Then he carefully, and casually, in case anyone was watching, carried the box into the house. Bartolomé shut the door after him.

Doctor Ortiz, with blackened hands, set the box on the table. They stood on either side of the table looking at it for a long time saying nothing. Finally Doctor Ortiz said, "Well, you had better open it and see what your father has left you."

The box consisted of a lower portion covered with a thin sheet of lead, and a lid also covered with lead. The lid fit tightly over the lower box. Bartolomé eased off the lid, and his mouth fell open. He couldn't speak and motioned furiously with his finger for Doctor Ortiz to look into the box. Doctor Ortiz leaned over the table and looked in. He stood back and stared at Bartolomé, while tears carved trails on his dusty face. Bartolomé's mouth finally moistened and he swallowed, "My father was a wealthy man! Yet, we lived on so little most of the time. Why?"

"I cannot explain why, but I can guess. After meeting your stepmother today, I believe that your father was quite wise. He knew that she would squander the money if she became aware of its existence. I suspect also that he was training you. He didn't want you to grow up with a large allowance and spoil you. He also planned for the future—a lesson you should never forget. Here — it is now the future!"

Bartolomé said with a smile, "So I have had two teachers, you *and* my father. Well, I could have done worse! I have been doubly blessed. And now I am blessed again with this money in my time of need. Come, let's see how much is here."

Instead of dumping the contents of the box onto the table, they were deliberate about lifting out each coin and item of jewellery as if it were too fragile to hold. They sorted the items into piles on the table. Most of the coins were gold, but there were also a number of silver ones. The gold coins were mostly from Castile, Aragon, and France, but there were a few from England, Bohemia and Naples—marcs, florins, coronas, ducats, guilders, and even a *royal d'or Lyons*. They counted one thousand two hundred and sixty-three gold coins, plus many fine pieces of gold jewellery. Some of the jewellery included mounted precious stones—emeralds and rubies predominating. Using the coins alone, Bartolomé could have lived the rest of his life in modest comfort. "This is incredible!" he said. "I have never seen so much money in one place. I had no idea my grandfather or father had accumulated this amount of wealth."

"You are now the rich one," replied Doctor Ortiz.

"Well, first I must repay you for the clothes and the charcoal." He selected a handful of the silver coins that he thought would more than cover the cost of the clothes and charcoal, and handed them over.

Doctor Ortiz returned three of them. "Thank you. I will accept repayment for the clothes, but not the charcoal. Bettering your stepmother in a negotiation was worth every maravedí, and I now have enough charcoal to last me many seasons. In fact, I still have more to collect. There was so much in your father's shed; it wouldn't all fit in the cart. I will have to return tomorrow for the rest."

"When you go out tomorrow," Bartolomé asked, "can you enquire about the welfare of a friend of mine?"

"Of, course, if it will not risk your safety. Who is it?"

"It is Catalina, daughter of Doctor Abram Mendoza, a doctor who lives across from the apothecary's shop on Calle de la Curraba near the cathedral."

"Bartolomé! You must not let anyone know that you are in the city. It is too dangerous. You have seen the results of a woman being seduced by the wiles of the Inquisition. Can you trust this girl?"

"You are right, I must be careful. I can trust her, but not her parents. They were ready to hand me over to the Inquisition if I continued calling on their daughter. Can you at least find her house, and if possible, see if she is well? I will write a letter, and then after I have left the city, can you deliver it to her?"

"I won't make any promises. I am concerned for your safety, and I will not do anything that will compromise it."

They spent the remainder of the day around a pleasant meal working out additional details of their plan to get Bartolomé out of the city without betraying him to the Inquisition. They planned to have Bartolomé return to France with a cartload of various kinds of Spanish olives and olive oil.

Chapter 40
(Valladolid, 1559)

The next morning Doctor Ortiz collected the rest of the charcoal and then went out again to buy the first of the supplies for the journey. He visited the apothecary on Calle de la Curraba. He purchased some dried leaves and flowers of horehound and asked the apothecary, "Is there a Doctor Mendoza living nearby?"

"Doctor Abram Mendoza, and his wife and daughter, lived in the house across the street until just recently."

"Where did they go?"

"He was called to serve King Felipe and has moved to Madrid. He and his family moved away about two months ago. However, I can direct you to another doctor if you wish."

"No, thank you, I was enquiring for a friend who used to be a patient of Doctor Mendoza. Have a pleasant day."

Doctor Ortiz was relieved that Catalina had moved away from the city. He did not want Bartolomé losing his head over a girl. He might do something stupid and let the Inquisition capture him for a second time. They would not be lenient with an escaped prisoner.

When he returned to the house, he told Bartolomé what he had discovered, "There is no need to write a letter. There is no one to leave it with. Once you get out of Spain and are safely in a country or city where the Inquisition cannot reach, such as England or northern Germany, you could write to Catalina care of her father at the court. I am sure that it would reach her, but you had better consider this action carefully. The Inquisition has been opening letters coming into the country. If they read your letter to her, they might assume that she is a Lutheran sympathizer and arrest her. You could endanger her life. You had best forget about Catalina."

"I will never forget Catalina."

"When you arrive at your destination, you will meet local girls whom you will find attractive."

"I will never forget Catalina!" Bartolomé repeated with emphasis.

"Let's not argue about this. I have seen many a young man like you fall in love and just as quickly fall out of love."

Almost becoming angry, Bartolomé said, "I will never forget Catalina!"

"Ok, but for now can we work on your escape plan?"

Bartolomé calmed down and nodded in agreement to the request.

"I have been thinking," said Doctor Ortiz, "you will have to go outside. You cannot stay indoors for the next few weeks as we prepare for your departure. Your skin has turned white during your confinement in the cellar. If you tried to go past the guards at the gate right now, they would immediately suspect something. No merchant who has been travelling for weeks looks like he has been sitting in the king's palace all winter."

"How can I darken my skin? I will have to go out during the hottest part of the day, but that is when most people are about."

"I have been thinking about that also. That is probably the safest time for you to be outside. If we quietly go about our business in a crowd, no one will pay much attention to you. You will start to accompany me as a servant when I shop for the supplies. I will let it be known around here that I have a friend from France visiting me."

"What if the soldiers see me? I might be recognized and arrested?"

"We will keep our eyes open and stay away from the areas patrolled by the soldiers. We will also stay away from the neighbourhood where you used to live. I suspect that even if one of your old friends saw you as a servant or a French merchant he would not recognize you. There are sixty-thousand people in this city; you will be invisible unless you deliberately draw attention to yourself. Also, if we can keep this up for a few weeks, the guards will be less vigilant when it comes time for you to exit the city. They will have assumed you fled long ago."

"I am worried somewhat about your suggestion, but we'll try it. God sparing me, I will escape this city!"

Chapter 41
(Valladolid, 1559)

Over the next three weeks, Doctor Ortiz and Bartolomé made trips throughout the city to as many different suppliers of olives and olive oil as they could find. They bought different sizes of oak casks, pine cases and clay jars containing green, red, and black olives; as well as various types of plain and spiced oils. In case his neighbours wondered what was going on, Doctor Ortiz informed some in casual conversation that he had an associate from France staying with him who was buying the best Spanish olives and oil to take back with him. The neighbours nodded with understanding. Of course, the French would want Spanish olives! When they saw Doctor Ortiz with Bartolomé heading out to make their purchases, they nodded pleasantly to them.

They tried to be as casual as possible and to vary their routes and the times they left and returned. At first, Bartolomé walked on the inside of the cart near the buildings and kept his eyes to the ground. Within a few days, his confidence increased and he began to walk more freely and openly. However, he avoided eye contact with anyone they passed on the streets, for fear he might be recognized. When they were making the purchases, he remained with the cart and tried to be as unobtrusive as possible. His demeanour was that of a not too bright, listless servant—basically, he behaved like many servants of his day in the city. When Doctor Ortiz had negotiated a price for a larger barrel or cask, he would command Bartolomé to load it into the cart.

Only once during these three weeks did they come upon any soldiers. These, however, were marching in tight formation and ignored people passing and those standing watching. They also came upon a group of Dominican monks. These, in their aloofness, refused to acknowledge the presence of anyone who passed them. As Doctor Ortiz had thought, Bartolomé became essentially indistinguishable from the mass of people passing through the streets every day. To recognize Bartolomé, a person would have had to be especially observant, but most people were far too self-absorbed to recognize anyone who appeared to be beneath their station.

Bartolomé and Doctor Ortiz spent almost every evening addressing different aspects of Bartolomé's escape plan. They also discussed different aspects of theology. Bartolomé came to the realization that Doctor Ortiz was not convinced of the principles espoused by Luther and Calvin. His views were similar to those that had been held by Erasmus. Doctor Ortiz felt that there were areas in the Church that needed to be improved, but not the basic doctrines. He approached many of the topics they discussed with intellectual curiosity rather than conviction. This perplexed and bothered Bartolomé who, over his last year in Paris, had become fervently convinced of the Reformation's principles. At least Doctor Ortiz disagreed strongly with the reactionary approach of the Inquisition and Council of Trent. In general, he felt that there should be more room within the bounds of the Church for variation of opinion. Bartolomé did not need to fear that Doctor Ortiz would deliver him to the Inquisition.

One time, Doctor Ortiz said, "I recommend that you head east toward Zaragoza in Aragon. You can follow the old Roman road that winds through the Rio Duero valley. From Zaragoza, there are a number of routes north into France. One route, on the east, goes through Pamplona and will bring you to Bayonne. The other route crosses through the Pyrenees farther west. From there, you can reach Toulouse. I suggest you take that route, it is less likely to be as heavily patrolled by the Inquisition's spies, but still provides adequate roads."

"How long do you think it will take me to get to France?"

"Since you will be travelling at a walking pace, it will probably take between ten and fifteen days to get to Zaragoza. It will take about ten more days to reach southern France. You will have to carry enough food and water to last you at least five days over any given period of your journey. Part of your route will be desolate. The great plague that reached Castile and Aragon in 1350 wiped out many of the towns along your route. People have not resettled much of that territory. Every chance you get you will have to replenish your supplies, especially your water. Never pass up the opportunity to refill your water barrels, you won't know how long it will be until you will get another chance."

The work of loading and unloading the little cart helped Bartolomé regain his strength. His skin started to tan because he was outdoors much of the day. He really couldn't pass for a merchant who had been on the road for many months, but unless someone consciously thought about it, his lighter skin colour would not be too obvious. He also started to put on weight since he was eating wholesome food regularly again. The house and courtyard were crowded with small organized stacks of supplies. They concluded that they had purchased enough and were ready to carry out the next step of their plan.

They went south of the city to outlying farms to purchase an ox and wagon. Since access to money was not a problem for Bartolomé, they bought a three-year-old ox with yoke and harness and feed, and a used wagon that was in good condition. The wagon had four large wheels and was better built than an average farm cart. It had a steel strap around the rim of each wheel and a steel hub in each wheel that rolled on a steel spindle on the axle. If regularly greased, this wagon could carry a heavy weight and could be used to pull all the supplies to France. They could not take the ox or wagon back to the city, as there was no room to store them at Doctor Ortiz's house. So, they agreed on a day the following week when they would come to claim them.

Meanwhile, they split up the money and jewellery into separate packets to minimize the possibility of Bartolomé losing everything should he be robbed on the way to France. They hid one packet in the bottom of a barrel filled with grain that was going to be used to feed the ox. Another packet they put into a thin wooden box that they were going to attach to the underside of the wagon. Smaller packets were placed in hidden compartments in the bottom of leather bags in which he was going to carry his clothing and food for the trip. Doctor Ortiz had suggested these actions, because as he said, "When I travelled from Venice, through Helvetia and France I was robbed once. The robbers didn't stay around to search my goods. They were only interested in what they could get quickly. Then they ran off into the woods. From then on, I have always split up my money in the hope that I wouldn't lose it all again. In all my travels since then I have never been robbed a second time, but it is better to be wise than sorry."

Bartolomé had outfitted himself with a change of clothing that would go into his travel bags. He had also purchased a pair of near-new sturdy boots, eating utensils including a small hunting knife, a short sword, and a leather purse in which he would carry coins—mostly silver of different denominations, for his journey. This purse would be the 'give-away' should he be robbed. It would be a temptation for thieves and would steer them away from the treasure hidden in the wagon. They also bought a large used canvas and rope to tie over the supplies.

The day before they were to pick up the ox and wagon they went out of the city and stayed over-night with the farmer from whom they had purchased the ox. During both of their trips out of the city, Doctor Ortiz had brought along Flor with her little cart. He felt that this would draw less attention to them.

Very early the next morning they led the ox with its yoke to the place where they were to obtain the wagon at a nearby farm. Doctor Ortiz had Bartolomé practice hitching the ox to the wagon four times. He wanted to make sure that he could do it on his own and that he would look like he was experienced working with an ox-drawn wagon. Bartolomé led the ox into the city. The guards paid no attention to two rustics leading in a donkey pulling an empty cart and an ox pulling an empty wagon. They assumed they were coming into the city to purchase supplies.

Before they loaded the goods in the wagon, they attached the box with some of the money and jewellery to the underside of the wagon. They used ropes passing through holes in the box and wagon and pulled the box snug against the wagon. Then they loaded the wagon with all the barrels, casks, cases and jars; covered them with the canvas; and tied everything down. Bartolomé then stowed his travel bags and some of his water and wineskins under the seat of the wagon. He was ready. It was around noon, so they paused to have a final meal together and a rest during the hottest part of the day.

In the late afternoon, they headed to the southeast side of the city where Bartolomé would pick up the road toward Zaragoza, as Doctor Ortiz had recommended. Before they reached the edge of the city, Doctor Ortiz indicated that he would not go with Bartolomé to the gates. It was best if he went on alone.

"I don't want to admit it but I have become a lonely old man. I have enjoyed our time together; I will miss you very much, Bartolomé."

"And I, you. I can't thank you enough for how you have helped me. I don't suppose that we will ever see each other again in this life. I thank God you were my teacher, and are now my friend and helper."

"Let's not draw out this parting. I'm not one for emotional goodbyes. I wish you Godspeed."

At that, Doctor Ortiz placed his hand on Bartolomé's shoulder and said, "May God bless you and make his face shine upon you."

They hugged each other. Bartolomé turned away. He didn't want Doctor Ortiz to see the tears coming to his eyes. He gently prodded the ox with his walking stick, and headed for the gates of the city. This would be the first real test of his plan to leave Valladolid, and Spain, disguised as a French merchant.

Chapter 42
(Madrid, 1559)

Catalina received two letters from Margarita in an official packet that arrived from Valladolid. They arrived at the end of May. Catalina noticed that the letters were folded and sealed with a hard red wax. The wax was pressed with a mark that she assumed was Margarita's seal. She had not seen this form of sealing letters before, although being around the court she had heard of it for sealing official documents. She thought that it was unlikely that anyone had opened the letters and read them. She was glad of this; she didn't like the idea that Margarita's letters could have been read by anyone, especially a nosy monk from the Inquisition.

The first letter gave her all of the details about the *auto*. Catalina wept over the death of Bartolomé's father; became angry over the injustice of the Inquisition; cursed under her breath Fernando Valdes, the supreme Inquisitor General, and Baca; and prayed for the families who had lost someone at the *auto*.

In the second letter, Margarita wrote:

I tried after the auto to find a way to determine what had happened to Bartolomé. The guards now assigned to the Santa María de las Huelgas convent are new. I didn't recognize any of them. Their accents indicate that they are not from Castile, but from Seville in Andalusia.

I asked one of the new guards what had happened to Alvaro, the guard I knew. They would not tell me anything. One of the guards now at the porter's door became quite angry and threatened that he would report me to the Inquisition if I asked any more questions.

Something has happened that has made them wary. There have been rumours going about the city that some prisoners escaped from the cellar prison the night following the Inquisition. I have not been able to find anyone who will confirm this as true, so cannot determine who might have escaped.

We won't be able to get any more information out of the guards. I cannot think of any other way to find out what has happened to Bartolomé. All we can do now is pray for him.

Catalina was trembling as she read the letter. She was surprised at how open Margarita was in describing her visit to the convent. She breathed deeply and convinced herself that the Inquisition had not read it because the seal was still intact when it arrived. What distressed her most, however, was that she had no direct news about Bartolomé. At least he hadn't been executed at the *auto*. She hoped that the rumour that prisoners had escaped from the convent was true. She thought, "It serves them right, if they let prisoners escape!" She imagined that one of them was Bartolomé. She saw him grab a sword from one of the guards and lead the fight to freedom through a dozen guards. She burned each page of both letters in the candle she used as a light in her bedroom. The smell of burning paper filled the room.

Before she went to bed that evening, she pulled from its hiding place her *New Testament* and started reading at a random location. It didn't matter where she read; she wasn't concentrating or paying attention to the words. What was more important to her, at that moment, was that the book had been Bartolomé's gift to her. As she turned the pages, all she could see was his face and hands. His lips were moving as if he was talking but she could hear no words. She cried herself to sleep.

The next morning at breakfast with her parents, she told them about the *auto*, the possible escape from the prison, and the changes made in the appointment of the guards. Her parents were sympathetic. Her father had heard through official channels about the *auto* and was disgusted by it. Her mother asked casually, watching for Abram's reaction, "Did Margarita give you any news of Bartolomé?"

"No, but she told me that Juan Garcia was executed. Bartolomé was not there."

With tears welling in her eyes, Susana said, "We are sorry to hear about Bartolomé's father. I do hope Bartolomé is well. I know we have been hard on you about seeing him, but we never would have wished this evil on him or his father."

"I know that. I know that you were only concerned for my safety. I wish I knew what has happened to him."

Catalina was relieved that her parents had not lectured her about what might have happened to her if the Inquisition had arrested her. She loved them more because they had showed some concern for Bartolomé, but she didn't want to talk about Bartolomé—it made her so unhappy. Therefore, she changed the subject, "Father, what have you been doing with King Felipe so much lately?"

"King Felipe has called a number of his advisors together. He has included me among them. He is developing plans to build a new monastery and church. He says that he wants it to be the greatest monument to God on earth."

"Where is he going to build it? Here in Madrid?"

"That hasn't been decided yet. In fact, I have been meaning to tell you both that King Felipe wants me to accompany him while he looks for a site on which to build it."

"How long will you be away?"

"Actually, it is how long will *we* be away?"

"What?"

"Yes, King Felipe said that we could bring our families along if we wished. King Felipe's staff will be providing food and lodging for us. We will get to visit places around Madrid that we have never been to. It could be fun."

"Oh! This will be fun! I can't wait to tell Luisa! When do we start?"

"That has yet to be worked out. We have recently concluded the Peace of Cateau-Cambresis and ended years of open war with France. King Felipe is planning to seal the peace by marrying Elizabeth of Valois, the daughter of King Henry II. The trip to identify a location for the new monastery has to be worked around the wedding."

"I thought Princess Elizabeth was to marry Don Carlos, King Felipe's son."

"That is what we had been told, but King Felipe has decided to marry her himself. Don Carlos has almost daily hysterical fits followed by heavy fevers. I have been attending to him and don't think that he has much time left to live."

"When is the wedding to be? How old is Princess Elizabeth? Is she pretty? Can you get me an invitation to the wedding? I would love to see the ceremony ..."

"Slow down, my dear! The wedding is planned for June 22nd. I understand that Princess Elizabeth is fourteen. She should be arriving in Madrid in a few weeks. You can get a look at her yourself and judge whether she is pretty, although I hear rumours that she is. I will see what I can do to get you, and your mother, an invitation to the wedding. Haven't you had enough excitement for one day?"

"Thank you, Father, I love you. Oh! Please see if Luisa can be invited also — please"

He smiled at her, and she broke out in a big grin. Breakfast had ended better than it had begun.

Chapter 43
(Madrid and Sierra de
Guadarramas, 1559)

King Felipe wanted to begin the work of building the new monastery, but first he had to find the perfect location for it. He was growing anxious to start looking for a site. He pressed his advisors to get ready to accompany him. Their advice was that he should wait until after the wedding, but he was insistent that the work of God could not wait for him to get married. He reminded them of Jesus' parable about the banquet in Luke's gospel where people gave excuses. "I will not be like the man who said, 'I have just got married, so I cannot come.'" So, with a great bustle, the court prepared to accompany the king on his journey of exploration.

Catalina spent much of her time over the next few days considering what she would take with her on the trip. She decided that it was too dangerous to take along her *New Testament*. She also needed to pick her clothes carefully; she was not going to be able to take a maid with her, and she had to take clothes that would be suitable for travel and easy to put on. She also needed gowns that would be appropriate for appearing in the retinue of the king.

Luisa helped her select the best outfits. Catalina said more than once, "How impractical woman's clothing is! I would love to be able just to wear stockings and a jacket." They both giggled at the thought of dressing in men's clothing.

Luisa asked, "Why do you want to go on this expedition?"

"I get bored in the city. All the ladies and girls think about is men and music. Don't misunderstand me. I like to look at a handsome man, just as much as anyone else. I also enjoy listening to music, and I like to be dressed up in a fine gown. Yet, I wish we could be more serious sometimes and not just be entertained. I think that men prefer that we don't talk about war and government policies, exploration of the Americas, or the latest scientific discoveries. When we do, it seems to frighten them. Is it possible that they think that someday we might actually be able to do some of the things they can do?"

"You wouldn't want to fight in a war, would you?"

"No, I am no Joan d'Arc! But, I would love to go to the Spanish Americas. Can you imagine what it would have been like to sail to Hispaniola with Cristóbal Colón, or to San Juan Bautista with Juan Ponce de León? I think I am cursed! My father spared no expense having me taught the Latin classics, and my tutor, Master Tomé Diaz de Montalvo," she said the whole name to emphasize his importance, "taught me French, geometry, anatomy, logic, and — Enough! How many girls do you know who can tell you who Leonardo of Pisa or Fibonacci were? Now I am expected to have no more aspirations than the meekest farm girl!"

"Catalina! Calm down! I don't envy your wide interests, but I hope for your sake that you can find a way to use your head as well as your hands and heart. I can see now why you have such an interest in going with the king. Come, let's finish your packing and then go watch the young men play bocce on the new green that King Felipe had installed in Plaza del Cebada on Calle Mayor."

The journey began on June 5th. Almost two hundred people travelled with King Felipe. This included soldiers as personal bodyguards for King Felipe, servants, and advisors including nobles, architects, learned clerics, doctors, and educators. Many of these brought along members of their families and their own servants. Doctor Mendoza now served as King Felipe's personal doctor and as one of his advisors.

There were many carriages and wagons full of supplies. The retinue made a long procession as it left Madrid.

Catalina and her parents rode in their own carriage with a hired driver. Occasionally her father rode on horseback with King Felipe and others of the advisors so that they could discuss matters along the road. He was not much of an equestrian and preferred, whenever possible, to have a seat beneath him rather than a saddle. So, some of the time he travelled with Catalina and her mother. Yet, he was going to have to learn to be better on a horse if he was to accompany King Felipe on any other trips.

On the first evening of their trip, the servants set up pavilions. Beneath these, they laid boards on trestles to create tables, and set out benches at the tables. Catalina and her mother sat at the table with the others, although not near the king. Her father was closer to the king so that he could participate in the discussions about the first sites they had seen.

During the meal, a noble named Alfonso Conde de Bobadilla, a widower, kept eyeing Catalina. From that evening, throughout the rest of the trip, he contrived ways to sit across from or near her at meals, to ride near her carriage, or to walk near her when the sites were being investigated. Catalina didn't like him, and especially didn't like the lascivious look that came into his eyes each time he saw her. She tried to avoid him at every opportunity. Her encounters with the Conde de Bobadilla were the only unpleasant experience during the entire trip. Sleeping on a cot and travelling in a carriage for many hours at a time were inconveniences, but they were nothing compared with the difficulty of trying to stay away from the Conde de Bobadilla.

King Felipe wanted to find a solitary and peaceful place for the new monastery, but he didn't want it to be too remote from his new capital at Madrid. His plan was to look at various sites in the foothills of

the Sierra de Guadarramas. He considered one location where a monastery of the Hieronymites already
existed. The Hieronymites were a disciplined and
isolated order that limited their contact with the
outside world. They were overwhelmed by the visit
of King Felipe and his company, and were unable
to accommodate them when they camped there over
night. They had only a few rooms and a small courtyard available, so most of the retinue had to set up
camp on the exterior grounds of the monastery. King
Felipe decided that the site was too rugged and inac-
cessible, and they moved on.

They continued their journey by heading
northwest toward Segovia, on the road that led to
Valladolid. They considered many possible locations,
some of them with beautiful views looking down on
the plains below. The primary challenge with most of
the sites was that they did not provide a sufficiently
large area of relatively flat land on which to build the
massive monastery that King Felipe had in mind.

At one spot, near a hamlet called Escorial, they
found a site that could serve as a location for the
future monastery. It was a fast, one-day's ride from
Madrid and would take two days at the most. The site
was barren except for the leftovers of the exhausted
iron mines. The village derived its names from these
heaps of *scoria*, or slag, that early miners had left
behind. The site was level and could accommodate
an enormous building. Nearby was a forest teeming
with wild game, streams with fish, and a good source
of clean water. King Felipe's chief architect, Juan
Bautista de Toledo, was particularly pleased that he

found close by a source of pale granite, flecked with pyrite that could be used to make a building of grandeur. He thought it especially suitable for the edifice King Felipe desired to build. This was the best site they had seen thus far.

They stayed at the Escorial site for two days. Most of King Felipe's advisors tried to convince him that they had found the perfect site. They informed him that God had provided the climate, location, setting, and natural supplies for the very purpose of building the monument he had planned. King Felipe could not disagree with them, but he wanted to be sure that there wasn't a better site. He was consumed by this endeavour and pressed on with the search.

They continued moving north until they were on the northern side of the Sierra de Guadarramas. Then they followed a road heading northeast that wound along at the base of the foothills. On the morning of Thursday, June 15[th,] they were almost immediately north of Madrid on the northern side of the sierras. King Felipe's advisors recommended that they head home and prepare for his wedding. He, however, instead insisted that they go a bit farther north to Aranda de Duero. King Felipe was quite familiar with the monastery of San Pablo in Valladolid that had been built by Simon de Colonia. He liked Colonia's work and wanted to get ideas for the monastery that he planned to build. He knew that there was a church, Santa María la Real, in Aranda de Duero built in the previous century by the same architect, and he wanted to see it. None of his advisors carried their arguments any further, and the party turned north.

Late in the day, as they approached Aranda de Duero, they came to the crossroads south of the town. The road heading west led to Valladolid; the one heading east to Zaragoza. At the crossroads, they cut off the traffic heading east or west. Among those who stood on the right side of the road was a young merchant standing beside a fully loaded ox-drawn cart. He had just crossed the north-south highway when the king's procession arrived. He decided to pause and watch them pass, since walking away might arouse suspicion. He was dressed in a brown leather jacket over green stockings, and wore thigh-high boots. He had on his head a felt hat with a goose feather.

He watched from under his hat, the procession heading into Aranda de Duero. He tried not to look up, as he was wary and didn't want to make eye contact with the guards or any of the servants, but also because the sun was starting to set and was shining directly into his eyes.

Catalina's carriage passed the crossroads. She and her mother were sitting on the right side of the carriage to avoid the sun's rays. Susana was riding in the carriage facing backward with Catalina opposite her, facing forward. Catalina noticed the young man standing beside his wagon and she turned and looked directly at him. Just as they passed he looked up. For a moment, the carriage blocked the sun and they made eye contact. Then they had passed.

Catalina tried to turn and see him, but the back of the carriage blocked her view. A knot formed in her stomach and she felt a chill rush up her spine.

She shivered. Her mother noticed and said, "What's wrong, are you getting cold? Here is a travelling blanket, cover yourself with this. It can still become cool in the evenings, even though it is June."

"I am fine, Mother. I just saw something outside the window of my carriage that gave me a fright."

"What did you see?"

"A young man with an ox and wagon."

"Why would that frighten you?"

"He reminded me of — no, he looked just like Bartolomé. I know Bartolomé's face like I know Father's. Is it possible to have two people in the world who look the same?"

"You know that it cannot have been Bartolomé. It had to be someone who looks like him. You need to stop thinking about him so much — you are going to start seeing visions. Here, drink some water, maybe you have not had enough to drink today and are starting to become delirious."

"Mother! I am fine. I know what I saw. But can there be another person who looks just like Bartolomé?"

"I don't know, dear. Of course, we certainly couldn't stop King Felipe so you can find out. Let's hope we reach Aranda de Duero quickly, I am tired."

At that, Catalina turned to look out the window of the carriage and to think of Bartolomé sitting in prison. Under her breath, she gave a short prayer, "Father, if Bartolomé is still alive, please protect him. Please! Amen." She felt a blanket of peace wrap around her. Whereas a moment before she had felt cold, she now was warm. She knew with absolute certainty that Bartolomé, wherever he was, was doing well. God was looking after him. Her prayer had been answered.

They didn't talk again for the rest of the ride into Aranda de Duero.

King Felipe didn't stay long in Aranda de Duero. The next day, he arose before dawn and went to the church where he kneeled at the altar in prayer for about an hour. He then toured the church and made a brief call on the abbot at the local monastery. The sun was barely up and he ordered his party to head south. They arrived in Madrid before dark on Saturday. On Monday, the preparations for Thursday's wedding would be rushed along.

Chapter 44
(Valladolid and north of the
Sierra de Guadarramas, 1559)

It was late in the afternoon on Monday, June 12th, 1559, that Bartolomé approached the gate of the city, with some concern. Although he had a strong desire to leave Valladolid, he was fearful of being recaptured. He was concerned that he would not be credible acting the part of a merchant. He was thankful that he had learned a little about playing a role when he and Doctor Ortiz where purchasing the supplies, and he had pretended to be a servant. He arrived at the gate, and one of the guards asked him to stop. A heavily loaded cart draws considerably more attention than an empty one.

The guard said, "What is in your load, and where are you going?"

In halting Spanish with a French accent he answered, "I am — merchant. I take olives of many kinds and oil to France."

Another of the guards laughed coarsely and said, "How do we know you are really French?"

Bartolomé replied, in Spanish, "Excuse me, I do not understand?"

"Prove you are from France!"

Bartolomé, knowing that they likely would not understand a word, said in flawless French, "I have been living in Paris; I am on my way back there. I have a cart full of olives and olive oil. I will be able to sell these in Paris. Let me pass, please."

"You could be just pretending to be French. We cannot understand you; you may be just spouting garbage!" the rude guard said. Turning to his friends, he said, "Let's call Jose. His mother is French, and he knows how to speak some French. He can tell us if this fellow is telling the truth."

Bartolomé was starting to worry that he would be detained.

Jose was brought from the nearby gatehouse and asked, "What is the problem?"

"This fellow says he is a French merchant; ask him to prove it to you."

"You, there, how do we know you are telling the truth?" Jose said in halting French.

Bartolomé replied fluently, "I have been living in Paris, in the *Quartier Latin* near the River Seine. I am returning to France after having purchased a large supply of the highest quality Spanish olives and olive oil. Since the end of hostilities between France and

Spain and the alliance between the king of France, King Henry II, and the king of Spain, Felipe II, your excellent products have been much appreciated in France, as has French wine in Spain." He chose his words carefully so as not to lie. He also spoke slower than a Frenchman would normally speak so that the guard could follow him.

Looking at the other guards he said, "He is legitimate. We will let him pass, but first collect the export tariff for the city of Valladolid." He turned back to Bartolomé and said in French, "We require that you pay the exit tariff for merchants." He struggled with the next sentence, "Based on the size of your wagon, that will be six hundred maravedís."

Bartolomé was relieved that he was going to be allowed to pass. Yet, he did not want to appear too relieved, so he pretended to argue with the guard, "That is scandalous, you rob a person who is trying to make an honest living!"

"Pay! Or you can turn around," he yelled.

Bartolomé took out his leather pouch and counted out silver coins to pay the amount. He counted slowly to make it look painful. The other guards had a laugh at his expense.

As he left them, he was tempted to yell, "Don't spend it all on wine and women!" but held his tongue and prodded his ox to move forward. He did not look back. It took him quite awhile to calm down from that experience.

As he left the built-up area outside the city wall and reached the start of farmland, he offered a prayer of sincere thanks. It was then that he first realized that he was on his way to freedom, but he told himself that he would not celebrate until he had passed well into France. He reminded himself that he must still be very careful. The Inquisition could have spies anywhere from Valladolid to Antwerp—his chosen destination.

Bartolomé continued eastward looking for an appropriate place to camp for the night. Since he had left Valladolid late in the afternoon, he was not going to cover much distance the first day. After he crossed the bridge at the Duero he went about an hour farther through a landscape of natural grassland, spotted with shrubs and stands of oak, poplar, elm, beeches, and chestnut trees.

He found a location where a creek flowed toward the Duero through a small cluster of trees. He pulled his cart off the road somewhat into the trees, freed the ox and tethered it with a long rope so that it could find grass. He fed the ox some of the grain he had brought along. He also filled a pail with water from the creek and let the ox drink. He had to fill the pail a second time, since the ox knocked over the pail in its eagerness to get to the water. The second time, he wedged the pail between rocks so that it couldn't be knocked over.

He laid out some blankets under the wagon and draped some cloths from all four sides of the wagon to make an enclosed area for sleeping. He kindled a small fire and had supper. It was too dark to read so he just sat by the dying fire thinking of what he had been through over the past few months. He sadly remembered his father's death. His thoughts then wandered to Catalina. He wondered where she had gone and what she was doing. He became even sadder thinking about her. He felt small and alone. He quietly sang from Psalm 27 the words: "Though my father and mother forsake me, the LORD will receive me." Then he prayed and crawled under the cart to sleep.

In the morning after breakfast, he filled his water containers, including a barrel of water for the ox. He cleaned up his campsite and headed out. The region was sparsely populated. He had yet to meet any person since he left the farmlands around Valladolid. In the distance, he saw a herd of cattle but no herder appeared nearby. He plodded on through the morning and rested through the heat of the day. The afternoon was much like the morning and he camped again for a second night. However, this time he had not been able to find a creek before it became too dark to continue any farther.

The third day, Wednesday, in mid-morning he encountered some farms and nodded to a few folks as he passed by. He came upon a village at a ford through a smaller river flowing into the Duero. He purchased a few supplies, including two new sturdy wooden pails, since the ox had broken the one he had brought from Valladolid. He spent the hottest part of the day in the village sitting in the shade on the patio of a tiny inn. He was glad for human company, even though no one engaged him in conversation.

He decided not to spend the night in the village and continued his journey. Before leaving, he remembered Doctor Ortiz's words about filling his water containers. He was fully aware of the need after the experience the evening before when he had not been able to find a creek. So, he filled his containers from the town's well.

That night was much like the two previous.

Thursday, June 15th, promised to be a hot day. It was already hot at sunrise when Bartolomé had resumed his journey. He wore his light, brown leather jacket rather than his wool one, over green stockings. He had on solid thigh-high walking boots to protect his feet, and he wore the hat that Doctor Ortiz had bought him to provide shade. He had put a new goose feather in the hat when he had bought supplies the day before. He stopped to rest in the morning, earlier than he had on the previous days.

By mid-afternoon he was on the road again. He found that he was approaching a more inhabited territory. He stopped a farmer driving a herd of scrawny goats and asked where he was. The farmer informed him that he was in the outlying district of Aranda de Duero. When he reached the crossroads a few miles farther along, if he turned north, he would approach the town.

It was late in the day when he reached the crossroads. He had already decided that he would bypass the town. He did not want to draw attention to himself, and certainly didn't want to face guards again who might require the payment of a tariff. Just after he had crossed the road heading toward Aranda de Duero, he saw a large procession coming from the south. He stopped to watch it pass. He thought that if he just ignored the procession and walked away to the east it might arouse curiosity. Better to be thought of as a local who was interested in this party than be viewed as an uninterested foreigner.

There were many soldiers on horseback and carriages. Near the front of the procession, he saw King Felipe with a number of nobles and retainers on horseback. One of them looked oddly familiar. He couldn't place where he had seen the man before, but thinking about it briefly he realized that this should not surprise him. King Felipe had until recently lived in Valladolid, and he undoubtedly had brought along many of his staff from there. He had probably seen the man, whom he thought he recognized, around the city. In another context, almost two years before, he would have recognized this man as the doctor who had come to his aid outside a stable in Valladolid and in whose clinic he had spent a week—and more importantly, whose daughter he loved. Yet, on this day, in this situation, he could not think why the man with a tidy beard and elegant clothing looked so familiar.

He watched from under his hat, the procession heading into Aranda de Duero. He tried not to look up, as he was wary and didn't want to make eye contact with the guards or any of the servants, but also because the sun was starting to set and was shining directly into his eyes.

As one carriage passed the crossroads, Bartolomé saw two women sitting in it. The carriage blocked the sun, and his eyes took a second to adjust from the change of light of the setting sun and to the shadow cast by the carriage. But as he looked up, one of the women in the carriage noticed him standing beside his wagon. She looked directly at him. They made eye contact for a fleeting moment. The carriage with the women passed by, and he could no longer see the younger woman. He felt his spine tingle. He became hot and flushed. For less than a second those eyes had penetrated to the core of his being. He was stunned.

After the procession had passed, he stood unmoving and kept asking himself what it was about those eyes that had affected him so profoundly. Then he remembered that Doctor Ortiz had told him that Doctor Mendoza had taken up service with King Felipe. He said aloud, "Is it possible that Catalina was travelling in that carriage? But, why? Why would she be here? Should I follow the procession and find out?" He almost turned to head north. However, his better judgment took over; and he realized that if it was Catalina and he tried to talk with her, her father might betray him to the Inquisition. If he were recaptured, they would likely bind him with fifty chains to make sure he never escaped again. He pulled himself back to the present and gently prodded the ox to continue their journey toward Zaragoza and, hopefully beyond, to freedom.

The next two weeks went by much as the first as they wended their way through the Duero valley — walking — resting — walking — sleeping — filling water casks — buying supplies at villages — The landscape varied little. He saw grasslands and trees, a few hares and deer, and the occasional herd of cattle or sheep. He by-passed Soria and Calatayud as best he could. He was particularly nervous as he approached Calatayud as it was a major centre for the production of armour and armaments for the Spanish army, and he saw many soldiers and wagonloads of supplies as he drew nearer.

Chapter 45
(Madrid, 1559)

On Sunday morning after the family had attended mass at San Nicolás de los Servitas and was eating lunch, Catalina said, "Father, have you been able to get us an invitation to the wedding?"

"Yes, I have. I'm sorry I forgot to mention it. We have been so busy the past two weeks that it slipped my mind. I asked King Felipe about it one day when we were near Segovia."

"Father?"

"Yes. I know that tone. What do you want?"

"No, not *want*, need! I *need* a new dress for the wedding!"

"I knew this was coming. Yes, you can get a new dress, but is it possible to get one made in such a short time? It has to be ready by Thursday. Surely all the seamstresses in the city are fully occupied."

"Father you should know me better than that! I reserved a seamstress. In fact, she has started work already. I knew you would say yes." Her smile disarmed him.

She went over to him and leaned on his shoulder, placed her hands around his neck and kissed his bearded cheek.

"You scoundrel!" he said with a smile.

"What about mother, shouldn't she have one too?"

Susana replied, "I don't need a new dress made this week. Just like you I knew we would be invited to the wedding and had a dress made before we went on the trip with King Felipe."

At that, Abram with mock exasperation, said, "With you two thinking ahead, I will never have to worry about planning for the future. It is a good thing that my income has increased substantially since we joined King Felipe's household. I could never have afforded to keep you two clothed if I was earning what I used to in Valladolid."

"Oh, Father, you know that we are careful not to waste *your* money! Thank you for getting us the invitation, and for the new dress. But, what about Luisa?"

"Yes, she is invited also, along with her parents."

"Oh, thank you Father! I love you so much." She kissed him again and ran from the room to find Luisa.

The next day she and Luisa spent the morning with the seamstress who fitted Catalina's almost-complete dress. It was a sleeveless farthingale gown of burgundy velvet. The front of the bodice was tastefully low cut, and it was laced up in the back. The front of the gown touched the floor when Catalina stood in only her stockings; the back consisted of a pleated train. The edges of the bodice at the shoulder were trimmed with gold braids. The same material was used as a belt around the waist of the bodice. She had brought with her a loose fitting long-sleeved blouse of light see-through silk that she would wear under the dress. She put this on while the dress was being fitted. It bunched up around her neck and at the wrists in simple ruffles.

Luisa asked, "What do you plan to wear to cover your hair?"

"Just a garland of small flowers to match the dress."

"You will be the talk of the wedding. I hear that Princess Elizabeth of Valois is pretty. You had better be careful; you don't want to attract all the attention on her wedding day! You will make her your enemy. You know that royalty does not like having someone outshine them."

"Oh Luisa, everyone will be dressed up, including you! I will be just another face in the crowd, but thank you for your compliment."

The excitement in the city increased as Thursday approached. No one, at least no one that Catalina or Luisa knew, had yet seen Princess Elizabeth. Everyone wanted to know what she looked like.

Finally, Thursday arrived.

The wedding ceremony of King Felipe and Princess Elizabeth was held in La Capilla del Obispo, the Bishop's Chapel, at Plaza de la Paja. As Madrid's

largest and newest church, built in 1535, it was the
only place in the town of about twenty thousand suitable for the wedding of a king. As a new church, it
had pews. Catalina and her parents were sitting about
ten rows from the front, and they let her sit on the
aisle. She was going to be able to see everything! She
looked around and found where Luisa was sitting.
She winked at her. Then she wrinkled her nose, and
they both started to giggle. Susana placed her hand
on her arm and whispered, "Shh!"

The church smelled beautifully fragrant. It was
filled with so many flowers that it was difficult to see
the walls. The choir sounded heavenly.

King Felipe entered the church dressed entirely
in black. His blond beard was neatly trimmed on his
Habsburg jaw. He wore a long sleeveless jacket, a
billowing silk shirt with neck ruff and leather knee-
high boots. His clothes were perfectly tailored and
made him look taller than he actually was. He also
wore a sword in a sheath. The handle and sheath
were also black. The only colour in his outfit was a
gold medallion with the emblem of a golden fleece
attached to a blue and yellow ribbon draped around
his neck, and a fine inlay of silver on the sword
handle. He was followed by a number of his nobles
and clergy. Bareheaded, he took his place at the front
with the Bishop who was to perform the ceremony.

Princess Elizabeth of Valois walked to the front
of the church on the arm of the Duc d'Lyon who had
brought her to Spain. She wore a scarf and a golden
gauze veil covering her head and face. No one in the
congregation could see what she looked like. Her

dress was of a rich gold silk with large silver *fleur-de-lys* embroidered on it. The sleeves of the dress merged in back into a long train that flowed behind her. There were rows of increasingly large hoops under her dress from her waist to her feet. Since her feet and legs were entirely hidden inside the hoops, it looked as if she floated down the isle on a river of gold. The effect was mysterious and magical.

After the wedding ceremony and mass were complete, the bishop blessed the couple and they rose to their feet. Queen Elizabeth stood slightly taller than King Felipe. With her back still to the congregation, she removed her veil to reveal hair the colour of harvest wheat. Every eye was on her, and she knew it. She turned slowly, gazed at the congregation through chicory-coloured eyes, and honoured them with a blazing smile. Every jaw dropped, every heart stopped. She was the most beautiful sight they had ever seen. Catalina remembered Luisa teasing her when she was being fitted for her new dress and thought, "No one will steal the glory from Queen Elizabeth!"

King Felipe held out his right arm, and Queen Elizabeth placed her left hand gently on his arm. Together they moved down the isle in a slow march. Music rose to the rafters and everyone was proud to be part of the greatest kingdom on earth.

Eventually the guests found their way to the alcázar for the wedding feast. The main hall had a rough stone finish, since the castle had been used until a few months before as a military fort, not a palace. However, on this evening, it was decorated with French and Spanish flags, blue and yellow, and gold- and silver-coloured banners to symbolize the compact between King Henry II and King Felipe. Candelabras hanging from the ceiling beams contained candles of the same colours. There were also many large sprays of flowers in stands and on the tables.

Catalina and Luisa were able to find seats together at one of the long tables that had been set up on the floor near the dais for the royal couple.

The meal was served in many courses. The first course consisted of a light soup with spiced parsnips, followed by roasted partridges and pigeons. Between each course there was dancing. Two young men, one the son of a principe, the other of a marques, approached with a flourish of their caps and asked Catalina and Luisa to join them in a dance. Luisa jumped up with excitement, but Catalina resisted. Luisa whispered to her, "Come on, this will be fun."

"I don't know ..."

"Just come and dance! It is just all for fun."

"But Bartolomé ..."

"Come!"

With a sense of reluctance and guilt, she joined the dance.

The first dance of the evening was the Pavane, which the Spanish claimed was invented by Ferdinand Cortez in Padua, though the Italians claimed it came from Pavana around 1508. After many curtsies, retreats and advances, the ladies rested their right hands on the backs of their partners' left hands and the slow, sliding procession began—step, step, double step, step, step—forwards and backwards in 4/4 time. At synchronized points, the men would strut like peacocks and the ladies would sweep their trains or gowns in acceptance. A few of the more adventuresome couples added energetic fleurets. Catalina and Luisa didn't know their dance partners, other than as nodding acquaintances, so were not inclined to try anything fancy. Having grown up in aristocratic circles, Luisa had participated in this dance before. Catalina had never performed it, but her natural fluid rhythm and instincts allowed her to anticipate the changes in motion by watching the others.

At the end of the dance, their partners bowed graciously to the girls and returned them to their seats. The next course of the meal was served. It consisted of heavier fare, including roasted pork and venison. On the tables were bowls with a variety of olives and leeks, sliced cucumber, breads, and pastries. Catalina had already eaten enough during the first course, so only had a few olives. She was staring into the distance deep in thought when Luisa asked, "What are you thinking about? You don't seem to be with us tonight. Aren't you enjoying the party?"

"I was thinking about Bartolomé. I can't really enjoy a party when I remember that Bartolomé is in prison and his life is in danger. I wish I knew how I could help him!"

"Bartolomé wouldn't want you sitting and fretting."

"I feel guilty flirting with these peacocks when I have sworn my love to Bartolomé, and I miss him! I really wish he were here with me. I would give up all of this — I would even go to prison — if I could be with him."

"Catalina! Don't say that! You have no idea how bad things are in the Inquisition's prisons. You don't want to be there, but we shouldn't talk about such things here. You don't know who could be listening. See that bishop at the end of that table," she pointed discreetly, "and those monks there," she twitched her head, "they are spies. Smile! Don't let them see your unhappiness; you might attract attention. Don't spoil King Felipe's evening, or mine, because of your unhappy thoughts. Catalina, I love you and really do pray that things work out for Bartolomé, but there is nothing you can do right now to help him. So, try to forget him — just for a few hours. Dancing here doesn't mean a thing! No one could infer that you were being courted."

The next dance started, and Luisa joined in. Catalina asked to be excused. She watched Luisa fondly and started to smile when Luisa made provocative gestures. She knew that Luisa was doing it just to bring her out of her bad mood.

Luisa returned and collapsed onto her seat. "That was fun! It was faster than the last dance."

The food, wine, and dances continued in a blur.

Catalina joined in the dancing again. She admitted to herself that the faster canaries and galliards with their creative improvisations were fun, as Luisa had declared.

As it grew late, Catalina was starting to feel tired. She had eaten little since the first course and had had only one cup of wine, but the excitement of the day was catching up to her. She was thinking about how she could leave without being too obvious. Her exit, however, was interrupted by a most unpleasant event. A rather drunk and overweight middle-aged courtier approached and asked her to dance. She had noticed him at the head table earlier in the evening. He was busy stuffing his face with food and hadn't participated in the dancing, so she had forgotten all about his presence. It was Alfonso Conde de Bobadilla. She turned paler than usual.

She said as graciously as she could, "I am sorry, but I am very tired and was just leaving."

He replied in a threatening tone, "You have honoured *all* the young men with dances tonight, you won't allow me one?"

"I ..."

"Come! The music is starting, let us join in."

With skin colder than winter winds from the Pyrenees and a pit in her stomach that almost made her vomit, she got up slowly from her seat. She had to concentrate hard to stay focused on the dance and overcome her panic. Even so, she made a number of false steps and more than once bumped into the person in front of or behind her. At the end of the dance, the Conde returned her to her seat and bowed. He almost fell over and stumbled away in embarrassment. Catalina grabbed Luisa's arm with force, "That was awful. He is a pig! I can't stand the man. Why won't he leave me alone?"

"I would normally be flattered if a Conde asked me to dance, but I agree with you that this was no honour."

"I have to get out of here. I don't want to see that man ever again!"

Just as she was preparing to leave, the orchestra started to play a new piece by Juan del Encia and the servants swept in with platters of roasted pheasants with the feathers put back and sculptures made from marzipan. These were placed on the tables, followed by trays of tarts and custards.

Catalina couldn't leave at this point. It would be an insult to the host. She ignored the food entirely and sat in a deep gloom. When the bowls of rosewater and towels were supplied, she hurriedly washed her hands, kissed Luisa on the cheek, and left as quickly as she could. She almost ran to her home near the alcázar.

She could not sleep. Her thoughts were in turmoil. What had started out as a hopeful day with the prospect of a wedding and the splendour of a royal feast had turned into fear for Bartolomé and dread of the Conde de Bobadilla. She was feverish, and tossed and turned all night in her bed.

The following Tuesday Abram returned home late. Catalina was already in her nightgown and was just about to go to bed, but when she heard her father coming in, she went downstairs to see him. He sat down and removed his boots. It was clear that he had had a rough day. Catalina asked, "Father, is everything fine?"

"Yes, my dear. I have something we need to discuss, but it can wait until morning. Here, kiss me and head off to bed."

"Father! How can you expect me to go to sleep when you say there is something we have to discuss and you look so serious? What is it?"

"Yes, Abram, what is it?" asked Susana.

"Catalina, it will be your seventeenth birthday on Sunday, isn't that right?"

"Yes, Father, but why does that make you so serious? That should make you happy. You will get to buy me a present," she said with a smile.

"I have just returned from a meeting with King Felipe. His recent wedding has turned the hearts of many in his court to romance. A number of his staff have announced wedding plans for July."

"But I enjoy a wedding," said Catalina. "why would that make you so serious? Please get to the point!"

"Some are asking why you aren't married yet. Most women as beautiful as you are married by their sixteenth birthday."

"But, Father, you know that I promised Bartolomé that I would marry him. I am betrothed, and I will wait for him."

"I am afraid that you will never see Bartolomé again. I know you don't want to hear this, but you need to face reality. If he hasn't already been, he may soon be executed by the Inquisition."

"Father! Don't say such things. Bartolomé is alive. He will be set free. I know it!"

Abram, starting to lose his patience, said, "You cannot marry Bartolomé. You must forget him. A noblemen was at the meeting I had with King Felipe this evening, and — he — he has asked me for permission to marry you."

Catalina turned stone cold. She tried to speak, but could force no words out. Susana came over and helped her down onto a chair. Catalina finally whispered, "Who?"

Abram replied, "Alfonso Conde..."

"No!" she screamed, and ran from the room.

Chapter 46
(North-Eastern Spain, 1559)

From Calatayud to Zaragoza the road was well travelled and busy with transport and commercial activity. It was on this road that Bartolomé met his travelling companions. They would accompany him for the rest of his journey into France. They were real French merchants heading north. When he heard them speaking French, he approached them and hailed them. On hearing his Parisian accent, they greeted him warmly. They never bothered to ask where he was from or about his background. They were more interested in what he was transporting and what he planned to earn from the resale of the goods he was carrying. No one in the group seemed to have a second name or an appellation of locale. He introduced himself simply as Barthélemy, and within minutes was part of the group.

Bartolomé discovered through listening to their talk and asking a few guarded questions that the merchants made two trips per year through the mountains. They had common rendezvous points so that they could travel as a group through the most dangerous areas. He had happened to run into this group of merchants just after they had left one rendezvous. More would join them in Zaragoza.

Bartolomé had joined part of a subculture that he did not realize existed. It was one of shared adventure and camaraderie on the open road that at the same time allowed for total anonymity. He thought it interesting that this was one part of European society in which it didn't matter what a person's background was. He could have been a priest, monk, pauper, runaway feudal servant—or escapee from the Inquisition. No one cared. He found this quite refreshing. Most areas of European society were based around class and caste. A new entrepreneurial class was arising that might be able to break the stranglehold of the traditions that had been in place for over a thousand years. And yet, to these men, mercantile goals appeared to be secondary. The primary goal seemed to be the journey itself.

Beyond Calatayud, the road began to travel through a more rugged terrain, rather than the flat and gently rolling valley land he had been in from the time he had left Valladolid. After Zaragoza, the route north began to climb into higher altitudes as they worked their way through the foothills of the Pyrenees and then into the mountains themselves.

Once, when they were fording a rough river, a wheel broke on Bartolomé's wagon. He was thankful to have the company of the merchants. They felt it was their duty to get him rolling again. They all helped unload his wagon, stacking all the barrels, casks, cases, and jars securely above the riverbank. A number of them were able to support one corner of the wagon, as they led the ox to pull it carefully out of the water.

On the shore, they unhitched the ox from the wagon. Then they set up stones and cases to hold the wagon upright and removed the broken wheel from the axle. Bartolomé was surprised at how proficient they were in this work. They also had the right tools for the job. He had never thought to bring tools with him. There was a village nearby, and they took the broken wheel to a wheelwright. He replaced the broken spokes and straightened and reset the steel band around the rim.

The merchants lost a day in their journey, helping Bartolomé with this repair, but it didn't seem to bother them at all.

Even though it was summer, the days were cool and the nights cold, as they worked their way through the pass. Bartolomé wore both of his coats and his cloak much of the time. It also rained quite often. He found that his hands were always cold. Yet, he was willing to put up with the lack of comfort to experience the new sights.

As they followed the road, which was more like a trail, as it wended its way leading to the mountain pass, Bartolomé would look down into the valleys below. He could see the route they had come. The villages and monasteries appeared to be tiny below them. He thought about how the world must look as

God surveys it from Heaven. The words of Psalm 14 came into his thoughts: "The LORD looks down from heaven on the sons of men to see if there are any who understand, any who seek God. All have turned aside, they have together become corrupt; there is no one who does good, not even one."

As they climbed higher, the lowland forests were replaced with pines and cedars. He saw animals he had never encountered including martins, mountain cats and even a bear. At night, they heard wolves howling. Bartolomé was glad to be with a company of travelling companions.

This was Bartolomé's fifth trip through the Pyrenees. On the previous occasions, however, he had taken more well-travelled routes. He had also been inside carriages. On those trips, he had not paid much attention to the spectacular views and the variety of the flora and fauna of the area he was passing through. He realized that really to see one's own country a person should walk through it, and he should take the less-travelled routes. He was profoundly thankful for this opportunity, and at every new vista or site his heart soared in private thanksgiving to the Creator.

On a number of occasions, one or another of the merchants was able to shoot a deer or a wild goat with a flintlock. Almost every night they all feasted on roasted meat. In the mountain villages, a number of the merchants purchased fine processed furs. The most expensive were ermine and wolf. Bartolomé knew nothing about furs and learned much just from hearing them discuss the merits of this or that fur, but he did not purchase any himself. He was not sure he would know how to go about selling them when he arrived in France. However, he did dream about the furs. He planned to go beyond his bachelor's degree and continue his schooling. Someday he would wear the ermine-lined hood on his robe as a master or a doctor at the university.

The only other adventure that happened on this journey occurred when they were still in the Spanish Pyrenees. They were passing through a steep and narrow valley when a band of six robbers stopped them and demanded their purses and other valuables.

In total, there were nine merchants in their company, including Bartolomé. They did not yield, for they felt that they could defeat the robbers. Bartolomé himself did not have a gun and had no real experience fighting with a sword. The closest he had come to a sword fight was in games as a child. However, the merchants with him seemed keen on taking on the bandits. Before Bartolomé realized what was happening, there were pistol shots and the noise of muskets and two of the outlaws lay on the ground, dead. The horses of two others had been shot. The remaining four rode off quickly on two horses.

One of the merchants had been shot in the arm. A musket ball had cut a groove through the man's outer arm, and it was bleeding heavily. Bartolomé took charge. He pressed a piece of linen on the wound until the bleeding eased somewhat. He told one of the other men to continue pressing the cloth on the wound and commanded others to make a fire while he collected Plantain and Chickweed leaves. He was able to find a Comfrey plant and asked one of the men to clean the root. Later when he remembered this incident, he was thankful that he had paid close attention to his studies of herbs with Doctor Ortiz.

Bartolomé shredded the Plantain and Chickweed leaves into a cooking pot and added finely cut pieces of the Comfrey root. He poured into the pot enough olive oil to cover the plant material and set the mixture over the fire and left it to stew for a couple of hours.

He recalled hearing how Doctor Mendoza had cleaned his head wound with diluted wine. So, he got some wine from his supplies and diluted it with water. The wounded man had to be held down when Bartolomé poured on the alcohol. Then, he temporarily bound the arm to stanch the bleeding.

After his herb concoction had cooled, he strained the mixture through cloth. He then added four spoonfuls of honey and stirred quickly. He soaked a few squares of clean linen in this solution and placed them on the man's wound as a patch. He covered the patch with a piece of leather and bound the arm with a strip of cloth. Then he said to the wounded man, "Leave this bandage on for five days and your wound should heal nicely."

When the wounded man was resting comfortably, the other merchants congratulated Bartolomé on his medical knowledge and quick action. They enquired where he had learned how to take care of a serious wound. He explained only enough to satisfy their curiosity without revealing too much of his background. "My tutor used to teach us about the use of herbs and my fiancé's father is a doctor." They were all measurably impressed.

They buried the two dead robbers near the trail and covered their grave with a cairn. Bartolomé wasn't sure if they should place a cross on the cairn. He wondered if it was right to give robbers a Christian burial, but he didn't challenge the merchants. They were very superstitious, and he heard them discussing the importance of the cross or the souls of the robbers would be left forever in Purgatory.

The merchants gave Bartolomé the better of the two horses that had been found in the woods after the robbers had fled. Thy said it was a reward for his service to the wounded man. It looked like a pure-bred Andalusian. Its saddle had elaborate ribs and a tailpiece in the style used by the Conquistadores. It was obvious that at one time the saddle, and probably the horse, had belonged to a Spanish nobleman.

Bartolomé knew quite a bit about horses from his youth, and he looked over the gift. Its coat, mane and shoes were all in good shape. He doubted that the robber had taken good care of the horse. This could only mean that it had recently been taken from its original owner. Bartolomé wondered what had happened to him. Had he been killed during the last war between Spain and France? Or, had the same robbers they had just encountered killed the owner and taken his horse? Or, had his horse just been stolen on a raid into Spain? Bartolomé wondered if one of the outlaws who had been shot was the culprit, and if he had been served with justice by meeting his demise with a bullet in the chest.

The horse was solid black except for a white diamond on its forehead. Its large dark eyes looked at Bartolomé in a friendly way as he was examining it. He said, "You remind me of someone I love dearly. She has black hair just like you and wears a white scarf, just like your diamond." The horse shook its head. "So I am going to name you 'Catalina'. And, I will love you like I love her." The horse acted as if it understood and let out a little whinny.

Bartolomé got the pails from the cart and filled one with some of the ox's grain and the other with water. He offered them to the horse. She responded with eagerness. Later when they came to a village, he purchased a brush and comb and a proper saddle blanket for the horse. He enjoyed taking care of the horse and riding it when he had the opportunity. He could not, however, lead the ox-drawn cart from on the horse until they reached better roads. Therefore, until they were well into France, he still had to walk beside the head of the ox to guide it. He tied the horse to the cart so it could follow behind.

Late in the evening on the day in which they had encountered the robbers, Bartolomé was trying to determine how long he had been on the road. He worked out that he had been travelling almost a month. It was now Friday, July 7th. He had left the city of Valladolid on June 12th. The date of July 7th wouldn't leave his head. He checked with one of the other merchants, the one with the most education, "What day do you reckon it to be?"

"Let me think," he counted on his fingers and related it to the stages of their trip, "I believe it is Friday, the 7th of July."

"That is what I get also."

Then it dawned on Bartolomé. It was Catalina's birthday! She had turned seventeen that day. He was convinced that God had given him the horse, on this very day, as a sign that someday he would see Catalina again. The horse was a token of a promise from God. Hope swelled in him and his joy beamed from him for the rest of the evening.

The merchants were perplexed by the strange emotions of their quiet travelling companion. They just attributed it to the gift of the horse. And so it was, but they would never know how deep the reason lay. That night Bartolomé prayed more earnestly for Catalina than he had in quite awhile. He asked God to protect her and to bring her back to him in his time.

They completed their traverse of the pass and arrived at the base of the foothills, in Gascony, on the French side of the Pyrenees, about a week after he had received the horse. It was then that Bartolomé realized he had finally escaped from Spain.

At one of their rest stops he knelt prostrate with his head on the ground and thanked God for bringing him safely through. The merchants seeing him thought that he was just a happy Frenchman who was glad to be back in his native France. If only they had known how difficult it was for a proud Spaniard to admit he was happier to see France than Spain.

When the party reached Toulouse, the merchants indicated that they would separate and go different directions. None of the merchants were heading to Paris. Goods from Spain destined for the northern part of France were usually brought in via boat to Le Havre. The merchants told Bartolomé that they would meet again at the fairground in Toulouse in a month and travel back to Spain. They planned their second annual return trip before the snows came to the Pyrenees.

Bartolomé decided that Toulouse was as far as he would travel with his load and said goodbye to all his travelling companions. It was an emotional time parting from them. Their experiences had bonded them in a way that Bartolomé had never experienced.

He went to the summer open markets and a number of the year-round covered markets around Toulouse and sold all the olives and oil, and then the ox and cart. He didn't bargain; he just took whatever he was offered for the items. Yet, when he tallied up his costs on the journey from Valladolid, including the cost of purchasing the ox and cart and supplies, of feed and food, and the repair of the wheel on the wagon, he determined that he had earned approximately double what he had spent. This surprised him. He thought that if he had had experience negotiating he could have sold his goods for much more than he had received. He also realized that if he had purchased the olives directly from the producers rather than having bought them in Valladolid, he probably could have made three or four times his costs. He under-

stood why merchants carrying goods in both directions were willing to face the hazards of dangerous
travel through the mountains and why travelling
merchants, as a class, were prosperous throughout
Europe. However, he wasn't tempted to become a
merchant, even though he had dismissed the idea of
working for King Felipe as an ambassador.

Bartolomé also sold his horse's saddle. He wanted
to get one in the French style. Spanish horses were
seen throughout France, but Spanish saddles were
rare. He didn't want to attract attention to himself
unnecessarily. He then purchased three sets of new
clothes. He outfitted himself with new undergarments, stockings, white blouses, trousers that buckled
just below the knees, and matching doublets, a cape,
riding boots and leather shoes with silver buckles. He
topped it all off with a hat that consisted of a colourful
rolled circular brim with a puffy soft crown, accented
with a fancy plume. He would no longer dress like
a travelling merchant. Rather, he would dress like
a member of the rising European, educated, middle
class.

His final purchase was a sturdy and healthy
donkey with panniers in which he could place his
belongings. He would lead the pack animal behind
his horse. He planned to travel by the most direct and
safest route to Paris and stay in inns rather than sleep
under a wagon as he had for the past six weeks.

He stabled his horse and donkey and went to a
clean, respectable inn in Toulouse. He had his first
real bath with hot water in many months, dressed in
one of his new outfits and sat down for a pleasant

supper. Then he bedded down in a real bed. He had come a long way from the vault in the cellar of the convent at Valladolid. God was merciful!

Chapter 47
(Madrid, 1559)

Susana entered Catalina's room. Catalina had been crying again.

"Catalina, can we talk?"

"I don't want to talk! You know that I don't want to marry the Conde de Bobadilla. Why did Father agree to this?"

"Catalina, there are many things in life that we don't want to do, but still have to. If you were a soldier and your commander told you to attack an impossible fort, you would be expected to. If you were a priest and your bishop assigned you to a new parish, you would have to go. If you were a youngest son without any inheritance, you would have to enter a monastery. Our situation as women is that we are often used as the token in an agreement. Think of Queen Elizabeth, for example, who is the daughter of a king and had to marry King Felipe."

"But I am not a princess. That is expected of princesses. I don't want to marry the Conde. I love Bartolomé. I promised Bartolomé that I would marry him."

"Catalina, I know you love Bartolomé, but very few women get to marry the person they love, and..."

"You did!"

"Yes, I was blessed in having the privilege of marrying your father by choice, and I have been blessed having him as a husband. — It doesn't help to talk about our marriage; it only makes your situation seem worse. I know of many arranged marriages that have worked out well. Think of the Manriques. They didn't meet until their wedding day. Look at them! After thirty-five years of marriage, they are like eloped newlyweds."

"It may be so, but what about Rodrigo and Constanza? Their marriage is a disaster. It is rumoured that Rodrigo has mistresses in three cities. And your brother is a cuckold. Arranged marriages don't work out!"

"Catalina, don't speak that way of your Uncle Jose! You cannot draw conclusions from those examples. There are marriages, arranged or out of love, that work out; and there are other marriages, arranged or contracted at the choice of the parties that are nothing but an empty shell. Marriage is what you make of it."

"That is true, but there has to be something there to start with. With the Conde de Bobadilla, there is nothing! He is fat! He is ugly! He is old! He is a drunk!

No marriage can be worked out from that beginning. I am going to run away and become a nun."

"I understand how unhappy you are. For a moment put yourself in your father's position. He has no grounds for refusing the Conde's request. If he refuses to allow the marriage, it will be considered an insult. We have told you that the Conde is a favourite of King Felipe. He knew King Felipe's father well and has contributed a large sum of money to the Church, to the Inquisition, and most recently for King Felipe's monastery project. If the Conde spoke to King Felipe to discredit your father, he would be sent from the court in disgrace—or worse."

"I would rather die as a Lutheran than be married to that pig! I am to think of Father's and your needs and position, but you don't have to think of mine! Where is there fairness in that?"

Somewhat exasperated, Susana replied, "I have never claimed there was fairness in this proposal. In fact, I have been explaining to you that even if unfair, it is what is required and expected. I don't think this conversation is going to conclude with a happy ending, so I will leave you for now. Please join us for supper. I know that your father would be happy to see you."

"I will eat in my room, if I eat at all! Maybe I won't eat, and then I can die. Death would be better than being married to that man!"

The arguments between Catalina and Susana continued over the next two weeks. Catalina stayed in her room, and although she was already thin, she ate little and lost weight. Her eyes were constantly puffy from crying, and she was exhausted from lack of sleep.

In exasperation, Abram went to visit her in her room. "Catalina, as your father, I could order you into this marriage. I could stand here and yell at you. I could have you whipped for disobedience, but I know you too well. You are strong-willed and free-spirited. So, that is not how I am going to deal with you. I am going to say three things. I don't want you to interrupt me. First, I miss having you visit me in the alcázar and helping me with my work. Second, I know you don't like what has happened, but your crying and fits of anger cannot change it. You may as well accept the fact that you have to marry the Conde de Bobadilla. — wait," he waved his hand, "I am not finished — Third, I love you very much and am sorry that events have transpired the way they have. I cannot undo the fact that we are now highly visible in King Felipe's court."

"Father! How can you say you love me when you agreed to this marriage," she paused. He did not reply, so she said, "Answer me!"

"Catalina, I won't try to convince you of my love. That is a useless exercise, but I want to give you an illustration that might help put my love into context. Put yourself in Jesus' position. In the Garden of Gethsemane he prayed for release from the cross. He went to the cross and asked the Father why he had forsaken him. Do you think the Father didn't love Jesus even though he had to put him through the terrible ordeal of the crucifixion? Can I not love you, even though I know that this marriage is a terrible ordeal for you?"

"Father, you don't even believe in Jesus. Why would you use this example?"

"Maybe I don't believe, maybe I do. Even so, as it is written, it is an illustration of Jesus doing the Father's will when the consequences are most painful. Do you believe God will take care of you?"

"Yes, Father, you know I do. I really do believe that God will take care of me."

"Then trust him, like Jesus did. He will work out things—and always for the best."

Catalina sat quietly. She was quite surprised to have heard her father using an example from Scripture to teach her a lesson. She could not remember him ever doing this before. She was truly confused. "Father, I will think about what you have said."

Abram put his hand on her shoulder, bent over, kissed her gently on the top of her head, and quietly went from the room.

"Susana, I think I have made some progress with Catalina."

"How?"

"I surprised her, and myself, by giving her an example from the Bible."

"You did?"

"Yes, it seemed so appropriate to the current situation. I know that Catalina is suffering greatly. So I used the greatest example of suffering ever recorded in literature or history—the death of Christ."

"What makes you think this will work with her?" she said, as her eyes misted with tears.

"Because she is an intelligent and thoughtful young woman, logical arguments have an impact with her. Just give her time, and she will come around."

Abram was right. Later that evening Catalina joined her parents. She said, "I have resigned myself to the marriage. I will, however, never enjoy it, and I will not get involved in planning it. It will not be a happy day for me. It will be the saddest day of my life, but I will no longer fight against you. I realize that we are all victims, you and I, and that we have no choice in the matter."

Susana went over to Catalina and held her close, "Catalina, let's not worry about planning a wedding right now. We are just glad to see you come out of your room. What would you like to eat?"

"Whatever you had for supper, but I don't care about food right now. Can you send María to fetch Luisa? I haven't seen her in many days, and I really want to talk with her. How I wish Margarita were here. She would know how to cheer me up. I miss her music so much. I miss her. I miss Bartolomé. I am so lonely!"

When Luisa arrived, Catalina explained everything to her. Luisa had been quite concerned about Catalina. Each time she had called to see her, all she had been told was that Catalina was very ill and was not able to receive guests.

"So you really have to marry the Conde de Bobadilla?"

"Yes, I have no choice, isn't it awful?"

"I don't know. He is not a young man. Maybe he will die in a few years and you will be left with a large estate. When you are rich, and a widow, you can marry whomever you want."

"I hadn't thought about that, but what about my promise to Bartolomé? I told him I would love him forever."

"You aren't breaking your promise. You are being forced to do this against your will. If Bartolomé is as much of a gentleman as you say he is, wouldn't he understand the obligations of obedience to parents and king?"

"Yes, he would — but ..."

"Catalina, you told me that Bartolomé's father was put to death by the Inquisition. I know this is a terrible thought, but what chance is there, really, that he won't be also?"

"It is terrible to think about it. I pray for him every day. Yet, you are right. The Inquisition is becoming more and more — wicked — Oh, don't ever tell anyone I said that!"

Luisa took hold of Catalina's hand and said, "Don't worry, what we say here is our secret."

"I told my parents that I would not plan the wedding and that I would not be happy being married. So, I want to ask you to do something for me?"

"What?"

"Will you help my mother plan the wedding? That way I can stay out of it, but you can secretly make it the way I want it."

"What a sneak you are!" For the first time in over two weeks, Catalina smiled.

"I want Margarita to come and sing. I will write to her and ask her. You can suggest to my parents that having her come would be a good idea, as it would cheer me up."

Luisa stayed over that night with Catalina, in her room, and the girls spent many hours discussing the wedding. Catalina, in spite of herself, started to get interested in the details and had many good ideas.

The next day Catalina suggested to Susana that Luisa would help her plan the wedding. Susana was grateful for the offer.

Abram spoke with the Conde de Bobadilla, and he allocated a considerable sum of money for the wedding. The wedding was scheduled for a Thursday the last day in August and was to be held in the La Capilla del Obispo. The Conde wanted it held on a Thursday and in the same place that King Felipe and Queen Elizabeth had been married, as a compliment to his sovereign. With Luisa's assistance the wedding planning began in earnest.

Chapter 48
(Madrid, 1559)

King Felipe was away most of July. He had chosen Escorial as the site for his new monastery and was eager to get construction underway. He drove his staff hard in the work related to designing the building and preparing the site. Both the Conde de Bobadilla and Abram were with King Felipe, so Catalina, to her relief, did not see anything of the Conde for many weeks. She was pleased about this, but she was not pleased about her father being away. She wanted to get back to working with him so that she could keep herself busy and her mind occupied. She continued to pretend to ignore the planning of the wedding, but was effectively controlling it through suggestions planted with Luisa.

Catalina wrote to Margarita and asked her to come to Madrid at the end of July. She suggested that she could help Luisa and Susana with the wedding planning, and she could introduce her to the court. The letter to Margarita didn't arrive in Valladolid until the first week in August, so Margarita had to rush to get ready and obtain transportation to Madrid. Her older brother acted as her escort. He was pleased to have the opportunity to visit Madrid. This was the first time Margarita could remember that her brother actually presented himself as a gentleman and that she was truly thankful to have a brother.

The reunion between Margarita and Catalina was bittersweet. They were thrilled to be in each other's company. Even so, Catalina cried steadily as she told her all the details of her forced marriage to the fat old Conde. Margarita asked if he was rich and made the same suggestion that Luisa had: if he died within a few years Catalina would be left a rich widow. Catalina didn't view marriage as a stepping-stone to a rich widowhood; she wanted to marry the man she loved, and no one else.

When Luisa arrived and the introductions were made, Luisa said to Margarita, "I feel like I have known you for years! Catalina has told me so much about you. I do really want to hear you sing and play your lute!"

"Thank you. I have brought my musical instruments with me, at Catalina's request. I also have heard all about you from Catalina's letters. It is so good finally to meet you. I am glad that you have been taking care of Catalina when I haven't been here."

To Catalina's relief, the girls got along well, and quickly they were the best of friends. Catalina was almost happy. It was great to have two such good friends. If only she didn't have a constant pain in her stomach!

That evening when Luisa had gone home, Catalina asked Margarita for news of Bartolomé. There was none. She could find no way of gaining information, especially without raising suspicions. The inquisitors were extremely secretive. Catalina helped Margarita make her bed in a guest room and then went to her own room. That night she had a difficult time falling asleep. And when she did, she slept poorly. She awoke in the middle of the night and couldn't fall back to sleep. Not knowing what time it was, she got up and lighted a lamp in her room.

She went to her dowry chest and took out her *New Testament*. She sat on her bed holding the book and caressing the leather cover. Her thoughts went back to the day she had received it from Bartolomé, and gentle tears flowed from her eyes. She loved Bartolomé dearly, so dearly that she ached when she thought about him. She got down on her knees and prayed, "Father in Heaven, please, you know I love Bartolomé. Please, if this is a selfish love wipe it from me. But, Father, if it is a holy love, please show me why you let me love like this and yet I have to marry the Conde. If that is your will, Father, I will do it. I won't complain any more. Please forgive me for the way I've been acting. Forgive me for being so unco-operative with my parents. Please, Father, take care of Bartolomé wherever he is. And, Father, don't let him be put to death. Thank you for allowing Margarita to come. Thank you for my good friends Margarita and Luisa. Please calm my heart, and stomach, now. In

Jesus' name, amen." Since her talk with Bartolomé two years before, she had never again prayed to a saint or Mary, or in their names.

She blew out the light and climbed back into bed. She lay staring into the darkness. To her surprise, so she discovered the next day, she had fallen asleep immediately and slept soundly.

She awoke much rested, and the hollowness was gone from her stomach. She was happy for the first time in over a month. When she realized this, she concluded that God had answered her prayer

After she had dressed, she went to Margarita's room and they went together to breakfast. They found Abram already sitting at the table.

Catalina rushed over to him and said, "Father, I didn't know you had come home."

"I got in very late. I heard from your mother that you have not been sleeping well lately, so I didn't want to wake you."

She kissed him on his cheek and sat down. Margarita silently joined them at the breakfast table.

Abram turned to Margarita, "Margarita, my dear, it is good to see you. Your presence always brings music into our household." Margarita blushed at the double meaning.

"Thank you. I am so glad I could visit. Please, Doctor Mendoza, tell me what it is like to be serving with King Felipe."

"Well — let me think — King Felipe is a thoughtful man. When you talk with him about any subject, he listens intently and often smiles. He doesn't talk much, but when he does speak, his words are weighed and deliberate. He rarely gets angry, but it is rumoured that it is a short distance from his smile to his dagger."

"Oh dear, is he ruthless?"

"He has the reputation for being a bloodthirsty tyrant. I suspect this is because his armies have been so successful. He is absolute in his decisions and cannot be contradicted. It has been said in the court recently that the only person who has challenged him is Catalina." He smiled, "Has she told you that story yet?"

"No. Catalina have you spoken with King Felipe?"

"I forgot to tell you about it in a letter. There has been so much going on. I will tell you later. Father, please continue."

"King Felipe works very hard managing the world's greatest empire. He pays attention to the smallest administrative details. He does not trust even his most able advisers and loyal servants. He double- and triple-checks everything. One thing I really appreciate about him is that he disregards the traditions of rank and privilege. Wherever he sees talent and ability, he promotes it. Sadly, because of this there is much infighting among his staff. The court is riddled with factions, secrecy, and discord. There is considerable discontent among the nobles with hereditary titles. Many of them are hardly as capable as a delivery boy, but they expect to be treated as trusted advisors."

Catalina added proudly, "Father has become one of King Felipe's direct advisors. King Felipe always listens to his advice."

"He may listen, but he does what he wants! For example, a number of us on his staff have been working with the architects who are designing the new monastery that is under construction in Escorial. I have been giving advice on the layout of the clinics and kitchens. Yet, in the end, King Felipe makes all the decisions. It is amazing what he has conceived. It will be the largest monastery ever built, possibly the largest building ever. It will have sixteen separate courts and fifteen cloisters. The architects' assistants have been calculating the amount of stone and wood that will be needed. They have estimated that there will be almost one hundred miles of corridors with two thousand windows and one thousand two hundred doors. Can you imagine walking from here to Valladolid and never going outside?"

Margarita said, "Do you think, Catalina, that you will be able to get me into the court? I have never seen King Felipe, except from a distance when he rode by with his retinue. He was in Valladolid so rarely."

"You are the daughter of the alcalde of Valladolid. I am sure that counts for something, even in a court that doesn't always pay attention to rank. Once they hear you sing they will be falling over themselves to invite you to their gatherings." Margarita blushed again.

Catalina introduced Margarita to the court, but she didn't have an opportunity to see King Felipe until a few days before the date of Catalina's wedding. He was away again at the site, supervising preparations for the foundation of the monastery. Abram was excused from this trip because of the pending wedding of his daughter at the end of the month.

The three girls came home to Catalina's house one evening about two weeks before Catalina's wedding and told Susana what they had done and seen in the court that day. They had been introduced by some of the young men to a new game that had been imported from Italy. It consisted of a table with a leather boarder. They used a smooth stick to hit an ivory ball into other balls made of ebony. The objective was to knock the ebony balls into pockets at the side of the table. Catalina said the game was called 'billiards'.

"It was fun to play, but we — I at least — were clumsy. I kept hitting the white ball in the wrong place, and it would jump over the ebony balls or right off the table. The young men had fun laughing at us, but we laughed with them."

Margarita said, "It was fun except that all the men kept sneezing. It made it hard to concentrate when hitting the ball."

"Was the room dusty?" asked Susana.

"No, not at all," replied Catalina. "The men had little boxes filled with a white powder. They would pick up a pinch of the powder and breathe it into their nose and then start sneezing."

"What an odd thing to do!"

"Yes, very. I asked one of the young men what it was. He said that someone had brought it from the Portuguese court last year. It is called snuff. I think all the sneezing is rather unpleasant. It is almost as bad as the habit of burning those rolled up *tobacco* leaves and sucking in the smoke."

Catalina then informed her mother of Margarita's performance, "She sang a number of songs by Juan del Encina including, *Triste España sin ventura* and *Una sañosa porfía*, and played her lute and a new musical instrument that was given to her by — as a gift. It is called a 'violin'. She also sang *Anchieta's Con amores, mi madre* and *Al alva venid, buen amigo*. Mother, they have never heard such good singing! The court was very pleased. Didn't I tell you that Margarita was the best?"

Margarita shyly said, "I was so nervous. I thought I was going to be sick."

"But you made everyone cry with your beautiful singing. They all want you to come back and sing again."

Luisa agreed, "Margarita, you are even better than Catalina said you were. I was so moved by your singing that I thought I was floating through the hall."

Susana interrupted their reminiscing, "Come girls, we have a considerable amount of work to do for the wedding. We still have to make most of the favours for the ladies who will be attending."

"Doña Mendoza, why do we make these favours?" asked Margarita.

"It is an idea that some of the female courtiers brought back from England when King Felipe returned after the death of Queen Mary. Apparently unmarried English girls had a tradition of tearing pieces of the bride's wedding dress to bring them good luck in marriage. To stop this, brides in England now give out sewn favours as a token for luck. I don't recall anyone ever tearing a bride's dress in Spain, but the idea of giving out a little gift to each of the ladies in attendance seems to have caught on quickly since King Felipe's recent wedding. Anyway, it provides a nice memento of the wedding."

They all sat around the table and sewed. Catalina was so happy being with her best friends that she even helped. She had completely forgotten her vow that she would not get involved in the wedding preparations.

Chapter 49
(Paris, 1559)

By the middle of August Bartolomé had arrived in Paris. He went directly to the home of Nicolas Beranjon. The family was quite surprised to see him. Symonne was the most delighted. It had been about a year since he had seen her. She was now sixteen and had blossomed into an attractive young woman. She also didn't seem to be as silly as he remembered. She was courteous and considerate in her attention to him and did not fawn over him as he had expected. This was a welcome change, and Bartolomé noted it with interest. "I could certainly grow to like her," he thought, beginning to forget the vehemence with which he had told Doctor Ortiz that his love for Catalina would never fail.

When he had arrived, Bartolomé had given only the barest outline of what had transpired over the past year. So, after he had changed from his travel clothes and joined the family, and their resident students, for supper, they requested that he tell the entire story in detail. They were truly distressed to hear of his father's death and the death of the other Protestants at the hands of the Inquisition. They were also amazed at his escape from prison and intrigued at his adventures travelling disguised as a merchant. Symonne was mesmerized by his account. A knight who had just won an all-European jousting competition wouldn't have been a greater hero in her eyes.

After supper, Nicolas had difficulty getting his wife and daughter to leave the table—even with direct suggestions that they find something to do. After a time, Nicolas asked Bartolomé to come to his library where they could have some privacy. Nicolas asked Bartolomé, "What do you plan to do next?"

"When I left Valladolid I was planning to go to Antwerp. I have heard there is a sizable congregation of Spanish refugees from the Inquisition there. I was thinking it would be good to meet with them."

"I suggest that you should make some enquires before you go there. The situation in Antwerp is not as it was when Charles was Emperor. There are rumours of increasing conflict between Protestants and Roman Catholics in Belgium. King Felipe's arm extends to the Lowlands."

"I haven't heard about that. One thing that attracted me to Antwerp was the publishing industry. There have been a number of translations of Protestant material coming from there. With my skill in languages, possibly I could help in some way. Since I can no longer work as an ambassador for Spain, I thought I could work in one of the publishing firms, possibly even as a translator."

"You wouldn't consider settling in Paris, or elsewhere in France, would you? I also hear that Spanish refugees have settled in Lyons."

"After my experiences, I want to get as far away from the Inquisition as I can. I have also considered London or Geneva; King Felipe's reach does not extend that far! Cassiodoro de Reina escaped from the Inquisition in 1557 and went to London. He is now the pastor of the Spanish congregation in that city. There is also a Spanish congregation in Geneva. I could settle in one of those cities."

"Please take all the time you want to consider your options. You know that you are welcome to stay here as long as you like. I would like to encourage you to settle in Paris."

"Thank you. I do appreciate your hospitality. I will accept it and stay here until I have had time to make plans for the future."

He continued to live with the Beranjon family as a boarder. He ate breakfast and supper, most of the time, with the family. He particularly enjoyed the discussion times among the boarders and with Nicolas. However, he did not really feel at home with the Beranjons or in Paris.

The day after his arrival, Bartolomé went to the office of Claude Lachy who helped him sell the jewellery he had brought from Valladolid. He asked Monsieur Lachy to invest most of the proceeds from the sale of the jewellery and the money his father had hidden in the box under the charcoal shed, and to give him a small monthly stipend. He had quite a bit of money invested and did not have to worry about exhausting the capital. It would continue to grow.

Bartolomé did not want to be idle, so he asked Claude Lachy if he could provide him with work. Lachy was able to hire Bartolomé as a law clerk, and he was given the responsibility of processing investment contracts. He did not find this work particularly demanding or interesting, but it would do for the present. He did not resume his duties tutoring Symonne. Her parents felt that she had had enough education and were more interested in getting her married to a suitable husband.

Shortly after he had arrived in Paris, Bartolomé began thinking about how he could contact Catalina. He remembered what Doctor Ortiz had told him about the danger Catalina would be in if the Inquisition associated her with an escaped heretic. He also was not sure how he could get a letter to her since he had no idea where she lived. He probably would have to send a letter via her father in the court in Madrid. He might not deliver it to her if he knew the letter had come from him. Finally, he decided to write to Margarita and ask her if she knew how to get in touch with Catalina. At first he wrote:

> *Margarita,*
> *I am the person who gave you the violin. I*
> *am well. I am trying to locate a mutual friend*
> *of ours. If you can give me any information,*

I would appreciate it. I live with my family in Paris.

Godspeed.

He did not sign the letter. He hoped that Margarita would understand his reference to 'my family' as the household he had boarded with and remember his address from the letters he had written during his previous year in Paris.

He did not send the letter immediately. He tried to think out different scenarios. He decided that if the officers of the Inquisition read that letter, they would find it too cryptic and their curiosity would be aroused. They would want to know more about whom it was from and who was the mutual friend being spoken about. This could put Margarita and Catalina in danger. So he recast the letter, and wrote:

Dear Margarita,

I hope that you have learned to play the violin. How is your family?

I have been doing well and have been living with the family I lived with during my studies at the University of Paris.

Please send my greetings to Catalina. Ask her to write.

Godspeed.

He signed it, "Barthélemy."

Before he sent the letter, he prayed that it would not endanger the lives of either Margarita or Catalina.

Nicolas and his wife knew that Symonne loved Bartolomé. They also liked Bartolomé because he was a sensible, capable young man and a devout Protestant. They began discussing privately how they could entice Bartolomé to marry Symonne. They didn't know about Catalina, and Bartolomé's engagement to her. Since Bartolomé had never told the family about Catalina, Nicolas started to pursue more seriously the course of having Bartolomé settle in Paris and marry Symonne.

One evening after supper, when the students had left the table, Nicolas broached the subject of Bartolomé's future. "Barthélemy, what do you plan to do next?"

"I am not sure. I have been feeling restless and have been continually thinking about how best to answer that question."

"There are lots of opportunities for someone with your training and talents here in Paris."

"I know that, but I just don't feel that this is where I should settle."

"Why is that? Have you thought about marriage? If you were married, you might feel more settled."

"Yes, I have thought about getting married." Bartolomé didn't want to say any more because he did not want to tell Nicolas about his engagement to Catalina.

"Would you consider marrying Symonne?"

Bartolomé wasn't surprised by the question, but he didn't answer immediately, so Nicolas continued, "She likes you very much. You have never given any signs of encouragement to her, so I don't know what your feelings are toward her."

"I have known for quite some time that Symonne likes me. At first, when I was her tutor, I attributed her attention to me as childish infatuation. Now I can see that she is much more serious in her affection for me. It hurts me somewhat because, until now, I have not been willing to return her affection."

Nicolas became encouraged by Bartolomé's choice of words and replied, "Would you consider marrying Symonne?"

"I don't know — I don't want to give you, or her, any false hopes. Nevertheless, I have grown fond of Symonne and, since my return to Paris, have considered marriage to her as a possibility. I believe that she would make a good wife, and since she has been raised as a Protestant it would make it easy for us to share a common faith. I could consider marrying her, but please do not think I am making an offer of marriage, or asking your permission. I have to sort out some outstanding obligations in Spain and would like to give more thought to the entire matter of my future before I take such a serious step as marriage. Give me some time. You can pray that I will make the right decisions. However, I really do not want to discuss this matter further as I find it unsettling." Bartolomé was very concerned that his love for Catalina might be waning and he wanted to find out if he had any hope of contacting her before he made any decisions with respect to Symonne.

Nicolas appreciated Bartolomé's position and respected him for his honesty and sincerity, so did not pursue the topic any further. He changed the subject, "Do you remember that you still have your books stored here?"

"Yes, I was thinking of registering to take a couple of courses at the university after Epiphany. So, I will likely need the books. In the meantime, if I could reclaim the book that you gave me as a gift, I would like to start reading it."

Nicolas retrieved the copy of the commentary on Romans by Doctor Jean Calvin and handed it to Bartolomé. They parted for the night.

Chapter 50
(Madrid, 1559)

In the last two weeks of August, the traditional summer festival *La Fiesta de La Borbolla* was in progress throughout the city. The main events were to be held on the last Saturday of the month—five days before Catalina's wedding.

The Conde de Bobadilla had asked Catalina to attend the festivities with him. He sent the request via a letter delivered by one of his servants. She had asked the servant to wait while she wrote a reply. The Conde offered her excellent seats at the afternoon bullfight where young men of the court would fight the bull from horseback. Catalina had heard much about this spectacle, and because she had never attended one, she was tempted to take him up on his offer. However, she declined the request specific to the afternoon events saying that she wished to spend the time with Margarita. This would be their last Saturday together before the wedding. She did, however, agree to attend the evening banquet with him.

Catalina, Margarita, and Luisa spent the morning together wandering through the open market and carnival. They wore their most colourful dresses to join the crowds. They watched madrigals, a morality play, and acrobats. They joined in some of the spontaneous dances. Margarita even played her lute with some of the itinerant musicians. She received appreciative applause.

For lunch, they purchased fish and cheese, and drank a delicious sweet red wine. Then they went back to Catalina's house for a rest.

After the rest, they began the process of helping one another dress for the evening banquet.

Luisa was to be accompanied by the son of a conde who had been showing her favours. Catalina and Luisa had arranged for an escort for Margarita. Margarita had not met him, but both Catalina and Luisa had assured her with many promises that he was a nice young man, who was polite and liked music. She was especially nervous and just about drove Catalina and Luisa to distraction making sure that her hair was properly set.

Luisa and Margarita would not be able to sit with Catalina at the banquet. She would be at the head table with the Conde. The girls were somewhat jealous that Catalina would be sitting with royalty. She responded, "Don't be silly, I would rather be sitting with you. I am just doing my duty, as I promised my father I would."

Catalina's parents were also attending the banquet, by invitation of King Felipe himself.

Both Luisa's and Margarita's escorts had been instructed to call for them at Catalina's house. Margarita blushed darkly when she was being introduced to her escort, but the young man was considerate and immediately made her feel comfortable.

A fancy carriage, with silver trim and pulled by four white horses, was sent by the Conde to pick up Catalina. She was embarrassed by all the attention, and thought it quite unnecessary since she could have walked to the alcázar faster. But the Conde, being rather heavy, could not walk more than the length of a row of houses. After the carriage had picked up Catalina, it returned to the Conde's residence, and he climbed into the carriage with some difficulty and some assistance from one of his servants. He kissed Catalina's hand and she greeted him cordially. They rode in silence for the few minutes it took to reach the alcázar.

They arrived in style at the entrance to the alcázar and were given a royal welcome with servants bowing everywhere. Catalina smiled as graciously as she could and thought that she would have trouble getting used to all the simpering of the servants. She was just too open and straightforward in her approach to people.

A butler escorted them to the head table.

Shortly after they had arrived, King Felipe and Queen Elizabeth entered to the sound of an orchestra playing at full volume. Catalina looked discreetly through the hall and caught sight of where her parents, and Margarita and Luisa, were sitting. She was pleased to see that Margarita was chatting with her escort. It would have been a disaster if they had not found each other's company satisfactory and had had to sit the entire evening without being able to talk with each other.

Wave after wave of dishes were brought into the hall. Entertainment, music and dancing were interspersed between the courses of the meal.

The Conde only asked Catalina to dance once. He seemed to be rather tired, looked pale, and was short of breath. Catalina thought that the heat of the sun at the bullfight must have worn him out. A few of the young men had asked Catalina to dance. She graciously declined so as not to insult the Conde.

Near the end of the meal, the Conde was speaking discreetly with King Felipe, at whose left hand he was sitting. Suddenly the cup of wine he held dropped from his left hand and clattered on the floor. Catalina was sitting on his left side, and her dress was splattered with the spilled wine. The Conde's arm dropped at his side, his face became distorted, and his forehead was soaked with perspiration. He tried to speak but was unable to. His eyes glazed over and he fell over backward onto the floor. In an instant Catalina was at his side. She held his head and in a loud voice yelled, "Father! The Conde is sick, please come quickly!"

Doctor Mendoza came over as quickly as he could get through the crowd that had rapidly gathered around the table. He pulled down one of the wall hangings, folded it, and placed it under the Conde's head that had been resting on Catalina's lap. He felt for a pulse, checked the Conde's eyes, and said, to no one in particular, "The Conde has had a stroke."

King Felipe commanded the servants, "Some of you men come here and carry the Conde to my chambers." King Felipe, Abram, Catalina, and a few of the more senior courtiers accompanied the men carrying the Conde. The Conde was placed on a bed in King Felipe's sleeping quarters.

Doctor Mendoza called for water and opened the Conde's shirt. He tried to cool off the Conde. Catalina sat in a chair to the right of the Conde and rubbed his hand. Doctor Mendoza then spoke with difficulty, "I don't think the Conde will live much longer. Please call for a priest immediately." The priest arrived within seconds. He must have been prepared, outside the door, in case he was needed. He administered the Last Rites.

Doctor Mendoza spoke softly, "He has died. Nothing more can be done for him." Catalina began to weep quietly, still holding the Conde's hand. After a few minutes, one of King Felipe's senior advisors gently escorted her from the room. She was feeling week and dizzy, and he arranged for some maids to see that she was taken home. As they led her through the main hall, the banquet was still in progress but was somewhat subdued because of concern over the Conde.

Margarita and Luisa saw the maids leading Catalina into the hall. They rushed over to her. Luisa asked, "What happened?"

"The Conde had a stroke. He just died."

"That is awful, are you feeling okay?"

"I am feeling weak, but that is all. Can you take me home, please?"

They both nodded and Luisa said to Margarita, "Please tell our escorts that we must leave to take Catalina home."

She went to them and they returned with her and offered assistance. Luisa had taken charge and said, "Thank you. But I think that it will be best if Margarita and I take Catalina home alone. I am sorry but we must go." The young men nodded in understanding.

Luisa and Margarita each supported Catalina, and they left the hall. The evening was still warm, but the fresh air revived Catalina, so she felt able to walk on her own by the time they had reached the house. They found that Susana was already home and waiting for them to arrive. The girls explained to her what had happened to the Conde.

When they had gone upstairs, they sat at the table and Catalina said, "I can't believe what has just happened."

Luisa replied, "Didn't I tell you that the Conde might die?"

"Yes, but you said he might die *after* we were married, not before. I never expected anything like this!"

Susana said, "That is often the way with Death. He sneaks in when least expected."

Margarita bubbled, "Now you won't have to marry the Conde."

"That is true. I didn't want to marry him, but I did not wish him ill. I *never* prayed for his death. In fact

I had come to accept the reality that I was to marry him."

Susana replied, "It was obviously not God's will that you marry the Conde."

Catalina continued, "I am too numb to be relieved."

Abram came in and sat with them. He sat with a glazed look in his eyes. "I always blame myself when a patient dies, but our knowledge about the human body is so limited. We don't know what to do when a person has a stroke. Rarely can we save him. And when a person does survive the stroke, he is usually paralyzed for the rest of his life. I hate Death!"

Catalina replied, "That is what happened to Bartolomé's grandfather. He had a stroke and was partially paralyzed. Bartolomé told me all about him."

"You will never forget Bartolomé, will you?" asked Susana.

"No, Mother. I can't!"

It took great effort for them to change the subject, away from death to other matters.

The next day the three girls began the process of undoing the wedding preparations. They had dozens of letters to write to inform people that the wedding was cancelled. Some gifts that had already arrived had to be returned, the cooks and bakers were paid for their efforts thus far, and their further services cancelled. It was unpleasant explaining to each of them about the death of the Conde.

They all attended the Conde's funeral. It was one of the largest spectacles the town of Madrid had ever seen.

Near the end of September, Margarita's brother arrived to escort her back to Valladolid. Catalina held her close, and they both cried.

Catalina said, "You are such a good friend to me. Thank you for all your help."

"I will miss you."

"You may come anytime to visit. Maybe you will be asked to come back to sing and play your lute. And maybe you will marry someone here and be able to live in Madrid! Then we could see each other all the time."

"Catalina, we don't know what is going to happen. Promise me you will continue to write."

"Of course! You know that I will."

After more tears, Margarita left and Catalina went to her room, sat on her bed, and cried softly. She felt so alone. Her thoughts turned to Bartolomé, "Oh God, where is Bartolomé? Will I ever see him again? Please take care of him." She was exhausted. She put her head on a pillow to think, and a moment later was asleep.

Chapter 51
(Madrid, 1559)

On the last Sunday in September, Catalina was sitting with Abram and Susana at a late breakfast. She had gone to early mass and returned to have breakfast with them. Abram had told María that she could have the day off. She had scuttled out of the house as quickly as a beetle hiding from the sun when a rock is overturned.

Abram then said to Catalina, "Your mother and I would like to speak with you."

Catalina's heart almost stopped beating, "Father, you are not going to tell me that I am to be married to another courtier, are you?"

"No, my dear, I will not make that mistake again. I promise you that you can pick your own marriage partner — as long as I approve of course." He smiled. "I hope that you really can marry the one you love, and I will not interfere again. I promise!"

"Father, are you apologizing?" She beamed him one of her blazing smiles.

"Well — I suppose I am, but there is more — it will likely shock you ..."

"What could be more shocking than when you announced our move to Madrid or that I was to marry the Conde de Bobadilla?"

"I will let you be the judge of that. I have been reading an interesting book lately. I found it a number of weeks ago when I was unpacking another one of the boxes of books that I still have to open. I have run out of shelf space, so I may not be able to unpack them all until we move into our new house. But, I digress. The book must have been among the ones I acquired when I purchased the library of the French nobleman from Languedoc. If I am not mistaken, I believe that you also discovered a book from that collection, a French-Latin edition of the *New Testament*. Am I correct?" Catalina nodded. "Well the book I found was written by a Frenchman who now lives in Geneva."

"Father! You are deliberately dragging out this story. What are you trying to tell me? You have piqued my curiosity. Get to the point. And since when can you read French? I am the only one in this household who can read French." She gave him a teasing smile.

"I didn't say the book was written in French. I said, it was *written* by a Frenchman. Watch that you don't make illogical deductions!" She grinned, remembering her tutor's instructions. "The book I have been reading is in Latin. I think you would enjoy it very much."

"You are going through all this to get me to read a book! All you had to do was hand me the book and say, 'Read this, you will find it interesting,' and I would have consumed it."

"Catalina, someday I may be able to teach you to be patient, but I guess today isn't going to be the day. So, as I was saying, I have been reading a book. It is entitled *Institutio Christiane Religonis* and was written by Doctor Jean Calvin."

Catalina's eyes opened wide as she said, "I have not heard of this book, but I have heard of the man. His name is often mentioned along with that of Martin Luther's. A spit and a curse often accompany his name. Father, isn't he among the Protestants whom the Inquisition says we must avoid? His book is probably banned. Have you been reading a banned book?" She gave the sly smile of someone who was sharing a secret.

"Yes, this book is one of the most hated of all by the Church. If the Inquisition were able to, they would burn every copy in existence and snuff out the life of everyone who has read it. It is probably the most powerful polemic against the position of the Church of Rome ever written. Doctor Calvin generally gives a clear, logical presentation of the truth rather than just attacking falsehood. The deliberations of the Council of Trent are largely focused on an attack against the doctrines found in this book."

"Father, aren't you in great danger if you read this book?"

"Yes, but I am in no greater danger than you with your Spanish *New Testament*."

"So we are both *heretics* now?" She liked the sound of that.

"Yes. Now what is more important to me, and your mother, and I believe it will be to you also, is that reading this book has convinced me that the Christian religion is true. This book is so full of the majesty and grace of God that it swept me from earth to heaven. I have really become a Christian, and a Protestant one at that."

Catalina couldn't believe what she was hearing. She sat in stunned silence, with her mouth wide open. She looked from her father to her mother and back again. Susana nodded; indicating that what Abram said was true. Then Catalina started to cry, and said, "Father! You were so right. This is the most shocking news you have ever told me, but it makes me so happy." She got up from her chair and went over to Abram, kissed him, draped her arms around his neck and rested her head on his chest. He gently rubbed her hair, and he started to cry also. Susana seeing them both crying couldn't contain her tears, so she joined them.

Catalina finally spoke, "What a mess we are!" They laughed.

"I have prayed for this for many months. Thank you, God! Now if only I could hear about Bartolomé, I would feel complete."

"Catalina, I have been very hard on you regarding Bartolomé. I know you love him. We will join you in praying for him. May God grant that he still lives and somehow can be set free."

"Thank you Father. Thank you Mother. It is such a relief to me that I don't have to love him against your will."

Her father began to speak again, "Catalina, there is still more that we must discuss."

"What more could there be?"

"Do you remember when I informed you of our Jewish ancestry and how concerned we were about being visible to the Inquisition?"

"Yes?" She said warily, not sure what would come next.

"I really was afraid of the Inquisition. I really did fear being thrown into their prison. I didn't stand for anything on principle, and I was afraid I would be called to make a defence of my faith—which didn't exist. Now that I have real faith, I am even more afraid of the Inquisition."

"But they don't need to know that you are a Protestant."

"The problem is now that I am one, I want to live as one. Have you noticed that your mother and I have not gone to mass for the past few weeks?"

"Yes, I noticed, but there have been many times you have missed mass. You were often busy with a patient or had some other excuse."

"I often had an excuse because I had no interest in going."

"Now I cannot go because I believe, from my understanding of what I have read in Doctor Calvin's book, that the mass is not true worship. I believe that I must associate with Protestants. However, there aren't, as far as I know, any other Protestants

391

in Madrid; and there certainly doesn't seem to be a meeting of them. Also it is impossible for me to continue to work for, and with, King Felipe. He feels that his royal power must be used to preserve the nation of Spain for the Roman Catholic religion. His whole life is now focused on ensuring that he is not the ruler of a nation of heretics. I cannot stay in his service and hold the views I now hold. I cannot be a hypocrite, working to further King Felipe's kingdom and being adamantly against his goals."

"So, Father, what is to be done?"

"We must leave Spain."

Catalina almost fell out of her chair. "Leave Spain? Father, you have changed. I never would have thought I would hear such a thing. You are so full of surprises."

"Are you in agreement with this suggestion?"

"Father, does it matter what I think?"

"Truly it does. I am still feeling the pain you experienced with the prospect of an arranged marriage, and I don't really want to force you to leave Spain if you don't want to. Yet, I hope that we can be united as a family and all want to move to a safer place where I — we can openly live as Protestants."

"Other than being concerned about being even farther away from Bartolomé, I am prepared to leave Spain. I have always wanted to travel. I don't remember much of it, but I did like it when we were in Italy. I am willing and even eager to go somewhere new. Where were you thinking we should go?"

"Your mother and I have been discussing this. Haven't we Susana?" She nodded. "We were thinking of either London or Geneva."

"But neither of you know any English or French, wouldn't that be difficult?"

Susana interjected, "We are willing to learn a new language so that we can be safe."

"Learning a new language," Abram said, "is the least of our worries. We have to figure out how to get out of Spain without arousing suspicion, and I would like to be able to take with us enough money and sellable goods such as jewellery so that we can make a start relatively easily somewhere else. I am thankful that my chosen profession is transportable. A doctor who is any good can find patients and earn a reasonable income just about anywhere."

"I would love to go to England," said Catalina, "but thinking practically, maybe we should think of Geneva first. Since I am now almost fluent in French I could at least help us in our travels through France and Helvetia."

"That is true, and very good thinking. Yes, we should consider that. Have you any other good ideas like that to help us escape from Madrid?"

"What if you told King Felipe that you wanted to go to Paris to do some more studying, would he let you go? You have always said that you wanted to go to the University of Paris to study medicine. Is there some way you could arrange that?"

Susana responded, "Abram, Catalina's suggestion is a good one. We could go to Paris and from there make our way to Geneva."

"Yes, we can do that. I will have to come up with a truly plausible reason for wanting to go to Paris. Let me think for a moment." They all sat quietly.

"I think what I should do is request that I be allowed to spend a short period, say a month or two, working with one of Paris' famous doctors. I am aware of a book on surgery written by the French professor, Ambroise Paré, which suggests treating wounds with soothing ointments instead of boiling oil. Jacobus Sylvius was in Paris when he wrote a book on anatomy. But I think I heard that he died. Then there are other Frenchmen, Peter Ramus and Jean Fernel, who might be appropriate. I will ask among my fellows, without raising suspicion, and find a reason for going to Paris."

Abram followed through on Catalina's suggestion and within a week had come up with a reason for going to Paris. He decided that he would propose going to learn surgical techniques from Doctor Ambroise Paré who, besides dealing with puncture wounds, appeared to be the leading expert in Europe on fractures and dislocations. Also, his recommendations for the use of ligatures to stop bleeding from veins and arteries during and after amputation intrigued Abram. He could use these new techniques as an opportunity to make his appeal for permission to go to Paris real, since military surgeons could apply his techniques. He approached King Felipe and asked for permission to go to Paris.

On arriving home, he told Susana and Catalina how the meeting had gone. "I asked King Felipe for permission to go study with Doctor Paré in Paris. I also told him that I would plan to be away for three to four months depending on the time it would take for the journey and on the weather. I am surprised at how easy it was to gain his agreement."

"Father, I was praying that it would go well. It is just like when Nehemiah wanted to go to Jerusalem and had to ask the king for permission. God made it possible."

"Not only did the king agree that I could go, but he understood that you both would be coming along. I told him that you, Catalina, would enjoy a visit to Paris after the events surrounding the recent death of the Conde. He was quite sympathetic to your situation and asked about your health. You should be flattered that the most powerful monarch in Christendom even knows that you exist."

"Father, he is just a man like you. You told me that once. Shouldn't it mean nothing to me that he knows who I am? But, I have to admit I am flattered. However, considering his views about Protestants, I think that the less he knows about me, or us, the better."

"I told King Felipe that we would plan to leave immediately to avoid travelling in winter. We also discussed the death of Queen Elizabeth's father, King Henry II, who was mortally wounded earlier this year when he took part in a jousting tournament. He was celebrating the proxy marriage of Princess Elizabeth to King Felipe and was wounded by a lance splinter. King Felipe wants me to carry some official papers to King François II, King Henry's son, the new king of France."

"God be praised that it went so well!" said Susana.

"Not only has he consented, but he said that he will send an escort of four soldiers to see that we safely arrive in Paris. I accepted graciously as I did not want to offend his considerate offer. He also gave me this bag of coronas to defray our costs. He said that I could consider it payment for acting as a courier."

Susana again said, "God be praised!"

"We will have to be careful about what we take with us. We do not want to give anyone a hint that we might not be returning. We have to pack only small trunks to make it look like we are going for just a few months. We must leave our house as if we plan to return. We will have to leave María here. I have already quietly sold a few items of jewellery. With the money I received from that, plus what I already had from the sale of our house in Valladolid and what King Felipe has just given me, we should have sufficient funds to get to Geneva and become established there—if we are frugal. I think we should plan to leave within a week. Can we be ready?" Both Susana and Catalina nodded.

"Catalina, you must be careful that you do not suggest to Luisa that you are not coming back."

"But, Father, I will not lie!"

"No, my dear, do not lie. If she asks you questions, however, be guarded in your answers. For example, if she says, 'When will you return?' you can say, 'I do not know. My father wants to be in Paris for three months.' Don't say any more than that."

Abram limited them each to two trunks. Catalina chose her clothing carefully so that she would have practical outfits for travelling as well as ones suitable for engagements in Paris. She was thankful that she had had the experience travelling in the spring, so that she had a better understanding of what would be useful and what would not be. She placed her Spanish New Testament and the *Geographia* Bartolomé had given her on the bottom of one trunk beneath her undergarments. She would not take either book out again until they were safely in Geneva.

They departed Madrid on Wednesday, October 11th, 1559. Susana and Catalina travelled in their own carriage that was laden with the trunks. A hired driver drove the carriage. Abram rode another of their horses beside the four soldiers who had been assigned to their party by King Felipe.

Catalina had not received a letter from Margarita since she returned to Valladolid, and in the urgency of leaving Madrid, she forgot to write to tell her that she was going to Paris. When she did remember Margarita, she decided that she could write her just as easily from Paris and let her know where she would be staying.

A letter for Catalina did arrive from Valladolid the next day, but the maid could not forward it to her because she did not yet know where the Mendoza family would be staying in Paris. She also thought, "Anyway they will be back soon enough."

Chapter 52
(Paris and Geneva, 1559)

In was not until late October that Bartolomé received a letter from Margarita. Before he opened it, he sat at his desk and offered a prayer of thanks. Margarita said the following,

> *Dear Barthélemy,*
>
> *Thank you for writing. It is great to hear that you are well.*
>
> *I am sorry that I did not write sooner. I was in Madrid visiting with Catalina for her wedding. I found your letter waiting for me when I returned to Valladolid and am responding immediately.*
>
> *I hope I didn't frighten you with that statement about Catalina's wedding. Don't worry she isn't married! I will tell you what happened in a moment.*

*I wrote immediately to Catalina to tell
her that I have heard from you. If you want
to write her, you can send the letter via me. I
will forward it to her in my letter.*

*I have learned to play the violin. I even
got to play it before the royal court in Madrid.
Thank you again for the gift.*

*Now let me tell you about Catalina's
near-wedding ...*

... Catalina still loves you very much.

*Goodbye, and God bless you in the
future.*

Your friend, Margarita.

Bartolomé went through a whole spectrum of
emotions upon reading Margarita's letter. His heart
almost failed when he read about Catalina's wedding.
Then he laughed aloud when he read further and
found that he had been tricked by Margarita. He was
relieved that the Inquisition appeared not to have
made a connection between himself and Margarita
and Catalina. Their visit to him in prison could have
resulted in their arrest, but they had escaped further
official notice. He felt drained of all energy thinking
of what Catalina had been put through because of an
arranged marriage, but his strongest emotion was one
of thankfulness. He felt that he was close to finding
Catalina again. He got up from his desk, went to his
bed, knelt, and prayed a long prayer of thanks with
many requests for Catalina.

After he had completed praying, he felt release from the sense of unease that had been bothering him for many days.

He thought about writing a letter via Margarita, but decided instead to take a risk and write directly to Catalina in Madrid, care of her father. He could always write through Margarita later if he got no response from the direct approach. However, on thinking through the matter, he concluded that if Abram were not willing to give Catalina his letter, he would still be unwilling to consent to their marriage. He believed that if Abram could not bless their marriage it would be unwise for him to contact her through Margarita. He could not suggest to Catalina that she try to escape from Madrid on her own and come to France, or go to Geneva, if he settled there. He also determined that he could not realistically go back to Spain to get her. The only hope he had was that Abram had softened and would allow Catalina to respond to his letter.

He composed a letter first to Doctor Abram Mendoza and then one to Catalina. He re-wrote both letters many times before he was happy with the results. He decided that it was best to keep both letters brief. If he were able to reconnect with Catalina, there would be opportunities for filling in details. He placed the letter to Catalina inside the one to Abram. He sent them the next day by the fastest courier he could find. It was expensive, but worth it.

He figured that it would take less than two weeks for his letter to get to Madrid. There were numerous fast couriers going between the cities. If Catalina got the letter, she would write, and it would take two weeks more for the response to arrive. So, every day during the first two weeks of December when he would return to Nicolas' home in the evening, he would ask if there had been any letters for him. The answer was always the same, "No." The family began to become curious and concerned about his behaviour. Finally, Nicolas asked, "Why are you looking for a letter every day?"

"I wrote to a friend in Madrid. The response I receive will help me decide the direction of my future. It will be an important letter, if it comes." He did not give any more details, and it left Nicolas and his wife with the same concern and uncertainty as before.

By mid-December, 1559, Bartolomé's restlessness had returned and was growing worse. He had been thinking more and more about the continuing, and increasing, persecution of Protestants throughout France and the looming danger of conflict between Catholics and Protestants. He kept thinking about the possibility of moving to a place where it was safe to be a Protestant. The three places he thought most about were England, northern Germany, and Geneva. He did not consider the requirement to learn English or German an impediment, but rather relished the idea of learning another language.

Finally, he decided that he could no longer wait to see if a letter from Catalina was going to arrive. He determined that he would act. So, he asked Nicolas if he could speak with him privately. They went into

Nicolas' library. "I have decided," Bartolomé said solemnly, "to leave Paris."

"Why? Are you unhappy with us?"

"Not in the least. I appreciate very much what you and your family have done for me. You have been a shelter in a storm and a refuge for a wanderer. I have enjoyed greatly being part of your family and being able to participate in the stimulating supper discussions. I also have been blessed being part of your congregation here. I have learned much, but this cannot be my permanent home. I must settle somewhere else."

"I am disappointed to hear this. And what of Symonne? I have not brought up the matter since we talked a few months ago, but I would like to know your intentions toward her. I have the responsibility to see her settled in a good marriage, and I need to know where you stand."

"I will *consider* marrying Symonne — wait, don't begin to dance in the street — but there are some conditions. Once I am settled in a new city, and if I do not receive a response from Madrid, then I will think seriously about asking for Symonne's hand."

"But where have you decided to settle? I am not sure that I like the idea of Symonne moving away from Paris. Her mother was truly looking forward to the day that she would have grandchildren running around the house."

"I will probably settle in Geneva. I want to go there and see what it is like. The Protestants in Paris and throughout France are becoming more strident and militant. With the ascension of François

II, a fifteen-year-old incompetent, the Protestants have been agitating for more freedoms. I have a sense that the confrontations are going to escalate. If armed conflict should come, I don't want to be in the middle of it. My experiences at the hands of the Inquisition have made me wary of the dangers of living in a country where the king and his court are in partnership with the bishops and monks of the Church of Rome. Geneva is a Protestant city. I could live openly there without fear for my life. It would be a safe place to rear a family."

"I don't know if I want Symonne leaving us. She is our only child and very dear to us."

"I understand your feelings, but if you want me to be your son-in-law it will have to be on the condition that you bring Symonne to Geneva, or wherever I decide to settle. I would be happy if you also could leave Paris and join me."

"I cannot leave my city and my country, but I will give thought to the idea of taking Symonne to meet you. She would probably go with you now, if you were willing to take her."

"As I said, I await the receipt of a letter from Madrid. The contents of that letter will settle a number of matters for me. I will not offer marriage to Symonne until then."

"I understand. I will not discuss the idea with her at this time. I must not give her a hope that could be destroyed."

"After I have left for Geneva, can you please send any correspondence immediately to Guillaume Bonenffant on Rue de l'Hôtel de Ville, and ship to him my books and other personal belongings. He is a personal associate of Monsieur Lachy and handles Lachy's affairs in Geneva. While acting as clerk in Lachy's offices, I have had numerous opportunities to correspond with Monsieur Bonenffant and know that letters sent to me in Geneva will reach me if they are sent through him. Here, I have written out this information for you." Bartolomé handed Nicolas a piece of paper with his forwarding address and some money to pay for the shipment.

"When do you plan to leave?"

"Immediately. Tomorrow, if possible. I will be taking only my horse."

"What do you want me to do with the donkey?"

"Please give it to a poor family in the congregation who could make use of it."

Bartolomé did leave the next day, Friday, December 15th. He saddled his horse in the Beranjon's stable and put the few personal items he would carry with him, and a change of clothes into the saddlebags. He led the horse through the archway onto the street where the Beranjon family were waiting to see him off.

He gave Nicolas a hug and a hearty handshake, and said, "Again, I thank you for all your physical and spiritual help. I will be in touch about the matters we discussed, once I have had an opportunity to establish whether or not I plan to stay permanently in Geneva."

He gave a bow to Nicolas' wife and kissed her hand, "Your cooking and hospitality have been superb. You have treated me like a son. You are very kind and generous. Thank you!" She blushed and gave a small curtsey.

Then he turned to Symonne, "Symonne, I have been pleased to have gotten to know you. I will not forget you. Our paths may cross again. Pray for me on my journey." He gave her a polite hug. She controlled her emotions and kissed him gently on the cheek. Then she turned away, and tears filled her eyes.

Bartolomé turned and mounted his horse, touched the brim of his hat with a salute, and rode away. He rode hard and long most days, and covered the distance between Paris and Geneva in just over a week. His horse held up well. He thought that that was a credit to its Spanish breeding.

He found lodging and a place to board his horse. The next day he went to visit Monsieur Bonenffant, to whom he had written many times from Paris. Guillaume Bonenffant was pleased to see him and Bartolomé efficiently itemized what he wanted done, "First, I would like to transfer my investment accounts from Monsieur Lachy's to Geneva. Second, I would like to ask if you could help me find employment."

Guillaume Bonenffant responded, "Based on the contracts I have seen you prepare, and on Monsieur Lachy's recommendation, I would be happy to employ you. You may start tomorrow."

Bartolomé was quite relieved and said, "Thank you. I didn't expect it to be that simple. I will be very pleased to work with you."

He spent the rest of the day walking through the town. He discovered that a new university had just been founded where he could continue studying law and work toward a Master's degree. He also found the Cathedral St. Pierre where Doctor Jean Calvin preached, and a nearby church where the Spanish Protestant congregation met on Sunday afternoons.

Bartolomé began to listen to Pastor Calvin's daily sermons with interest, and was excited to have the chance to hear such a great preacher. He politely introduced himself to Pastor Calvin on the second day after hearing him preach, and told him of his escape from the Inquisition. Pastor Calvin was moved by Bartolomé's account, placed his hands on his head, and blessed him. Bartolomé felt as if he had been welcomed home by his father.

Bartolomé also attended the Spanish service on December 24th. The pastor of the congregation was Doctor Juan Pérez de Pineda, a godly man who welcomed Bartolomé heartily into their midst. He was overwhelmed by the kindness of the congregation.

During the following week, Bartolomé started to feel at home in Geneva. On Saturday evening, he composed a brief letter to Nicolas Beranjon:

> *I'm now twenty-one years old and will be twenty-two in a few months. It is time for me seriously to consider my future.*
>
> *I have found work as a law clerk. I have been to hear Doctor Jean Calvin preach and have met with the Spanish congregation. I like Geneva, and although I have been here only a week, I am sure that I want to settle permanently in this city.*

I have sufficient money from my grandfather's legacy to buy a house in the city and to support a wife and family. There is a new university here. I plan to register to study for a Master's degree. When I complete that degree, I should be able to obtain a better position than the clerk position I now have.

I have grown fond of Symonne during the last few months I was in your home. I know I could grow to love her, and believe that I would be a good husband for her.

If you are still willing that I marry Symonne, please pass on my request to her. If she agrees, please arrange to bring her to Geneva as soon as you are able.

Bartolomé planned to send the letter the following Monday.

That night he got only a few hours of restless sleep. Thoughts of Catalina kept him awake. He thought, "I have to accept the reality that Catalina's father did not give her my letter. It seems unrealistic to think that I will ever hear from, or see, her again. Beyond the fact that I would marry Catalina if she were here, I can't think of any reason why I should not marry Symonne. But, am I doing the right thing? How can I contact Catalina? Should I try again to reach her through Margarita? Would I just put them all in danger? How would Catalina get out of Spain, even if I could contact her?"

Early Sunday morning he spent over an hour praying that God would give clear direction.

Chapter 53
(Paris and Geneva, 1559)

The Mendoza family arrived in Paris in early November. Upon their arrival, Catalina went into a shop that looked as if it served decent folks. She explained that her family had just arrived from Madrid and was looking for accommodation. Her abilities in French were pressed to the limit, and at first she felt a bit shy trying to converse with the store clerks. They, however, noticed her accent and were impressed by her willingness to speak with them in French. They turned out to be quite helpful and gave her directions to a clean and respectable inn. Catalina wrote out the directions and gave them to her father. He rode with the soldiers, but beside the carriage so he could speak directly to Catalina who was inside.

As they followed the directions, Catalina and Susana tried to see the sights of Paris, but it was difficult with horses on either side and with trying to follow the directions. They agreed that their introductory tour to the city would have to wait until they were settled.

When they arrived at the inn, they found that there were numerous rooms available. November was not a busy time for visitors coming to the city. Catalina translated for her father as they negotiated two rooms, one for her parents and an adjacent room for her. They also found out where they could lodge the horses and park the carriage during their stay. Abram then thanked and dismissed the soldiers and driver, and gave them each an extra gold coin for their efforts.

After the porter had moved their trunks to their rooms and they had changed, they agreed that they should find a place to eat. Catalina went to the proprietoress of the inn and asked, "Where can we obtain supper?"

"I would be happy to prepare meals for you, and you can eat in my dining room."

"That would be very kind. We will eat here during our stay. However, we are quite excited about being in Paris and would like to take the opportunity to see the city. Can you recommend where we might eat near the river tonight?"

She gave Catalina directions to a couple of suggested places.

The Mendozas walked the short distance to the nearest recommended *bouchon*. It was tiny, with only four tables that could seat four people each. They were served an excellent meal of capon in a

Dijon mustard sauce, fresh bread, cheese, a cucumber salad, and a tangy French white wine.

After the meal, they walked through the neighbourhoods near the river and along the path beside the river before heading back to their inn.

The next day, Catalina and Abram left early. Catalina spoke with passers-by to find them a hired carriage. First, they delivered the papers that King Felipe had asked them to deliver to François II. They delivered these into the hands of a senior official at the palace. Then Catalina gave the driver instructions to take them to the university and they began looking for Ambroise Paré.

When they found his clinic, they were told that he was teaching and would return around noon. They decided to walk around the university and to return later. Catalina was thrilled with all there was to see. The city had an entirely different ambiance than Valladolid; it seemed to be running all the time. Valladolid crawled in comparison. Catalina thought about Bartolomé and thought she recognized some of the places he had described to her in his letters.

At noon, they returned to Doctor Paré's clinic and met with the doctor. Abram was able to converse with him in Latin and introduced himself as a doctor serving King Felipe II in Madrid. He explained that he would like to learn more of his techniques and that the Spanish Court was willing to reimburse the doctor if necessary. Doctor Paré suggested that Abram accompany him on his rounds, assist him in the work of his clinic, and sit in on his classes. The fee would be negligible. This was agreeable to both.

Catalina then said, in perfect Latin, "Would you mind if I came along also at times?"

Doctor Paré was so shocked to hear her speaking Latin that he could not refuse. Catalina laughed inwardly at her ability to catch people off-guard.

Over the next few days, she split her time between accompanying her father and Doctor Paré on their medical duties and touring the city with her mother to visit the numerous sights of Paris.

Susana and Catalina visited old churches, including two impressive ones built in the thirteenth century—la Sainte-Chapelle and Notre Dame. They also looked at some of the fancy administrative buildings, including the Hôtel de Ville built under the direction of François I and the Hôtel de Ferrare Fontainebleau with the Cardinal's apartments and gardens, and Le Louvre being built by Pierre Lescot.

They all walked, one evening, on the Pont Notre-Dame and looked at the new townhouses and workshops that were occupied, at high rents, by the goldsmiths. Catalina thought of Bartolomé's father when she saw the men at work at their small furnaces and displaying their wares. They were offered many fine items of jewellery but declined considering them. They were all quite aware of how carefully they had to manage their family funds until they were settled in Geneva.

As they toured the city, they were intrigued by the amount of outdoor art, such as the Fontaine des Innocents, that they found almost everywhere. Catalina said to her mother, "There can't be another city anywhere in the world with such a variety of architecture and so many impressive buildings and monuments, except possibly Rome. I can just remember seeing the churches and the ancient Roman ruins when we visited Rome. There seem to be as many in Paris."

When the Mendozas had been in Paris for about a week, Abram said, "We must begin to plan our escape to Geneva. As a first step, can you two start taking out the horses and carriage regularly? The horses have had a good enough rest from their long trip from Madrid and now need to have exercise. This is especially necessary if they are going to be able to take us all the way to Geneva. Also, if you start taking the carriage on day trips, and even overnight, we will not raise suspicions when we decide to leave entirely."

Catalina was thrilled to have the opportunity to drive the team, and she took her mother around the city and out of the city. More than once she received angry shouts from other drivers and dozens of catcalls from those who thought it very inappropriate for a lady to be driving a carriage.

When almost a month had passed, Abram announced, "I have learned sufficiently from Doctor Ambroise Paré, and we should plan to leave. I told Doctor Paré that I would be taking my family on a trip out of the city, and he should not expect to see me for some time."

They left Paris and began the journey for Geneva on Saturday, December 16th.

The roads between Paris and Geneva were of generally good quality, and the route was well travelled. The trip was uneventful other than that it rained on a number of days. On those days, Abram rode on top of the carriage, covered in a large oiled-leather cape; and his riding horse was tied to the back of the carriage. On clear days, Abram rode their horse and Catalina drove the carriage.

It took them just under two weeks to make the journey. Abram was sure that no one would notice they were missing from Paris, for at least a week. By then, it would be difficult for anyone to determine which direction they had gone when they had left the city. Yet, it was not until they were well into Helvetia that he was able to stop wanting to look over his shoulder to see if they were being followed.

During the journey, Catalina and Susana talked about their future. Susana said at one point, "I know that it will be hard for you to forget Bartolomé, but we are making a new start in a new town and a new country. This is a Protestant city. You will meet many young men who will believe the same things you do. You are very pretty and they will be attracted to you like bees to a flower. You should give them a chance. You will be eighteen next summer, will you consider marrying?"

"Mother, this is difficult. I promised Bartolomé I would wait for him. I wrote to Margarita while we were in Paris to tell her that we were there, and to describe some of the sights. I could not give her a return address. Once we are settled in Geneva, I will write to her again and ask her if she has heard anything about Bartolomé. If she has not, then I will give thought to allowing other young men to court me, but I will never love anyone else like I love Bartolomé."

"I understand, dear, but your father might have something to say about your writing to Margarita. You will not be able to send letters to her from Geneva without arousing suspicion. The Inquisition knows that it is a Protestant city. They would immediately suspect Margarita to be in sympathy with Protestants."

"How then can I find out anything about Bartolomé?" she said with distress in her voice.

"My dear, your father may be able to think of a way to get a letter to Valladolid safely. We can ask him once we are in Geneva and he is not as worried about being arrested by the Inquisition."

They arrived in Geneva two days after Christmas, and found a furnished townhouse to rent on Rue St Ours near the Parc des Bastions. It was made of limestone with heavy arches around the doors and windows. There was a small tree in a little courtyard in front of the main door. The street was generally quiet, and the courtyard with the tree gave the house a degree of privacy that was rare in the city. Catalina and Susana loved the place and, as best they could, started to make it their home.

Abram told Susana and Catalina, "We still have the proceeds from the sale of our house in Valladolid plus what I received from selling the jewellery. We have not had to spend any of that money on our trip. We have been able to live off the money King Felipe gave me before we left Madrid. And now I am going to start looking for employment. While I do that, can you look throughout the town to see what houses might be for sale? I realize that some of those offering houses for sale may not be willing to speak with you; they may only want to deal with a man. But you can at least find out what might be available. We do not want to pay rent if we can purchase a house at a reasonable cost. The house doesn't necessarily have to have a clinic in it like we had in our house in Valladolid."

Catalina replied, "Oh, Mother, this will be fun! I always like to spend Father's money." She flashed him her most saucy smile, and they all laughed. It had been awhile since they enjoyed a real good laugh together as a family. Abram kissed them both and went out. "Maybe we can buy this house. It would be so much fun to live right here."

Susana replied, "There is no harm in asking. Let's find out if the owner might be willing to sell it."

Abram began to make enquiries about setting up a medical practice. He discovered that Doctor Jean Calvin and Doctor Théodore de Béze had just founded the Schola Genevensis earlier in the year. He thought that there might be an opportunity to become involved in a new medical faculty. He soon found out that its primary focus was on the humanities, theology, and law. So, he switched his plans and offered to serve as a resident doctor for the students and faculty. He was accepted into this position with a small stipend. With the matter of initial employment settled, he then set about finding a suitable facility for his clinic in which he could set up his private practice. There were many people in the town who could speak Latin and he was starting to pick up the rudiments of French; so he was able to get along reasonably well without Catalina to translate for him.

Catalina and Susana had fun walking through the town looking at the houses. They liked the compactness of the Old Town and how clean it was kept. The people of Geneva were much more orderly than the inhabitants of Valladolid, Madrid, or Paris.

On their walks, they discovered that there was a Spanish congregation in the city. On Saturday evening Catalina told her father, "We have discovered a Spanish Protestant congregation that meets near Cathedral St. Pierre, on Sunday afternoons. Can we go there tomorrow?"

"Of course!"

"Father, this will be our first time attending a Protestant church. I am so glad that we can go together as a family!"

"Not only that, we don't have to be secretive about going. You can even carry your Spanish *New Testament* with you. The freedom is so liberating"

"I don't know how you feel, but I already like it here. The town is smaller than Valladolid, and much smaller than Paris; but I love it. I do not miss Valladolid or Madrid. I only miss my friends, Margarita, Luisa — and I miss Bartolomé."

Abram answered, "I feel like a heavy weight has been lifted off my shoulders."

"And I don't really care where I live, as long as I have you two with me, and you are happy." replied Susana.

"Then we are all happy here — almost, if only I had news about Bartolomé," said Catalina.

Chapter 54
(Geneva, 1559)

On Sunday afternoon, December 31st, 1559, Bartolomé arrived early at church to attend the service of the Spanish congregation and sat in the second row of pews near the pulpit. He liked to sit in the front of the church because he found he was not as easily distracted as when people sat in front of him. However, he didn't want to sit in the front row that day because during the service on the previous week the pastor kept staring directly at the people sitting in the front pews.

The church slowly filled with the congregation. The people were silent as they entered the church, and Bartolomé sat reading his *New Testament* and meditating on it while he waited for the service to begin. At two o'clock, the side door opened and the pastor came into the sanctuary accompanied by the elders; all were wearing black gowns. The elder leading the small procession carried a large Latin pulpit Bible and climbed the stairs of the pulpit to place the Bible on the lectern. After he had descended, Pastor Pérez, carrying a *New Testament*, climbed into the pulpit and called the congregation to worship.

People were still entering the sanctuary during the singing of the first Psalm. Bartolomé thought that people should be more respectful of God's house and organize their lives so that they could arrive on time. Then he rebuked himself critically, reminding himself that he did not know the reason for their lateness and should be more charitable. He did not turn to see who the latecomers were. To turn around would only distract him from the singing of praise, and he wouldn't have been able to see who it was anyway, because the congregation was standing. He redoubled his efforts to stay focused on the words that he was singing.

Among those who entered late were the Mendozas. They found a place for three to sit together near the back. There was a bit of shuffling as those currently occupying the pew had to allow them to pass and then shift around so as not to crowd the visitors. Catalina stood between her parents.

The congregation continued to stand for the opening prayer. Then the pastor encouraged everyone to be seated. During the reading of the Word, Catalina paid close attention. She had brought along her *New Testament*. The pastor gave the reference as Hebrews chapter eleven. As he started to read, tears came into Catalina's eyes. This was the first time she had ever heard the Word of God read in Spanish from a pulpit. Abram and Susana were also moved by the experience.

The pastor came to the words, "Women received back their dead, raised to life again. Others were tortured and refused to be released, so that they might gain a better resurrection. Some faced jeers and flogging, while still others were chained and put in prison. They were stoned; they were sawed in two; they were put to death by the sword. They went about in sheepskins and goatskins, destitute, persecuted and mistreated — the world was not worthy of them. They wandered in deserts and mountains, and in caves and holes in the ground." Catalina began sobbing heavily, and Susana put her arm around her and squeezed her tightly. Catalina laid her head on Susana's shoulder. With her free hand, she reached out and held her father's hand. He held her hand firmly and gave it a comforting squeeze. Both Abram and Susana knew she was thinking about Bartolomé.

During the sermon, Pastor Pérez referred to the fact that many in the congregation had lost loved ones through persecution. Catalina's sobbing could be heard throughout the sanctuary. Her tears wet the floor with those of more than half the others in the congregation. Bartolomé was among them, thinking of his father and his friends who had been executed about a year before.

The service ended. The congregation stood to sing the last Psalm, and the pastor pronounced the benediction. Everyone remained standing silently as he descended from the pulpit, carrying his *New Testament*, and as he walked to the back of the church building. He stood in the doorway to greet the congregation as they exited.

Bartolomé sat down and prayed privately for a minute before he finally arose to join the congregation.

When he stood up he greeted some of the folks that had been sitting near him, and they began to talk together. Out of the corner of his eye, he noticed a young woman at the back of the sanctuary who was being welcomed by those who had been sitting near her. She was taller than most Spanish women, had shiny black hair and wore a white scarf to hold back her hair. An elderly woman was still talking with Bartolomé and asked him a question, but he missed it entirely. In a daze, he ignored her and turned fully to face the back. His mouth turned dry as dust and his knees became weaker than water. He tried two or three times to say something—anything. Then he swallowed hard and, far louder than he intended, cried out, "Catalina!"

She turned instantly and cried out, "Bartolomé!"

They almost ran down the isle toward each other and would have knocked over everyone in their way if the people standing talking hadn't cleared a path for them. All talking ceased, and the entire congregation turned to watch a young man meet a young woman in the middle of the sanctuary. Catalina flew into Bartolomé's arms and he held her tight. They both were weeping. For many minutes, they just stood in the middle of the aisle, oblivious to the presence of anyone else, crying and holding each other.

They could not let go of each other for fear that they might be separated again.

Abram and Susana began to make their way over to the couple. The people watching began to talk again with one another. Abram and Susana stood silently beside Catalina until Bartolomé opened his tear-filled eyes and looked around. He noticed them standing there, and loosening his hold on Catalina slightly, said, "Doctor Mendoza, Doña Mendoza, what are you doing here? I never expected to see you in Geneva, and most certainly not at a Protestant worship service."

Abram replied, "Bartolomé, we are all Protestants now, and have escaped from Madrid. My *son*, it is good to see you. I am truly sorry that I had to forbid Catalina from seeing you or writing. I hope that you understand that, at the time, I had to protect my family from the Inquisition. I praise God that he has allowed you two to be reunited."

Bartolomé gently let go of Catalina and gave both Abram and Susana a hug. "Of course I understand. I probably would have done the same in your situation. I can't express how thankful I am to see you here. God is truly gracious!"

"Amen!" they all replied.

Catalina put her hand in Bartolomé's.

Bartolomé asked, "How did you end up here? I must hear your story."

Abram replied, "You will. But Bartolomé, your story is much more important. How did you get out of prison? How did you escape from the Inquisition?"

Before they could begin their respective stories, Pastor Pérez came over and welcomed the Mendozas. Bartolomé said, "Pastor Pérez, this is the family I told you about last week. This is Catalina! And this is her father, Doctor Mendoza, and her mother, Doña Mendoza. It is a miracle that God has brought them here!"

"So," Abram said, "let us hear *your* story."

"Yes, please, Bartolomé!" agreed Catalina.

Bartolomé gave them an outline of his adventures from the time of the *auto* and his escape until his arrival in Geneva. They stood in wonder listening to the account. Catalina was filled with so much emotion that she wept and laughed at the same time. Her heart ached with the joy of finding Bartolomé alive and healthy. She was also glowing with pride as he told his story.

"Bartolomé," Catalina said, "you have had quite an adventure! Our trip to Paris was boring in comparison. It is amazing that you escaped from prison and fought with robbers in the mountains!"

"Well, actually I didn't fight. I didn't have a pistol, and my short sword wouldn't have been of much use. I just ducked down behind my wagon and prayed!" They all laughed.

"I don't care. It was still dangerous. And you took care of the wounded man. Aren't you proud of him, Father? He could be a doctor like you!" Bartolomé stood tall as she gave him a kiss on the cheek. "Do you know Father was a doctor in King Felipe's court? King Felipe let him go study in Paris. That is how we escaped."

"It is interesting that you mention King Felipe. When I was following the route out of Valladolid along the Rio Duero, I saw King Felipe and his court heading north toward Aranda de Duero."

Catalina felt a chill go up her spine. "When was that?" she asked.

"Oh, sometime in the middle of June. Why?"

"Could it have been June 15ᵗʰ?"

"I suppose so. But, why?"

"Describe what you saw!"

Bartolomé describe the passing carriages.

"Tell me what you were wearing! What did your cart look like?"

Perplexed, Bartolomé thought back and described his clothes and his ox cart.

"You see, Mother! That was Bartolomé we saw! Bartolomé, we passed you that day. I was looking out the window of our carriage, and I looked right at you. A moment later, we had passed you and I could not look again to see if it really was you. Mother told me that I was imagining things."

"I remember that now. It seems so long ago. Yes, I do remember looking at a young woman in a carriage and thinking that she looked just like you. I also recall seeing a man on horseback riding near King Felipe whom I recognized but couldn't place. Now that I see your father with his short beard and not wearing an academic gown, I realize I was looking at him. This is all so strange. We passed each other and didn't know it."

"But I did know it! Right after that, I felt a warmth encompassing me that assured me that you were alive. I have never given up hope since that day. God gave me a sight of you to assure me and keep me going until this very day. He has rewarded my trust in him!"

Bartolomé then said, "I wrote to Margarita when I was in Paris. She said that she would write to you in Madrid. She also told me about your near-marriage experience. At first, she worded her letter in such a way that it made me think you were married. I almost died. But she told me later that the Conde had died. I was so relieved you weren't married."

Catalina smiled and replied, "I wrote to her also from Paris."

"We will have to write a letter to her and let her know that we are together at last. She will be surprised and pleased. We would not want her to receive a letter from Geneva; it could put her life in danger. So we can send it via Claude Lachy, in Paris."

Catalina replied, "Thank you, Bartolomé. I have been wondering how I could write to her from here but didn't know how to protect her from suspicion. You always have the answers!"

"Now I want to hear your story!" Turning to Abram, he said, "And I want to hear how you, Doctor Mendoza, came to accept Protestant beliefs."

Abram began, "I was reading Doctor Jean Calvin's *Institutio Christiane Religonis* ..."

"Doctor Jean Calvin! I heard him preach last Sunday and again today, and have gone to hear him during the week. You will have to meet him. He will be pleased to hear that his writings brought you to the truth. — I'm sorry, please forgive me for interrupting, I got too excited hearing about what you read, please continue."

At that point, Pastor Pérez, who had been listening to the entire conversation with great attention, interjected, "Come! We cannot stand here all afternoon. Come to our home and we can continue listening to the account of your arrival in Geneva. We are always pleased to hear of folks who have made it safely out of Spain."

Much of the rest of the congregation had departed by this point. Bartolomé and Catalina walked down the isle, holding hands. Catalina's heart was bursting for joy. She looked into Bartolomé's eyes and said, "Bartolomé, promise me you'll never leave me again."

"Catalina, I will never leave you again. I promise! I love you."

"I love you too!"

He pulled her to himself and kissed her.

They continued walking out of the church. Hand-in-hand they exited through the doorway into bright sunshine and a glorious future.

Author's Note
to the Reader

This novel is a work of fiction. It is not intended to provide an accurate history of the times it recounts. Many of the named individuals in the story were real people; for example, King Felipe II and his wife Queen Elizabeth, some of the prisoners in Valladolid, and the leaders of the Inquisition. But most of their actions and words were created for this story. Juan Garcia was a real person, and a goldsmith in Valladolid. He was betrayed by his wife to the Inquisition, and was executed at the *auto* on the gallows on May 20th, 1559. I do not know what his wife's real name was, or if she was a second wife. I do not know if they had any children. Bartolomé is fictional, and the representation of Damiana as a stepmother to Bartolomé is an invention that provides a 'wicked stepmother'. Catalina and her family and friends, Doctor Ortiz, and most of the people Bartolomé encounters are also invented characters.

I have attempted to be accurate to the historical context and avoid anachronisms in order to provide the correct 'feel' for the times. For example, technical innovations such as sealing wax and cultural innovations such as clothing styles are mentioned in their correct historical period. However, their presence in Spain around 1560 has not been established.

I believe that the following are the significant changes I have made to actual history:

- The Inquisition had a permanent base in Valladolid and did not return as I have portrayed it in the opening chapter.
- I have not been accurate in describing the imprisonment of the Protestants. In general, the Inquisition treated prisoners far worse than I have depicted the scenes. Prisoners were usually not allowed to share a cell, and were kept isolated from one-another.
- After Philip returned to Spain, he did not settle in Valladolid. However, he did not immediately make Madrid his new capital either. For about two years, his capital was in Toledo (about 70 kms) south of Madrid. He moved to Madrid after his new wife, Queen Elizabeth, became ill from pneumonia and it was believed that

Madrid offered a better climate for her. It was after his move to Madrid that he began the search for the site for El Escorial. I have compressed time in this instance to provide for the passing contact between Catalina and Bartolomé.

If a work of fiction needs a purpose, other than to be an enjoyable story to give us a break from our daily routine, then this story is a parable about God's Providence. In the late Middle Ages, and in the Reformation era, almost all people understood, and believed, that God works out all events for his purposes and glory, and for the good of his people (Romans 8.28)—whether or not they are pleasant in the short-term (e.g., enjoying a good meal, being robbed or being executed in a fire). In our 'enlightened' age, we have lost sight of the truth that God is in control, is working all things according to his plan, and will accomplish all of his objectives. Nothing that happens in this world is a mistake. This story reminds us that we are not masters of our own destiny; nor are we subjects of the Fates. We are living under the hand of God, and we can rejoice that ultimately good will triumph over evil.

Two books I found to be very helpful when working on this story are the following:

- Thomas M'Crie, *History of the Progress and Suppression of the Reformation in Spain in the Sixteenth Century,*

William Blackwell, Edinburgh, 1829; reprinted by the Hartland Institute, Rapidan, Virginia, 1998.

* Henry Charles, *A History of the Inquisition of Spain*, Volumes One, Two, and Three (Original edition, Macmillan, 1906-07).

In addition, I found an incredible amount of material available on the Internet. It is amazing what specific search terms entered into Google will retrieve. The amount of research I was able to accomplish from my computer, while in the middle of writing the text always surprised me. For example, I found a map of Roman roads in Spain, studied clothing styles in the sixteenth century and found pictures of churches in Valladolid from the sixteenth century. It is impossible to thank all the people who contributed the information used in this book because they are mostly the anonymous creators of the vast warehouse of information called the Web.

I cannot imagine the time it would take to write an historical novel if one had to find all the reference material through traditional paper sources. It is the same as trying to imagine how someone like Cervantes could have written his lengthy story without the use of a computer. While I was writing this novel, I read a novel about Johann Gutenberg and the invention of the printing press. I am continually aware of the way in which technology can be used for good or evil. My hope is that this story is an example of applying technology for good.

It is not easy to find friends who are willing to edit one's work and be truly candid with their comments. So, I truly appreciate the feedback that was provided by the early readers of this story. Marg Jackson, my wife Lillian, Cathy Dienesch, and Holly McCabe all provided significant editorial feedback. I thank them for their efforts and willingness to provide input as the book was a work-in-progress. I also thank my father for his thorough edit of the final manuscript.

Questions for Group Discussion

1. What themes are used in the story that are found in many other stories?
2. What are some of the significant cultural differences between sixteenth-century Spain and modern North America?
3. How are the four '*solas*' (*sola fide*; *sola gratia*; *sola christos*; *sola scriptura*: faith alone, grace alone, Christ alone, Scripture alone) of the Reformation woven into the story?
4. How does Bartolomé resolve his questions about truth and final authority?
5. How does the form of worship that Bartolomé participates in differ from the Roman Catholic form or that practiced by most churches today?

6. How do the protagonists respond to God's providences?
7. What are the various forms of escape recounted in the story?
8. What does this story teach about how the Church should apply tolerance?

Printed in the United States
61150LVS00001B/1-30

9 781600 344237